i am Elephant, i am Butterfly

Leslie Tall Manning

This book is a work of fiction. Names, characters, businesses, organizations, places, and incidents are the product of the author's imagination or used fictitiously. Any resemblance to actual persons, living or dead, events, or locales is entirely coincidental.

ISBN: 978-0-9600177-0-6 (Digital)
ISBN: 978-0-9600177-1-3 (Paperback)
ISBN: 978-0-9600177-2-0 (Audio)

Cover layout and typography by J. Kenton Manning Design,
Copyright © 2018.
Cover photo by Shutterstock.com.
Book formatting by Polgarus Studio.

Available at Amazon.com and other book stores.

Other books by Leslie Tall Manning

Upside Down in a Laura Ingalls Town
GAGA
Maggie's Dream

Enjoy a sneak peek of *Upside Down in a Laura Ingalls Town* at the end of this book.

This book is dedicated to my parents,
Edward Lay Tall and Lydia Argenti Tall—
whether because of or in spite of—
for unknowingly planting the seed so long ago.

A Cherokee Legend:

An old Cherokee is teaching his grandchild about life:

"A fight is going on inside me," he said to the child. "It is a terrible fight, and it is between two wolves. One wolf is evil—he is anger, envy, sorrow, regret, greed, arrogance, guilt, self-pity, resentment, inferiority, deception, false pride, ego, and superiority. The other wolf is good—he is peace, love, hope, joy, serenity, humility, benevolence, empathy, generosity, truth, and faith. The same fight is going on inside you, and inside every other person, too."

The grandchild thought a moment and then asked,
"Which wolf will win?"

The old Cherokee simply replied, "The one you feed."

Chapter One

Two-five-two.

Two-five-three.

Two-five-four...

Doctor Stan stared down at my feet and back up at the numbers on the slide bar. I wondered if he'd spotted the chipped toenails. It wasn't like I was a dirty person—I showered daily. I washed my wavy hair and my face. Even my ears. It was just too much trouble to reach my feet to file those dang toenails.

Little dandruff flakes sat in the bald spots between the even rows in Doctor Stan's gray hair. As his eyes came up to meet mine, I tilted my head toward the ceiling. A weird stain was spread out on some of the tiles. It looked like a coffee stain.

How could a coffee stain get way up—

"...real problem here."

What? My brain asked this, but my lips did not.

"I'll have to discuss the options with your parents," Doctor Stan said. "Step off the scale, please." He jotted something down on his clipboard. "I'll be right back."

He left the room.

I started to push myself onto the table, but changed my mind. The sanitary paper would stick to my legs, and I'd have to peel tiny fragments from the sweat on my thighs. So I stood there, in the middle of the room, in a faded blue patient's gown, waiting. I hated doctors' offices. And I'd seen my share. This room was no different, except that it had a first-floor window with a view of the parking lot. Through the slits in the blinds, I watched as a woman made her way around the front of her SUV and helped the girl—her daughter, presumably—out of the passenger seat. They had parked in the handicapped spot.

Handicapped.

I turned away and looked at the stupid posters on the wall. One of them was of an attractive Hispanic-looking family—mother, father, sister, brother—all holding hands as they stood on a rolling green lawn, beaming at the camera. The kids were skinny. Maybe they used to be fat, eating all those burritos and tacos and stuff, but then they lost a bunch of weight when they were promised fame in a poster on a doctor's office wall. At least their tans looked real.

The other poster was even more stupid than the first: a bunch of puppies in a fuzzy dog bed. What do dogs have to do with being a fat sixteen-year-old loser? Nothing, that's what.

The door opened. My mother entered the room first, followed by my father, and then Doctor Stan.

"Oh, Simone," my mother said, floating over to me and brushing the brown, uneven bangs from my forehead. I had cut the bangs myself. No one at home commented on my new style, so I assumed it looked okay.

My father said nothing. He plunked down on a chair in the corner like a giant turtle, his thick veiny neck sticking up out of his green golf shirt—a shirt tight enough to show his muscles left over from his quarterback days.

Doctor Stan leaned against the counter, rubbing the edge of his clipboard.

"If we don't take care of this now, who knows? Diabetes, arthritis, heart disease..."

"Simone is too young for heart disease," my mother told the doctor, nervously re-wrapping the hair tie around her dyed red ponytail. She wore a ponytail all the time, like she believed it made her look like a teenager by stretching her face and smoothing out her wrinkles. I didn't have the heart to tell her she still looked like a housewife and mother of two.

Doctor Stan turned to me. "I've offered your parents an option I think is right for you. The bottom line is this can't go on. You have to do something." He turned toward my mother. "You all have to do something. As a family. When your sixteen-year-old is only five-foot-five and weighs two hundred and fifty-four pounds, well, by today's standards, that's considered morbidly obese."

A coughing sound emanated from the green turtle in the corner.

"The place I have in mind is in the mountains," Doctor Stan said, mostly to my mother. "Near the Tennessee border."

"That's so far away," my mother told him.

"No, it's not," my father said.

"It's still in North Carolina," Doctor Stan said. "And it'll only be for the summer. Simone needs to spend time away from the life she knows now. Away from her friends..."

What friends?

"...her school..."

School's almost out for the summer, genius.

"…her usual routine…"

I have no routine, unless you want to include thinking about food, dreaming about food, drawing pictures of food on the damp mirror after my showers…

"Oh, Simone," my mother said again. She was putting on the waterworks now, her tiny cheerleader body trying to wrap its arms around all of me, but not quite succeeding. "A whole summer? I don't want to lose my baby."

"Is this really our last hope?" the turtle in the golf shirt said. "A *fat farm*?"

Doctor Stan held tightly to his stethoscope. "It's a *camp*," he said. "Physically, Simone is up to it. She'll have to undergo a psychological evaluation to make sure she fits the profile before being admitted."

"Admitted?" my mother asked, placing a hand against her cheek.

"Into their program," he explained. "It's very elite. They only take a handful of girls." Doctor Stan looked from my mother to my father, and then back to my mother. "I'll give you a brochure. Take it home, check out the website. Call them with any questions you have. Ultimately, this should be decided as a family."

Like the perfect poster family with the big white teeth and tan smiling faces?

"Why don't we let Simone get dressed," Doctor Stan said.

They left the room. My mother, dabbing at her wet eyes with a tissue, my father, scurrying out of the room before he accidentally looked me in the eye, and Doctor Stan, who closed the door behind him.

I gathered my clothes from the chair and laid them on the examining table, took off the ugly gown, and turned toward the mirror, naked, except for my C-cup bra and my granny-panties.

My body meant nothing to me. It didn't belong to me, as a matter of fact. It used to, back in the old days. Now, it belonged to that girl in the mirror. That freak. That girl who spent her babysitting money at the movies each week so she'd have an excuse to eat licorice and M&M's and buttered popcorn, all in one sitting. That one who, with a perfected nasally whine, could get her mother to hit any fast food drive-thru any time of day, any day of the week, and order everything supersized. That girl in the mirror was the freak, not me. She was the one who could feed a family in Haiti for a week on the food she devoured in a day. Who snuck into the kitchen in the middle of the night for stale doughnuts or chocolate milk. Whose mother thought her daughter was so mature because she insisted on doing her own laundry, but really it was so her mother wouldn't see the Hostess cupcakes and Little Debbie snacks hiding in her underwear drawer.

That girl in the mirror wasn't me. That girl in the mirror had devoured me. Swallowed me whole. That girl had an extra chin that made it look like her neck was missing. She had beady brown eyes that peeked out through a blown-up beach-ball face. She had a permanent sweat line above her lip, even in an air conditioned room. Anytime she moved, she could hear her thighs rub together, could feel the heat from the friction. Her belly button had sunken between the rolls of skin on her stomach, so deep she couldn't remember if she was an innie or an outie.

And that girl in the mirror could no way in hell have been me, because she was crying as she stood there half-naked, and I had made a pact with myself that I would never cry.

Chapter Two

I was rinsing the syrup off the last breakfast dish when my mother said to Bucky, "You're coming with us. We will support your sister together. As a family."

"It's not my fault she can't keep her grubby hands out of the fridge," Bucky said. He pushed his summer side bangs out of his eyes. "God, you act like I should be punished. Dad, tell Mom I don't need to come."

"Fannie," my father said, never taking his eyes off the sports section of the paper, "Bucky doesn't need to come."

"Why don't we leave it up to Simone?" my mother said as she poured bacon grease into an empty coffee can. Bacon grease I wouldn't smell for a whole summer. My lips trembled with fear at the thought of this. "Sissy," she asked me, "do you want your brother to come and support you?"

I observed my younger brother. At fifteen, he was already shaving those little wiry sprouts on the tip of his chin, though most of the time he missed a few. He leaned against the kitchen counter, his arms crossed like a prison guard. His newly discovered biceps bulged out from underneath his T-shirt. Soccer was his thing at the moment. That and girls. The girls loved Bucky right back. Funny, only a few years earlier, I was the popular one. Had curves in all the right places, knew how to wear makeup correctly since the eighth grade. I used to get invited to all the best parties, even the high school ones. I was pretty funny, too. When I had sleepovers, my friends would just about pee their pants when I threatened to beat Bucky's skinny ass with my lacrosse stick if he didn't leave us girls alone.

Now, he was the one with the friends, and I was the lame one who sat in my room on the weekends, staring at my posters of Logan Lerman, wishing I had a boyfriend, even if he wasn't as hot as my *Percy Jackson* hero, wondering what boy would gift me with my first real kiss, maybe invite me to next year's junior prom.

Fat chance. Ha-ha.

I told Bucky, staring into his dark mocking eyes, "Forget it. I don't need you to come along. Don't *want* you to. Even if you begged me, I would tell you to stay home." *Because you're a jerk, and you won't know how to keep your juvenile mouth shut when you see the girls up at that camp.*

"Hmmm..." Bucky said, rubbing the stray hairs on his chin.

My stomach fell. I had told him to stay home, so naturally he would rebel and—

"Maybe I will come along to Camp Fat Mama." He knew perfectly well it was called Camp *Kamama.* My brother smiled his perfect braces-are-finally-off smile. "You know. To support your endeavor."

Endeavor? Must have been a vocab word left over from the previous year's English class. Bucky rarely used three-syllable words.

I, on the other hand, lived for three, four, five syllables. I would look up extra words in the dictionary on Sunday nights just so I could use them around the house during the week. The kids I babysat for loved it when I threw out funny words like an English nanny: "Cal, your *la-bor-i-ous* (exhausting) attitude is making me *mal-con-tent* (disgruntled); or, "Miranda, I saw you take that cupcake, you *cir-cu-i-tous* (devious) thief!"

"Bucky, that's very mature of you," my mother told my brother now, praising him by touching his arm, disregarding his joke about the camp's name. She was an expert at disregarding anything that forced her to take sides; to take a stand for what was right.

Our minister had once mentioned in his sermon that there are three ways to handle stressful situations: fight, flight, or freeze. My mother was definitely of the frozen Popsicle variety.

I opened the back door and let in Muggs, our chocolate lab. I'd rescued her from the streets after a hurricane had blown through our town. Next to food, my dog was going to be the worst part about leaving for the summer.

Muggs followed as I huffed up the stairs to my room and locked the door behind me. I didn't want to go to a camp for obese girls. Why did I all of a sudden have to be hit in the head with the way I really was? With the truth of it all? I wanted to stay home where I could take Muggs for a walk to the other side of the neighborhood to by a push-up pop from the ice cream man; visit the food court at the mall; hit the DQ for my favorite Blizzard; head to Sonic for a couple of chili dogs they only carried in the summertime. I wanted to sink myself into chocolate brownies while re-reading some of the books on my shelf, alone in my room with Hamlet, Mrs. Haversham, and Lennie.

I said to Muggs, who lay sprawled out on my comforter,

"Their lives were tragic, but at least they lived the way they chose."

Muggs put her head on her paws and stared up at me.

Fighting back tears, I opened my closet and pulled out my large suitcase—we were only allowed to bring one—and put it on the bed beside Muggs. She watched with apprehension as I filled it with shorts and T-shirts, an extra pair of tennis shoes, and flip-flops. I picked out my faded denim baseball cap with the two crossed lacrosse sticks. I grabbed a wad of bras and underwear and shoved them in, then snatched the candy bars and Little Debbie's from the drawer. My plan was to hide them in my suitcase, but before I knew it, I had eaten them all.

"What?" I said to Muggs. "Don't look at me like that."

I tossed her a doggie treat from a dish on my dresser so she wouldn't feel left out. Then I washed the chocolate from my mouth, brushed my teeth extra hard, and shoved the wrappers into the bathroom air conditioning vent before dragging my suitcase downstairs.

***

My father cocked the rearview mirror a few inches upward so I could only see his receding hairline, and he couldn't see any of me. My mother turned around from time to time to give me a wilted smile. She was usually a chatterbox, but today she was pretty somber. Like she was sending her only daughter to prison. Or death row.

I glanced over at Bucky. His big lame head lay flat against the window as he slept, his mouth threatening to drool, which I hoped it did.

I turned up my music to drown out the thoughts trying to invade my brain. The camp brochure had shown a glistening lake with the sun setting behind it, ancient pines and cypress in the distance rising tall and proud. The brochure also showed a gazillion happy faces. Girls with wide grins pushing out their fat cheeks; girls with thunder thighs hiking up a hill; girls sitting on their beds, playing Monopoly or some other crappy board game.

"Camp Kamama," the pamphlet read. "A retreat where girls learn to love themselves through the spirit of nature and self-discovery."

Some summer weekends, when I was little, our family would visit the Blue Ridge. We'd go camping, hiking, fishing. I excelled at paddle boarding, swimming, throwing a Frisbee, starting a campfire, catching trout. During middle school, I went to lacrosse camp three summers in a row. Won all kinds of awards and trophies which my parents beamed over during those corny Family Days…

But that was back when the world still liked me.

The sudden altitude change made my ears pop as we left the foothills and headed into the mountains. I readjusted my ear buds. Beyonce, White Room, and some old-school rock kept me company as the wide open highway turned into two lanes, and the forest on either side grew thick, hugging the road. For the next half hour, I didn't see a house, a barn, or a gas station. I began to wonder if my parents were taking me to camp, or off to a secret place out in the woods so they wouldn't have to worry about me eating them out of house and home anymore.

They're punishing me, I thought, *and I deserve it.*

A dozen camp signs flew by on our way up the mountain: Outriggers, Skylark, Boy Scouts, 4-H, Protestant, Lutheran. I was feeling hopeful that the GPS would take us to the wrong camp when a sign appeared on our right: *Lake Kamama.* Beneath that was a poem, or a prayer, or a little of both:

To the Weary Traveler:
I will draw thorns from your feet.
We will walk the White Path of Life together.
Like a sister of my own blood,
I will love you.
I will wipe tears from your eyes.
When you are sad,
I will put your aching heart to rest.

My mother chirped like a twenty-year-old, "How totally awesome is this, Sissy!" She clapped her hands like we'd just won a kitchen makeover on HGTV.

We drove up the long dirt road, crunching a bed of pine needles.

"Are we here?" Bucky asked, wiping his wet chin with his T-shirt, 1980's punk music blaring from his ear buds which now hung around his neck.

"No," I told him. "We're still in our driveway at home. We planted all these pines while you were asleep."

"Shut up."

"Robert, there's a parking lot up on the right," my mother said.

"I see it," my father said. It was the first sign of life he'd shown in hours.

As my father followed the signs, Bucky leaned close to me and breathed, "I looked up the name of your special camp on the Internet."

"So, you finally learned how to type. Hoo-rah."

"Did you know that *Kamama* means *elephant*?"

"Does not."

"Camp Elephant. Someone was thinking."

I turned toward the window and mumbled, "Screw you."

A girl stood in the middle of the parking lot, motioning us to park where she pointed. She carried a clipboard and wore a large blue T-shirt that reached the hem of her shorts. The shirt had a smiling stick figure in the middle of it with the arched words *Camp Kamama* over its round head.

She looked a year younger than me. *Two-hundred*, give or take. I'd spent a lot of time calculating what overweight people weighed. Sometimes I turned it into a game. I'd see someone on television, guess his or her weight, and then look it up. Most of the time, I was spot-on. Maybe a carnival could hire me as a professional weight guesser.

"Welcome to Camp Kamama," the girl said as we stepped out of the car. "My name is Marion, and I'll be your guide for the next hour. Then it's on to meet the others."

"I thought we were just dropping her off," my brother said, glaring at me.

My mother said, "Bucky..."

"Oh, we'll have a terrific time together," Marion said, gaping at Bucky as she nervously tucked her short dark hair behind an ear. My brother ignored her in favor of kicking a pine cone across the parking lot. "Most of the other campers got here earlier," Marion went on, "so they've already had the tour. I have ya'll to myself. You'll get to check out the camp from top to bottom. Where we sleep and eat, and where the daily exercise takes place."

"Exercise?" I asked.

The brochure had called the camp a *retreat*. I'd pictured groups of girls making macramé plant holders and friendship bracelets out of gimp. Relaxing in hammocks while listening to the birds.

"Exercise...well, sure," Marion said, smiling. "That's what this camp is all about. There's swimming, the obstacle course, working in the community garden..."

"A garden," my mother said, "how wonderful."

"Let me check your name off the list," Marion said.

"Wheeler," my father told her. "First name Simone."

He took a subtle step backward as Marion stepped toward him, like being overweight was contagious. For every pound I'd gained over the last two years, my father had moved an inch away, until the inches had grown into miles.

"Got it," Marion said, checking off the name on her clipboard. She turned to me. "*Simone.* I love that name. Go ahead and put your suitcase on that cart over there. It'll be brought to your bunk. I'm your cabin counselor. We're in number ten. The closest one to the lake." She tucked the clipboard under her arm. "You can keep your watch and your iPod, but leave behind your cell phone and whatever other tech stuff you have. Up here, we live like pioneers. Only with indoor plumbing." She giggled.

I begrudgingly handed my cell phone to my mother and then stuck my lacrosse baseball cap on my head.

"Okay, power up," Marion said. "We have a quarter-mile hike into the camp. It's going to be a totally awesome day. By the time y'all say goodbye to Simone, it'll feel like you're leaving your daughter with family."

Chapter Three

The camp was spread out across fifty acres of hilly forest. Within fifteen minutes, my legs felt like they'd already hiked every inch and my bra and Crocs were wet with sweat.

"Oh, Sissy," my mother cooed. "I can't believe you get to stay here. It's like a spa." She grabbed my arm like a girlfriend and whispered, "Maybe I should find a way to sneak in."

I knew she was joking, but I also knew in reality my mother would never have to worry about spending time at a fat camp. She did yoga at the YMCA three mornings a week, played tennis with her girlfriends on Tuesday afternoons, and took a spin class some nights after dinner.

Jocks run in my family.

"I can't wait to see the obstacle course," Bucky said, his voice feigning enthusiasm.

"Follow me," Marion said.

For a large girl, she sure could move fast. I had to stop a few times to catch my breath, and my knees were beginning to throb.

Marion led us down a winding path to a section of forest far away from everything else. Along the way, we passed other girls trudging along the trails with their parents. Marion said hello to every one of them. A few minutes later, the path opened to a wide clearing. In the middle of the clearing sat a giant playground, with tires and a balance beam and monkey bars, and even a basketball net.

"The infamous obstacle course," Marion said. "After running this a couple of times, you'll be able to do it in your sleep."

I scanned the course and swallowed hard. I could feel Bucky staring at me, his stupid grin burning a hole through the side of my face.

"How about I take y'all down to the lake?" Marion said, as she led us away from the obstacle course and down another path. This time we stepped over tree roots and low branches that tried to trip us.

Soon, the lake lay before us, reflections of puffy summer clouds barely moving across the still water.

"Amazing, huh?" Marion said.

"Not bad," my father said, shrugging.

"This is enormous," my mother said, taking in the scene.

"A half mile straight across, and a mile from side to side," Marion said, like she was the one who had put it there.

Bucky wandered to the edge of the lake, picked up a stone, and tossed it in. The stone skipped two-three-four times across the flat surface until it disappeared from sight.

"What activities do you do here at the lake?" my mother asked, shooing a gnat away from her face.

"Most activities take place back at the camp," Marion said. "The lake is for reflection. You know, a place to chill out. The campers can reflect anywhere they want. Some girls choose to stay near camp, others like it closer to the lake. Good place to sit and think."

"Think?" Bucky asked. "What about swimming?"

I could tell my brother was disappointed that his imagination had been jilted, picturing a herd of fat girls bobbing up and down like overly inflated inner tubes.

"Swimming takes place in the indoor pool," Marion explained.

"What about fishing?" my father asked. "Sissy knows how to fish."

It was the first time in ages he'd acknowledged any of my talents.

"Sorry, no fishing," Marion said.

"What the hell does Kamama mean?" Bucky asked.

"Bucky," my mother said pouting, "language."

Marion didn't seem to notice my brother's rudeness. "It's Cherokee," she said. "It means *butterfly*."

My I-told-you-so look aimed at my brother was interrupted by echoed laughter.

Bucky squinted as he looked across the water. "Hey. There's a bunch of girls over there."

I followed his gaze. On the opposite side of the lake, we spotted specks of pink and blue and blond, like pieces of confetti moving in the wind.

"Don't pay them any mind," Marion said, her tone suddenly firm like a teacher or a principal. "There are a lot of camps up here in the mountains, and we all keep to ourselves."

"What kind of camp is it?" I asked, cupping my eyes to shield the late morning sun.

Marion's watch beeped. "Oh, my gosh," she said, glancing at her wrist. "I have to get ya'll back. They're gonna take roll in twenty minutes, and I haven't shown off the garden yet!"

Like a line of ducklings, the four of us followed Marion as she started back along the winding path, me trailing behind, the laughter from across the lake washing over my shoulders then fading away.

***

A row of log-style cabins were spaced about twenty yards apart, with winding dirt paths like fat anacondas weaving between each. I stepped onto the porch of cabin number ten. Above the screened door hung a long wooden sign with words burned into the wood:

May the warm winds of Heaven blow softly upon your house.
May the Great Spirit bless all who enter.

I peeked through the screen and counted ten single beds lined up in a row, a foot between each, like military barracks. At lacrosse camp we'd slept in bunk beds. Maybe at Camp Kamama they were afraid the weight of the girl on the top bunk would come crashing down on the poor girl below.

Next, Marion showed us the buildings that housed the cabin offices, the infirmary, and the classrooms.

"Classrooms?" I asked. "What are those for?"

"So you can learn about things like cooking and nutrition and communication."

"You mean, like school?"

"You have to go to school in the summer," Bucky said, seemingly amused by this idea.

Marion smiled at me. "You'll love the classes, Simone. They're the best part. I promise."

Was she high? The altitude had to be getting to her. No one in their right mind would think that going to school in the summer was the best part of anything.

Marion brought us to the backside of the cabins where the

cafeteria was located, and beyond that, the gymnasium, where the pool was housed. The last spot to visit was located at the edge of the compound, the only place in the whole camp besides the lake where no trees stood between us and the sun. An arched wrought iron sign above the gate welcomed us:

Come in peace, tend to me gently, and I will provide for you.

"Oh, my," my mother breathed as she stepped through the low wooden gate.

Countless rows of bushes and vines filled the garden. Some I recognized, like cherry tomatoes and blackberries. The garden seemed to stretch on forever, and I couldn't make out the hundreds of plants that disappeared into the distance, only that everything was green and lush. It was like being in a fairy tale where a farmer had planted magic beans.

"The girls grow everything you see here," Marion said. "Of course, the seeds were planted long before y'all got here, but the campers are responsible for maintaining it. If they don't, then they pretty much don't eat. Thirty grams of your diet will be from fiber, most of which you'll get from the garden. That's a good thing, since some of our campers are vegetarian."

Vegetarian? Was I expected to go without a burger or a hot dog for the entire summer? How would I survive without the taste of summer cookouts? I was sure at that moment that I would be left to rot here at Camp Kamama and they'd use me for compost, like in a dystopian novel.

Marion guided us between the vines of peas and robust raspberry bushes. "Of course," she said as her fingertips gently pet the leaves, "there's plenty of other food, too."

"Like what?" I asked, trying to stay calm.

"You know, organic chicken and turkey and fresh fish."

My body relaxed a little.

"But the garden is the most important part," Marion went on. "The director likes to think of it as the heart of Camp Kamama."

My father stooped next to a small plant by the fence. "What's this?"

Bucky sang in my ear, "*Cannabis.*"

I mouthed, "Shut up."

"Italian basil," Marion said. "We grow all of our herbs, too. You name it, and we probably grow it. We even have fruit. Y'all can't see from here, but behind those oaks back there are a couple of cherry trees, a grape vineyard, and an apple orchard. Behind the orchard, there's a greenhouse where we grow oranges, lemons, and limes."

"I'm impressed," my mother said. "What do you think, Robert?"

My father stood up, rubbing a tiny piece of parsley between his fingers. "As long as she follows the rules."

"Well," Marion said, "I'd better get y'all to orientation. Once everyone gets settled in, it'll be dinner time."

As we followed Marion out of the garden, my stomach growled. My mouth salivated. I was suddenly very hungry. Starving, in fact.

Then I realized with a sudden rush of fascination that I hadn't eaten since we'd stopped at Cracker Barrel nearly four hours ago. And I hadn't thought about food until now.

Chapter Four

It was like being beneath the claw in a glass case packed with dozens of identical stuffed animals. I stood in the middle of the bunch, mesmerized. There were so many girls who looked like me. They were all heavy like me, all with sun-licked cheeks like mine, and pudgy knees sticking out from the bottoms of XXL board shorts. I felt invisible all of a sudden.

And I sort of liked it.

The camp director stepped onto a small stage. She had two shiny brown braids which hung down past her rib cage. Covering the top of her head was a green and white bandana, tied in back at the base of her neck. She wasn't dressed like us campers, who wore T-shirts, summer shorts, and an assortment of brand-name tennis shoes and flip-flops. She wore a Camp Kamama T-shirt like the counselors, but it must have been three sizes too big, the hem at mid-thigh. And instead of shorts, she wore a long flowing skirt that looked like it was patched together with samples from the Fabric Warehouse remnant table. On her feet was a pair of cheap white tennis shoes decorated with puffer paint, little hearts and rainbows covering the canvas tops and sides, like she'd bought them at a *Hello Kitty* store. She wore no jewelry, no wedding ring or anything, and no makeup as far as I could tell. A smattering of freckles dotted her nose and cheeks, and her pretty smile was filled with even rows of white teeth. She looked healthy. And thin.

Compared to all of us who stood gazing up at her, she looked like an elf.

"I'd like to thank y'all for coming," she said, her soft voice entering the microphone. "Not just our new campers, but your families and friends who have shown support by being here with you today. Right now, I'd like each of you girls, each of our Kamama, to turn to those who brought you here, and give these lovely beings a thank-you hug. They are your Earth-angels."

I could feel the crowd shift as each girl hugged a parent, grandparent, or sibling. My mother reached out her arms and brought me to her. She smelled like peppermint gum and cherry lip gloss.

"You don't need to thank us, Sissy," she said in my ear. "We're your parents. This is what we do."

I wanted to say, *Mom, don't leave me here. I don't belong here. I belong at home, spending the summer with my best friends: Bojangles, McDonald's, Smithfield's, and the DQ*. But she seemed so proud of me, so I said nothing.

She let go of me and gently pushed me toward my brother.

No way was I hugging him.

"Thanks," I mumbled.

"Whatever," Bucky mumbled back.

I turned toward my father, but another family had separated us. He stood next to someone else's daughter, looking at his Nikes.

"I'll thank him later, Mom," I lied.

Ms. Diggs tapped the microphone.

"Now," she said, "each cabin has two counselors assigned. They are holding a sign with your cabin number on it. By now, y'all have met at least one of them. They will be taking you to your cabins in a few minutes to go over a list of do's and don'ts before dinner. Please show your counselors respect at all times. They are my eyes and ears, and they are crucial to the smooth running of Camp Kamama. But they aren't the only ones. I'd like to introduce a few people who will be an integral part of your lives for the next eleven weeks."

She pointed to a person down at her right. I could barely make out the top of her head.

"This is Katharine, my assistant director. She handles everything from the admissions process to advertising to trash and recycle pickup. You won't see her out and about too often, but she's here, doing all the behind-the-scenes work.

"Next, we have Wilhelmina, chef extraordinaire, in charge of making sure we have enough cooking supplies and fabulous recipes to keep the summer interesting.

"And this is Mary, our camp nurse and resident family counselor…"

As the director introduced the people who were undoubtedly here to change my life, I took another look around, scrutinizing the crowd more closely, noting that, except for the obvious common aspect that brought us all together, we did look pretty different after all. There were White girls, Black girls, Chinese, Hispanic, and East Indian. There were baseball caps depicting different teams, like the Orioles, the Yankees, and the Braves, or colleges like NC State and College of Charleston. Shoes were even more varied, some girls wearing Rainbow flip-flops or Crocs like mine, others wearing New Balance or Under Armour tennis shoes. Most shorts ended at the knee, but a few of the braver girls took to wearing those embarrassing short-shorts. Some wore sunglasses, prescription glasses, or no glasses at all. There were chunky watches, precious metal rings, tiny stud earrings, nose rings, and eyebrow hoops. Socks, no socks. Makeup, no makeup. Tats, no tats.

It was like a visit to the United Nations.

I waited through the clapping, and when the director got to her last guest, the crowd grew silent. I tried to see who Ms. Diggs was pointing to, but there were too many people in my way. It wasn't until person stepped onto the stage that I stopped breathing.

"...Jake Stonewolf, your athletics director..."

I could hear a collective heart skip a beat as Jake, all one-hundred-eighty pounds and six feet of tan, lean muscle, nodded toward the crowd of fat girls and their families. Dark hairless legs extended from his hiking shorts and disappeared into a pair of boots that looked like they were made for conquering the Appalachian Trail. He readjusted his red bandana, and when he slightly turned his head to the right, I could see a dark braid cascading down his back, almost to his tailbone.

I heard a girl behind me let out a "Holy crap." The one on my right grabbed her mother's arm and giggled.

Ms. Diggs continued: "Jake will be teaching y'all to swim like Olympians. By summer's end, you'll feel like you can take on the English Channel."

Even though the camp list said to pack a bathing suit, I did not. I didn't own one. At Belk or Target, the only suits that fit me were the maternity ones. When we went to Atlantic Beach or Hilton Head, I wore a tank top and a pair of shorts while boogie-boarding.

Now, as Jake nodded modestly, into my head poured a thousand excuses as to why I would not be swimming the English Channel anytime soon.

***

We left our parents to go free range while the bunk counselors took us to our cabins. We would meet up with them again for dinner, before we said our final goodbyes.

The inside of the cabin was damp and musty, the smell of mildew pushing its way through the scent of Pine Sol.

Each girl grabbed a bed she thought was rightfully hers, and I did the same, taking the one closest to the screened door. I always slept with my window open at home, even in the winter time, which drove my parents crazy, but I sweated at night. I needed to have some air circulating around me or I would melt.

A tan girl with strawberry-blond hair slid her suitcase toward me. She took off a cap with "Maryland is for Crabs" scrolled across the front, and plopped down on the bed next to mine. Her cheeks were flushed, and a wide circle of sweat cupped each armpit.

"I'm Charlene," she said, fanning her red face with her cap. "What do you think so far?"

What did I think? I thought I would have a stroke when we passed the cafeteria on the way to our cabins as the smell of dinner wafted into my sinuses. I thought there was no way in hell I could live without regular food for eleven weeks. That I would probably end up being part of the two percent the website had warned wouldn't make it the whole summer, begging until the director caved, calling my parents to come and get me, then stopping at the DQ on the way home as my mother's apology for making me suffer.

"Okay, I guess," I told Charlene.

"How much do you weigh?"

Wow. Just like that. Was that how it was going to be? How long would it take before we asked each other what we craved in the middle of the night? What our favorite fried food was? What we missed most about our refrigerators?

"About two-fifty," I told her, for the first time saying the number out loud. It tasted like wet dough on my tongue.

"Oh," she said with a wave of her hand. "I hit your weight over a year ago. I'm almost two-seventy now."

She said this like she was proud of weighing more now than she did a year ago. More than me, even. At least I'd nailed her weight.

"Where are you from?" Charlene asked.

"New Bern, North Carolina. It's about two hours east of Raleigh, not far from the beach. You?"

"Western Maryland. Hills and cows and corn."

The screened door opened. Marion and another girl—*a mere one-eighty*—stepped into our cabin. Marion held a pile of T-shirts, and the other girl held a clipboard.

"Hey, everyone!" Marion called. "We're excited, too, but y'all have to settle down if we wanna make it to dinner on time."

The room quieted like she wielded a machete.

"This is Karen," Marion said. "In case you don't know it already, she and I will be your counselors. We'll be sleeping in here with you. Our beds are the two in the back, with our suitcases on top. But don't think of us as Big Brother or anything like that. We're pretty kickback. At least, most of the time."

She looked at Karen.

"Hey," Karen said, taking a blond braid and swishing it over a shoulder. "We only have a few things to go over, so if you all want to get comfortable, we'll get started."

Beds squeaked.

"First, we have to do roll call," Karen said, holding up the clipboard, "to make sure no one's gone AWOL on the first day."

She counted out eight names, all accounted for.

"Good," Marion said. "Now I'll give each of y'all four T-shirts. There's a laundry service next to the pool. Each bunk has laundry day on different days. Ours is on Thursdays." She walked around the room and handed out the T-shirts. Everyone in our cabin had the same color: light blue. When Marion was through, she said, "We have a bunch of rules y'all have to follow at Camp Kamama, and we need to make sure you understand them."

A silent groan moved around the cabin.

"Look over the list," Marion said, as Karen passed out the sheets. "The rules are set in granite. Y'all need to sign on the bottom."

I scanned the list but barely paid attention. Camp was camp. Rules always included curfew, lights-out, bunk cleanliness, emergency procedures...most of it was no-brainer stuff, especially if you'd spent a good part of your life at summer camps.

One of the girls—*three-hundred*—raised her hand.

"Hi," Marion said. "Tell us your name and where you're from."

"I'm Hannah, from Virginia Beach. I didn't know we weren't allowed to write or call home all summer. Isn't that, like, against our civil rights?"

Marion said, "Camp Kamama feels that if ya'll call home, you'll become weak, and if you become weak, you might convince your family to come and get you. As far as civil rights go, I guess as soon as you sign the bottom, ya'll sort of give up those rights."

A girl about as wide as she was tall—*three-thirty-something*—with pale skin and mousy brown hair, raised her hand.

"Sue. From Delaware. It says here we aren't allowed to eat alone."

"Right," Marion said. "Y'all can only eat in the company of others, except power bars that the camp supplies. Anything else must be eaten in the cafeteria or during cooking class, unless approved by Ms. Diggs. All the girls in each cabin were specifically chosen to be together. So make sure when we get to the cafeteria, y'all pay attention to where your table is. That's where you'll eat for the rest of the summer. Together."

Another girl—*two-twenty, give or take*—raised her hand. She wore a pair of small glasses and a tie-dyed bandana on her head.

"I'm Sabrina," she said, pushing her glasses high up on her tiny nose. "From South Carolina. What is contraband?"

Marion's face grew serious. "Food of any kind is not allowed in the cabins, ever, for any reason. Or you can expect punishment."

The stocks from the days of the Salem witch trials popped into my head.

Another girl raised her hand. *Two-ninety*. A stack of *People* magazines sat beneath her bed next to her suitcase. "My name's Trish. From Asheville. Does that include candy and gum?"

Marion said, "Candy, gum, even the wrappers are banned from the cabins or anywhere else in the camp. Just like *when* you eat, *what* and *where* you eat will be regulated."

Marion wasn't being fun anymore. First there were all these rules and then punishment if we didn't follow them. No calling home. No eating alone. No freaking gum. I felt like I was in a women's prison, cell block H instead of cabin ten. I imagined sneaking out in the middle of the night with my suitcase and hitching a ride on the dark road down the mountain.

But that thought scared me more than the rules.

Marion's partner in crime, Karen, asked, "Any other questions?"

A tall freckly brunette—*two-forty*—lying with her feet raised on a pillow, said in a confident voice, "Diane. From Florida, the sunshine state. I have a question for ya. When the hell is dinner?"

Everyone, including Marion, laughed.

"In a few minutes," Marion said. "Your families will be eating outside in the picnic area, and y'all will be at your assigned table in the cafeteria. But before we head over, I have to warn you: dinner won't be what you're used to. So don't freak out. The last thing Ms. Diggs needs is a bunch of campers rioting on the first day."

Chapter Five

We walked along the winding path. Charlene stayed by my side, her "Maryland is for Crabs" hat back on her head. As we made our way to the cafeteria, I spotted my parents and Bucky at one of the outdoor picnic tables. I caught my mother's eye and waved.

"Are those your parents?" Charlene asked.

"Uh-huh. And my alien brother."

A smile crossed my face when I saw what the families were eating: meatloaf with gravy and mashed potatoes and something green on the side. Generous helpings, too. Marion had really scared me earlier, but this meal looked wonderful. It made me feel all squishy inside.

When we stepped inside the cafeteria, nearly every chair was occupied. But even though there were girls as far as the eye could see, the room was mostly silent.

"This way!" Marion sang. She reminded me of that extra peppy girl in the movie *Grease*. I wondered if she knew how to do cartwheels. She led us across the room, and Karen followed at the rear. I walked right behind Marion. Another good reason to have my bed by the door: first one in line at mealtime.

When it came to food, I could be quite clever.

Marion took us to the last empty table. Its centerpiece was a roofless miniature log cabin with the number ten painted in black on the side. The inside had been divided into compartments holding napkins, pepper, and olive oil.

No salt. No mustard. No ketchup.

"Let's sit next to each other," Charlene said.

What did I care who I sat next to? I'd be paying way more attention to meat loaf and mashed potatoes than Charlene from Western Maryland.

"Sure," I said, shrugging.

Marion led us to the back of the cafeteria, where orange plastic trays were stacked two feet high, and cheap metal forks, knives, and spoons sat in individual cubbies. The white plastic plates had three separate sections, like giant peace signs.

"Y'all can get one spoonful of whatever you want, one for each section of your plate," Marion said, holding up a number one with her finger, that serious voice taking over again. "No more than *one spoonful* per section. If you break the rule, you won't get dessert."

Dessert! I nearly screamed. *Hallelujah!*

I slid my tray along the metal track, trying not to drool. But when I peeked through the glass, my stomach fell and the happy spit swirling in my mouth dried up. Where was the meatloaf? And the gravy? All I could see were gobs of cooked vegetables.

"I'm not a vegetarian," I told Marion.

"Me neither," she said, as she reached beneath the glass and scooped out a spoonful of green beans, then a spoonful of peas.

"But this is nothing but vegetables."

"It's your first night. Ms. Diggs feels it's important to introduce you right out the gate to all the things we grow. We'll have some meat tomorrow."

Tomorrow? I couldn't wait until tomorrow. I was hungry *now*.

No wonder the room was deathly quiet. I wasn't the only one going through withdrawal. I glanced over my shoulder and observed the sad faces as campers picked at their spinach and corn and beets.

OMG. Even my mother doesn't cook beets.

I craned my neck to see if dessert was really offered, or if Marion had been pulling my chain. But she'd told the truth. There it was, sitting in that big aluminum tub, moving by itself as it often does: Jell-O. Lime freaking Jell-O. I thought I would cry, right there in the cafeteria line.

"You'll be fine," Charlene said from behind me.

"How do you know?" The words came out mean, but I didn't care. I felt like a bear just out of hibernation, starving, and in no mood for chitchat.

"Because I was here last year," Charlene said. "You'll get used to it in about two weeks. The meals I mean. The exercise? Well, that's something I've never gotten used to."

Charlene had been here before.

"Five percent come back again," she went on. "Two percent never make it through an entire summer."

I could feel the pressure of the girls behind me, ogling the skinny beans and the spongy squash, waiting for me to choose. I grabbed the serving spoon, but before I scooped up a bunch of stewed tomatoes, I again scanned the roomful of hungry overweight girls, and wondered in a panic which ones had been here before, once or twice, or more, and what the odds were I would be just like them.

***

I sat in between Charlene and Vanessa—*two-eighty*—a beautiful black girl with her hair wound up high in a bun.

Ms. Diggs' soft crackly voice came over the loud speakers: "Please bow your head in silence as we thank this food for giving us vitality in body, mind, and spirit. Thank you, food, for giving us life."

That was it. That was the whole prayer.

We dug in. My dinner had vanished in fifteen seconds. Maybe less.

I slurped up my Jell-O as Charlene on my right and Vanessa on my left chattered happily in my ears, but I was still grumpy. The brochure said we'd be getting up to 1,200 calories per day. What I had just consumed amounted to about ten. How could anyone sustain themselves on that? Even back when I played lacrosse I ate more than this. Maybe Ms. Diggs' goal was to make us look like *Survivor* contestants before summer's end. Make us look like her.

After everyone had eaten, Ms. Diggs said, "Counselors, please show your campers our recycling and compost bins, then let them meet with their families to say goodbye. Our bonfire reception at the lake will start in one hour."

"Will there be S'mores?" I asked Marion as she showed us to the compost bin outside the back door.

"Oh, Simone," Marion said with a laugh. "You're funny. S'mores are illegal around here. Rice cakes and green tea."

I didn't even know what rice cakes were, exactly, except that they had no business calling themselves *cakes*. And green tea? OMG. And whoever heard of a bonfire without S'mores? Wasn't that sacrilege regarding American tradition?

I had to be dreaming. That was it. I was caught in a nightmare. Tomorrow I'd wake up, crawl to our family's kitchen table in my favorite SpongeBob pajamas, and sit down to a hearty breakfast of pancakes, overcooked bacon, eggs fried in the grease, and a large glass of whole milk. That was breakfast. That was real life.

***

My mother cried, even though it should have been me. I let her hug me as long as she needed.

"I love you, Simone," she told me, burying her face in my thick hair. "I know you'll do fine here. Just fine."

Instead of telling her I loved her, I said, "Please take care of Muggs. She's going to go crazy without me."

After another squeeze, she released me and walked around to the passenger side of the car. "Say goodbye to your brother," she added before getting in.

Bucky was already in the back seat.

"Later," he said, shutting his door before I had a chance to ignore him.

That left my father and me.

"Well," he said. He coughed and then leaned into me and offered a hug that was filled with all kinds of uncomfortable stuff. He pulled away quickly and got into the driver's seat. My mother rolled down her window and waved a teary goodbye as my family drove out onto the darkening dirt road leading out of the camp. I stared at the tracks the Volvo had left in the dirt.

"You alright?"

Charlene clicked on her flashlight.

"Sure," I said. "Why wouldn't I be?"

The sun was setting, and we stood among the shadows of blue and pink and orange. A cool wind blew through the trees.

"Some girls have a hard time letting go," Charlene said.

"Especially when it hits them that they won't have their families to placate them for the summer."

"I've been going to summer camps since I was eight," I told her. "They're all the same."

"You think so?"

I walked beside her as she led us toward the sound of voices echoing through the trees.

"Look," Charlene said. "Marion and Karen, they've been coming here for three years, which is why they're counselors now. And counselors have to act, you know, superior to the campers. If you really want to know about this place, I can give you some honest answers."

We walked side by side, our feet crunching the twigs and needles. The scent of pine logs burning nearby entered the air. A Demi Lovato tune played in the distance, her voice floating through the trees like a ghost-song.

"What would I want to know?" I asked.

"Well, like the diet thing. You think that's going to be the hardest part. Or the exercise, which totally sucks. But really, those are a joke compared to the rest."

"The rest of what?"

"Losing weight," Charlene said. "Becoming balanced in mind, spirit, and body, as Ms. Diggs says, doesn't begin with food."

"It doesn't?"

She shook her head. "You have to get healthy on the inside before you can get healthy on the outside."

"You mean, like, with diet pills?"

I'll admit I was a little confused.

"Pills?" she said, stopping in the middle of the path and pointing the flashlight between us. "No way. That might be the way some doctors handle it, but not here. At Kamama, you reflect, think about things, talk things out, go to powwows—"

"Girls?" A woman's voice came from a dark silhouette on the path behind us. A dim light from the direction of the lake made its way through the trees. "It's me, Mary."

"Camp nurse," Charlene whispered.

"Get on down to the bonfire please. They're taking roll."

"Yes, ma'am," Charlene said.

"Yes, ma'am," I repeated, as we headed carefully down the slope toward the lake, Charlene's flashlight bouncing up to the trees with each heavy step.

The beach was alive with fire, the flames reaching high into the air. The moon hovered above the eastern edge of the lake, its plump reflection casting a yellow image on the water's surface. Girls were everywhere. Some sat on beach chairs, others on towels on the sand, and some wandered around, flitting from one group to another. Already girls were forming little clusters.

I stayed glued to Charlene's side as she introduced me to campers from all over: Stephanie from upstate New York; Helen from Georgia; Betsy from Florida; Petra from Canada.

"You've already met Vanessa," Charlene said, taking the pretty black girl by the arm. "She's in our bunk."

Vanessa and I said hi to one another.

"Vanessa is working things out," Charlene said. "Aren't you, Vanessa?"

"Have you been here before, too?" I asked her.

Vanessa nodded. "A bunch of us have been here before. You were lucky they chose you. The odds of getting in are slimmer every year." She snorted a laugh. "*Slimmer*. Get it?"

When the cabin counselors had finished roll call, rice cakes and cold stainless steel bottles filled with green tea were handed out. I looked at my bottle and read the words on the side, printed in neat black Sharpie: "Camp Kamama: Simone Wheeler."

"Cool," I said. I had seen one like it at Target for over ten dollars.

Vanessa said, "My mom says these are way better than that plastic crap. She's all into that environmental stuff."

"The camp tries to stay away from anything throwaway," Charlene told me. "Keep this through the whole summer. If you lose it, you can only earn another one by cleaning the swimming pool."

Thinking of swimming made me think of our instructor.

"That Jake Stonewolf is something else," I said, the comment popping out on its own.

Vanessa nodded. "Mmm-hmm."

"I know, right?" Charlene said. "I think he's more buff than last year."

"His hair got longer, too," Vanessa said, uncapping her water bottle and peering into the liquid darkness. "I wonder how my mama would like it if I brought home a pet Cherokee instead of a papier-mâché squirrel."

A voice came over a loudspeaker hidden in the shadows of the trees.

"Ten minutes until bunk time."

"Time to get cleaned up," Charlene said. "We have about an hour before bed."

I looked at my watch. It was only nine o'clock. "We go to bed at ten?"

"Rule Number Seventeen: lights out at ten on the dot. Remember the contract?"

"Guess I skipped over that one," I said.

"Well," Charlene said, "there'll be some nights you won't be able to keep your eyes open that late."

Vanessa said, "Some nights you'll fall asleep at dinner."

"I doubt that," I told them. "At home, I go to bed around midnight and get up at six-thirty every day."

"That's your other home," Charlene said. "For the summer, this is home. Ms. Diggs and Mary are your moms, Jake is your dad, and all these girls are your sisters. Including me."

"And me," Vanessa said, yawning.

As I sipped the bitter green tea, a flash of light from across the lake caught my eye. Without thinking, I walked to the water's edge. Charlene and Vanessa followed.

"Looks like they're having a bonfire, too," I said, nodding toward the flickering orange and yellow light in the distance.

"Goody for them," Charlene said.

Vanessa shook her head. "Mmm-mmm."

I thought about all the different camp signs we had passed on the way up to Kamama. I wondered if the camp across the lake was one of the Christian ones, or maybe one of the sports ones.

"Are they the enemy?" I asked.

I had gone to my first lacrosse camp just before middle school, and there was another camp less than a mile's trek through the woods. A dance camp. The battle was on the second one of the girls from the other camp painted the word "DYKE" across the front of one of our cabin doors. I don't think we even knew at the time what the word meant, but the war lasted the entire two weeks of camp, each camp trying to outdo the other's prank.

"*Enemy* is too good a word for them," Charlene said.

"What did they do?"

"It's not what they *did*," Vanessa said. "It's who they *are*."

I strained to get a better look. In the dark, even with the

brightness of the nearly full moon, I could barely make out the flames over there, let alone any people.

"Who are they?" I asked.

"Felines," Charlene and Vanessa whispered at the same time.

"Cat people?" I asked, my mind picturing a character from *Batman*.

Charlene laughed. "*Beautiful* people. You know, girls who were born that way."

"No matter what they do," Vanessa said, "their lives will turn out perfectly."

Charlene said, "Most of them are rich."

Vanessa added, "And spoiled."

Charlene suddenly grabbed me by the wrist and put her face close to mine. She sang in a whisper: "The girls at Camp Felina love to eat their canned Purina; they purr and meow and cry like cats, but deep inside they're really rats."

Vanessa laughed.

Charlene let go of my wrist. "I know Camp Kamama says the lake is a choice spot for reflecting, but it's not worth it. How can a person reflect with that business going on over there? Those perfect little bodies showing off their itty bitty bikinis, making the girls at our camp feel even worse about themselves. It's like a freaking beauty pageant over there. When it's time to reflect, follow the marked paths on the Kamama map. Seriously."

"Listen to Charlene," Vanessa said. "She knows what she's talking about." She screwed the cap back onto her water bottle. "I'm gonna hit it, girls. Check you back at the bunk."

Vanessa disappeared into the dark beyond the dying fire.

Charlene glanced up at the moon and yawned. "We should head back as well. I still have to take a shower. I haven't stopped sweating since I got out of the car this afternoon."

"Me neither."

"Well," Charlene said as we followed her flashlight beam up the path, "you might as well get used to it. It's gonna be one helluva long, sweaty summer."

Chapter Six

Before the sun had barely tapped its fingertips against the cabin windows, a song blasted through the screened door, nearly pushing my heart through my chest. I sat up, forgetting for a moment where I was, then looked around at my bunkmates as they, too, were startled into consciousness.

Through speakers somewhere up in the trees blared a song from the eighties, "I'm Walking on Sunshine." My mom sometimes played that and other throwback music while she did housework.

"That's our wake-up call," Marion said over the music. She got out of bed and stretched. She had slept in her Kamama shirt and shorts from the day before. I noticed that a lot of the girls did. I wore my SpongeBob pajamas—not because they reminded me of home, but because they were super comfy.

"Get dressed, y'all," Karen said. "Breakfast in an hour."

"An hour?" I heard myself ask under my breath.

"Yup," Charlene said, pushing her feet into a pair of slippers. "After sunrise yoga."

"Yoga?"

"Girl, you really didn't read much about this place did you?"

"I—"

But Charlene was already shuffling her way across the cabin floor to the bathroom.

I sighed as I changed into my Camp Kamama T-shirt and a fresh pair of shorts. I slid on my Crocs and waited in line for the bathroom. As the loud song finally faded, Marion hiked us down to the lake where leftover kindling was the only sign that there had been a bonfire the night before. A large white bird swooped down over the lake toward the other side.

I told Charlene, "I've never done yoga before."

"That's okay. You'll get the moves down in no time."

"What if some of us don't want to do it?"

But Charlene didn't need to give me an answer. Of course I would want to do it. Jake Stonewolf was the instructor.

Somehow, he and the counselors effortlessly got all one hundred or so girls to line up in long straight rows across the narrow beach.

I glanced toward the other side of the lake, positive I would see a pyramid of cheerleaders, the prettiest one on top watching us through a pair of binoculars, ready to pass down information to the girls below. But the other side of the lake was empty and still. I found myself envious that the Felinas got to sleep in and would probably wake up to a happy breakfast.

"If you prefer to do this barefoot," Jake said as he slipped out of his sandals, "then go for it."

I slipped off my Crocs and let my feet sink into the soft cool sand.

"Sit down, please, and cross your legs," Jake said.

It was funny to see so many girls plunk down on their rear

ends in unison. I felt like part of a water ballet team.

Jake explained how to sit lotus-style, back straight, cross-legged, with each foot on the opposite thigh. Hardly anyone near me could perform this task. I heard Charlene and our loud bunkmate, Diane from Florida, cuss under their breath, but I held in my angst. Somehow, I managed to cross my legs, though within seconds my toes began to tingle from lack of circulation.

"I'm going to teach you how to breathe properly," Jake said in his deep voice, a voice that was somehow monotone and sexy at the same time. "Close your eyes, and listen to your bodies."

A few counselors walked around to make sure we were breathing.

"Breathe in for ten seconds, then breathe out for ten seconds. In through your nose, out through your mouth. Slowly. Deliberately. Listen to your breath as it comes into your lungs, and goes out again. Air is life. Treat it with respect."

I had to stifle a giggle. This all seemed so silly, like a scene from one of my mother's 1980's videos of women in Spandex touching their toes while their sweatbands hold back their Aqua-Net hairdos.

But after a moment, the giggles melted away, and for the next few minutes I did as Jake asked: I breathed. My body relaxed as my spine curved a bit, my shoulders dipped, and my head rolled forward. I wasn't asleep, and yet I was. I could hear birds and critters in the nearby woods, but I could also hear my own breathing as my lungs filled, then released. In and out, in and out. I was suddenly floating above the sand, like a feather that isn't in any hurry to land. I felt the girls around me, could hear their breathing too, but I didn't feel separate from them. It was like we were all part of the same organism.

As I was getting ready to float above the lake, Jake Stonewolf's voice came to me.

"...slowly...good...that's it...now open your eyes."

We opened our eyes.

The sun had changed positions.

Jake motioned for us to follow his lead. Together we stood and shook out our legs and feet.

"Imitate what I do," he said.

He started bending his body in ways I had no idea such a tall, muscular man could bend. Leaning over, with his arms dangling down, he touched the sand with the palms of his hands. My hands made it to a place just below my knees. Not too bad for a girl who hadn't exercised in two years except in her own one-woman race to the fridge. Standing again, Jake bent his right leg so his knee pointed outward, and placed the bottom of his right foot against the inside of his left thigh. "Tree Pose," he said, bringing the palms of his hands together in front of his heart. "Grow your branches," he said, raising his arms up and out toward the sky. He performed his tree imitation for thirty seconds on the uneven sand, never moving an inch. I never even got my foot onto my thigh, though I did make it as high as my calf. A few girls fell over into the sand.

Tim-ber!

I am proud to say I was not among the fallen.

We spent the hour bending this way and that, like the green rubber Gumby that hung from my aunt's rearview mirror. The sun crested the tops of the pines, and growling stomachs broke through the morning quiet.

When our Cirque de Soleil contortionist tricks were finished, it was time to eat. *Thank God*, I thought. Anymore time without food and they'd have to roll my weak body like a beach ball to the cafeteria.

Cabins ate in numerical order, so sleeping by the cabin door was a waste of time. As cabin number ten, we had to wait until everyone else had their food. The positive side was that I got to see what breakfast consisted of before my tired, hungry brain was thrown into shock. That morning's treat was a bowl of oatmeal, the portion perfect for Little Miss Muffet or Baby Bear, with honey and raisins and cinnamon. On the side we got one piece of whole wheat toast covered with dark berry jam, a small cup of yogurt, and our choice of grapefruit juice or green tea.

Grace was said.

My food was gone in less than a minute.

Charlene said, "Eating slowly makes you feel fuller faster."

Vanessa agreed with her mouth full: "Mmm-hmm."

I thought about whether or not that was true as I rubbed my finger against the inside of my bowl, hoping to scrape out another thimbleful of mush.

Ms. Diggs' voice came through the speakers: "Counselors, please show your campers how the daily scheduling will work."

Karen pushed some trays out of the way as Marion set her clipboard on the table. She tapped different parts of the page with a pencil. "Y'all started with sunrise yoga, then breakfast, like the rest of the camp," Marion explained. "But this is where you'll separate. The cabins double up. First you go to cooking class, then on to the obstacle course, then reflection, then lunch. After that, we meet in the garden, then on to swimming, then expression time, where you can do something in the crafts room like make jewelry or draw or whatever, or tool around in the music room. After that, you go to powwow. Then it's dinner and whatever they have planned for us afterward. A copy of the schedule is posted outside the office door, and outside our cabin door. Any questions?"

"That's a lot of stuff to fit into one day," Diane said in her confident loud voice. She reminded me of my former lacrosse coach. "How much time do we have between each?"

"Fifteen minutes. All meals last forty-five minutes, and all activities are an hour."

"What about other stuff?" Sabrina from South Carolina asked. She sure did like her tie-dye. Today, it was her knee-high socks, covered in smears of green and red and yellow, which she wore with a pair of Dr. Scholl sandals. She looked like an editor for some 1960's magazine. "Like kayaking?" she added.

"Don't worry," Marion said. "They just want y'all to get used to this place first. The altitude and all. There'll be plenty of off-site activities starting in a week. Anything else?"

No one said anything.

"Good," Marion said. "While we were at yoga this morning, a backpack was placed on your beds. Karen and I each have one, too. Every bag has a name tag. Inside there's a map, sunscreen, bug spray, a whistle, and some other stuff. Sort of like a gift basket. Except that you'll be carrying this bag with you every day for the rest of the summer, along with your water bottle. Don't lose anything. Be sure to fill up your water bottles ahead of time, either with water or green tea, since y'all will need to stay hydrated. We don't want anyone fainting out there."

Chapter Seven

My backpack started to feel like fifty pounds before I even stepped out of the cabin. It was not only filled with all those goodies Marion had mentioned, it also contained a small flashlight and a pair of ankle weights. By the time I reached the cooking class—AKA the Kamama Café—sweat had soaked the top of my shirt.

We were combined with cabin number nine, so the twenty of us would be spending the summer cooking together. Charlene, Vanessa, Diane and I collected together outside the doorway.

"You're gonna love this," Charlene said.

Vanessa nodded in agreement.

Diane said, "I've never cooked anything but microwavable Hot Pockets. I sure hope they know what they're doing, having me in their kitchen."

The Kamama Café was a long narrow room. Taking up two-thirds of the space were five round tables and a bunch of chairs around them. All of the tables had pale pink tablecloths and real flower centerpieces. Near the doorway was a long line of wall pegs with hanging aprons like the ones we used to wear in kindergarten for finger painting. The walls were covered in framed paintings of flowers and hillsides and sunsets. Watercolors, oils, gouache. On shelves sat dozens of mixing bowls and stacks of dishes. From the ceiling hung a rectangular wire rack with large s-hooks that held onto a variety of pots and pans. Some were Teflon, like the ones we had at home, others were copper. Six stoves, with ovens underneath, squatted at the far end of the room. Above them were a bunch of oak cabinets. A long narrow island with four deep sinks ran parallel to the stoves. Off to the side, a narrow table held three microwaves, and along the wall opposite, there stood two large stainless steel refrigerators, the kind with freezers on the bottom.

The instructor, Wilhelmina, was tall and willowy, her bleached yellow hair cropped at the neck, a bunch of friendship bracelets around both wrists. She wore a tall white chef's hat on her head and an apron around her neck with stains spattered across a picture of a French street scene. Below her apron, a pair of tan muscular legs looked like they belonged to a professional tennis player.

"She's pretty chill," Charlene said as we dropped our bags on the floor underneath the hanging aprons.

"I heard she likes playing dead rock and roller CD's while we cook," Diane said.

Charlene nodded. "A little Led Zepplin to help you make smoothies, a little AC/DC to help you make quiche."

"She's been in some magazines," Vanessa said. "Invented something called beet juice reduction."

I nervously took a chug of water from my bottle as Wilhelmina waited for us in the center of the room. She clapped her hands and out poured a Western North Carolina drawl. "Girls, let's settle down. Please grab an apron from one of the pegs and put it on. Every time ya'll come into this room that will be the first thing you do."

While we slipped into our aprons, the instructor continued.

"For those of ya'll who don't know me, I'm Wilhelmina, but call me Willie. My dad wanted a boy, so he called me that, and it sort of stuck in my gut.

"By now y'all have heard bits and pieces of what'll take place in this room during your time here. Some true, like how many of y'all will become incredible chefs, and some that are out and out lies, like we spend our precious time making caramel apples and deep-fried Twinkies. I can also tell that some of you are intimidated by what you see around you, the stoves, the beautiful cutlery…"

"What's *cutlery*?" I whispered to Charlene.

"Knives."

"Oh." A new word to add to my list.

Willie went on. "Some of you may think you've got zero talent when it comes to cooking. Or maybe you hate the thought of preparing food because it takes you away from your Twitter account or your Instagram page. But you'll change your mind in this room. Cooking expertise does not come from imitating what you see on YouTube or in a *Gourmet Cooking* photo. It doesn't need to be stressful, or fattening, or gluttonous. My main goal is to get y'all to see how easy and fun it is to eat right. That preparing some of your own meals, even for your whole family, will give you an incredible feeling of being in control. Your love for fatty foods will begin to disappear as you discover there are other great foods to take their place.

"Creating here at Café Kamama will come from a place

within yourselves that perhaps ya'll cannot yet see. A place that is deep and personal, and maybe a bit shy. But it's a place to tap into while in this room without fearing any negative consequences.

"Now, let's talk science. A calorie is a unit of energy. When I tell you that a certain food contains a certain amount of calories, I'm describing how much energy your body gets from eating or drinking it. Your optimum caloric intake while on any healthy weight-loss program should be around 1,200 calories a day. Any less than that and you risk low sugar, messing up your hormones, and so on. Ten grams should be from fat, fifty grams from protein, and at least thirty grams from fiber. You must always remember that no matter what type of program you choose, your body needs calories for energy. Calories are what keep us alive.

"Lastly, I don't do this gig with any sort of regulated outline other than the caloric guidelines." Willie leaned in to us and whispered, "In other words, I teach this class however the hell I want."

The room let out a laugh, Diane's the loudest.

"So," Willie said, "around here y'all will find everything one needs to create meals that are not only quick and easy, but healthy. Nearly everything we cook comes from the Kamama garden. We have specific recipes we'll be using, but ya'll will also have a chance to experiment."

"Cool," someone whispered behind me.

"This camp has a lot of rules, I know," Willie went on, "and they apply in this room as well. In addition to that list, there is one more y'all must obey: be honest with what it is you are trying to create. Oh, sorry, one last rule." She held up a large whisk and hammered it against the air. "Be neat, or don't eat." She laughed as she walked toward the back of the room. "The first thing ya'll are going to do is take a little tour with me. Don't be shy. Come on over to our kitchen, and I'll introduce you. Y'all aren't here to sit idly. Y'all are here to create!"

We clustered around the island.

"Girls, meet some of the best friends you'll make this summer: our appliances!"

She made us touch the stoves, open the ovens, turn the tap water on and off, hold a couple of pots and pans in our hands. She picked up a long chopping knife, twice as long as the largest one my mom had, and caressed the sharp blade with her finger. She told us she would do all of the cutting in the beginning, that we would do the actual cooking.

When we were through with the tour, Willie went to a cabinet and pulled down the largest bottle of olive oil I've ever seen, then asked a girl over by the wall to hand her a large frying pan. Willie unscrewed the cap from the oil, went to the stove and turned it on, then placed the pan on top.

She turned toward a girl near the back of the group.

"Darling, would you press play on that old contraption back there?" Willie pointed to a worn silver boom box.

The girl pressed the button. Ancient rock and roll music blared through two tiny speakers.

"For my first trick," Willie said as she adjusted the flame beneath the pan, "I'm going to show y'all how incredible dishes can be created without grease or white sugar or salt. How eating what you cook can be done with finesse, and joy can be discovered in the process."

Chapter Eight

As we left the cooking class, Charlene grabbed my arm.

"Spoiler warning: this next activity sucks."

Obstacle course.

"Last year," she said, "I tried to ditch early on. You know, thinking it was like study hall, when you miss the first day, and the teacher thinks she has the attendance sheet wrong. But around here, that doesn't work. I hid in the bathroom for a while, but when that got boring, I took a walk by myself in the woods until they busted me."

"Were you punished?" I asked.

"No dessert for a week."

"Jell-O? Big deal."

"I thought the same thing…until they took it away from me."

I wondered what excuse I could give that no one had yet thought of. Something physical that would keep me from running around an obstacle course. Could appendicitis be faked? Could I give myself a fever? Feign menstrual cramps? That last one had worked once to get out of gym class, but only because we'd had a male substitute.

Charlene and I walked with our group down the path to the course. On the sidelines stood Ms. Diggs, wearing a pair of tan Capri pants with her oversized Kamama T-shirt, those funky tennis shoes, and a pair of ankle weights. Her long hair was still tucked under a bandana, but it was knotted into a bun at her neck.

I glanced at the course behind her. It looked different than when Marion had introduced it during orientation. Now, there were more obstacles. *Way* more.

"She looks too tiny to teach this," I whispered to Charlene.

"Don't let her fool you."

"Okay, girls," Ms. Diggs said, clapping her hands for emphasis. "We only have so much time. Grab your ankle weights from your backpacks, then put your packs on that tarp over there. Make sure your name tags are visible so you don't mix them up."

By the time most of us had managed to Velcro our ankle weights—Charlene and I took turns holding each other up while strapping on the two-pounders—Ms. Diggs had already begun.

"Woo-hoo!" she called.

We turned in her direction. Like a wild horse let out of a pen, she scrambled up and over a short wooden fence, then a second. She ran over to a sandy area and fell to the ground like a front-line marine. Before her lay a twenty-foot tunnel that looked like it had been stolen from a kid's birthday party, made of orange parachute material and held together by a giant coil. The bottom section of it was buried in the sand to keep it from rolling away. When Ms. Diggs reappeared from the other end, she hopped onto a balance beam two feet above the ground. Along the fifteen-foot beam she pranced like a ballerina, grinning like a kid.

"Go, Ms. Diggs!" Diane hollered, and all the girls, me included, began to cheer her on.

Ms. Diggs made a silly dismount off the balance beam, then stopped in front of a row of four long foam blocks. Each one stood about a foot high. She swung her arms back in a wide arch, bent her knees, and jumped over the first. Within seconds, she had jumped over all four. With her shaking fists in the air, she shouted, "Woo-hoo!" again.

"She's like a miniature Iron Man," I said, laughing.

"Iron *Woman*," Charlene corrected.

"Iron *Freak*," Vanessa added.

We continued to cheer as Ms. Diggs climbed the ladder that led to the monkey bars. She glanced behind her as if someone were chasing her, then, like a monkey, she swung across the bars, never falling, never stopping to catch her breath. I was running out of air just watching her.

She dropped from the last monkey bar to the ground and ran to a round cement spot in the middle of the course. She picked up one of the jump ropes from a pile and shouted, "Girls rule, boys drool!" We counted with her as she jumped ten times, quick as a hummingbird. She threw the jump rope down, and we cheered her on to the next spot, another cement area, this one a rectangular blacktop with a white line painted at one end and a basketball hoop at the other. From a large tub she drew a basketball, stood on the line dribbling for a moment, then threw it. Into the basket it went.

I was astounded.

She missed the second one, much to the chagrin of her cheerleaders, but then made the third, and continued on her way. By now, we girls were thinned out in a long line that bordered one side of the course, following her progress.

"Go, Ms. Diggs! Go, Ms. Diggs!"

I laughed again, trying to ignore the inner voice reminding me I wouldn't be so cheerful in a few minutes.

On the course, Ms. Diggs moved to a soft spot of earth and picked up one of a dozen Hula-hoops.

"Count to ten!" she ordered.

"One…two…"

That Hula-hoop spun around her body like a planet orbiting at warp speed around the sun.

"…nine…ten!"

Next was the tire course. I used to run the tires during lacrosse practice, but now the thought made me nervous. I could barely *see* my feet, let alone stomp in and out of those tires. Ms. Diggs' feet dipped in and out, over and over, like a professional football player's. Not once did she trip. Not once did she *almost* trip.

After the tires, she dashed over to a zigzagged row of twenty orange cones. Around the cones she zoomed in crazy eights, never touching a single one, never losing her balance, even in those drugstore tennis shoes.

She rounded the last of the cones and ran to a high bar that sat nestled between two tall trees. She stood on a small step beneath the bar, jumped up, and grabbed the bar with both hands. She began to do pull-ups.

We girls stood on the sidelines, counting, "One…two…three…four…"

While we counted, I observed Ms. Diggs. There was something so determined about that face. Something so incredibly intense.

"…ten!"

Ms. Diggs dropped to the ground and ran to a large blue mat in the far corner of the course. She fell onto the mat. I thought for sure she had collapsed from exhaustion, but she was far from collapsing. She lay on her back with her knees pointed toward the sky, folded her arms behind her head, and performed sit-ups. Again the girls chanted the numbers, and when we reached twenty, Ms. Diggs stood up, sprinted to a tall tree stump, picked up a rubber mallet, and banged it against a large cow bell that was hooked to the side of the stump. She gave a wide bow.

The girls cheered. Ms. Diggs beamed. Her smile nearly took over her reddened freckled face.

"That was totally amazing," I told Charlene.

"She'll do this five times today," Charlene said.

"Five times?"

"She has to show each group how it's done. Even later on, when the girls have the course memorized, Ms. Diggs'll sometimes join in."

I thought Ms. Diggs was super human. That maybe she had bionic parts or was taking steroids. Her personality was like a real-life version of Miss Frizzle, from the *Magic School Bus* cartoon I loved as a kid. I was waiting for her to say, "Get busy—make mistakes!" and then take us on a joyride through the galaxy.

"Where do you think she gets her energy?" I asked Charlene.

"I'm sure you'd find the energy if you almost died."

"Died?"

I was suddenly pushed into the middle of the group as we were forced into a long line.

"Shortest in front, tallest in back," Ms. Diggs said. She wasn't even out of breath. "That way nature decides who goes first. Tomorrow we switch from tallest to shortest. Those of you in the middle, enjoy."

As the bunch of us worked to get our height in order, I fell somewhere in the middle. But I didn't have hope for too much enjoyment regardless of my height.

Before I could see where Charlene, Vanessa, or Diane had landed in the lineup, a loud whistle blew, the front of the line started to diminish, and I was forced to follow the rest of the pack through the course. I could hear Ms. Diggs' voice grow louder and glanced over to see a megaphone, the kind the cheerleaders used at school, held against her lips. As if she wasn't loud enough on her own.

As I struggled to get over the two short fences, my shin scraped against the wood, drawing a spot of blood. I felt my thighs rub and burn as I crawled through the tunnel, but was relieved not to have become stuck. I fell off the balance beam four times before I made it to the end. The jumps looked easy enough, but I ended up knocking down two of the foam blocks. I looked behind me to see a counselor picking them up again for the next girl. The monkey bars made me the most nervous. I hadn't played on those things since elementary school. I climbed the ladder and stretched my arms until I had a hold of the first rung. Another girl—*three-fifteen*—dangled three rungs in front of me, kicking her legs but not moving forward. Another in the lead would fall, jump up to catch the bars, then fall again. The girl in front of me slipped and landed hard on her butt. I had barely gripped the first rung when I followed her to the ground.

"Keep moving!" Ms. Diggs shouted. "You don't want to get kicked in the head!"

I took her words seriously as I scrambled on all fours in the dirt, dodging the spastic legs hanging from the bars, reaching my hand out to help the girl in the front get to her feet. Somehow, I made my way to the jump ropes. I thought this would be the easiest; after all, jumping rope had once been part of my lacrosse training. But I was wrong. By the time I'd counted to ten, I thought I would puke.

The next part, the free-throws, was a bit calmer. I picked up the basketball and made the first shot. Then I made the next. And the third. No one cheered for me, each girl caught up in her own crazy world of obstacles, but I heard a silent cheer inside my head, and oddly enough it sounded like my father's voice.

Pushing the voice away, I moved on to the Hula-hoops, but the plastic ring never made it higher than my knees. Nearly spent, I stumbled to the tires. I tripped on the second to the last one, my stomach making contact with the tire's edge. I made it to the cones, slipping in the dirt, but catching myself before I did a face plant. I managed half of one pull-up and three sit-ups, and by the time I'd made it to the finish line, fainting or having a stroke felt like a strong possibility. My heart was trying to climb out of my chest. I bent over with my hands on my knees then sucked down water from my bottle.

While the rest of the girls finished their way around the course, and just as I was about to collapse onto the dirt in a celebratory moment of personal achievement, Ms. Diggs' encouraging yet authoritative voice bellowed through her megaphone. I believed she was going to praise us. Tell us how amazing we were, how impressed she was. That we had worked harder than any other group she'd ever witnessed at Camp Kamama, and we'd be rewarded with sugar cookies and a nap.

But that is not what happened.

"Again!" she shouted through the megaphone. "You don't think you're only going to do this once, do you? We have another twenty minutes to kill! Woo-hoo!"

I tried not to let the water rise up from my stomach, sucked in a few deep breaths, and once again hauled my butt over the first of the two fences.

Chapter Nine

"Reflection time," Ms. Diggs sang as she handed each of us a power bar before shooing us away like little flies. "Think, pray, write, sing, be one with yourselves."

"Bye, guys," Vanessa said as she headed up the hill.

Diane gave a weak salute as she trudged behind Vanessa. I don't think she had any breath left over to actually say goodbye.

"Later, Simone," Charlene said as she picked up her backpack and swung it over a shoulder. "Don't forget to drink lots of water, and wear your whistle."

My ribs were in spasms, my cheeks on fire. I managed to ask, "Where are you going?"

"Last summer, I found a private spot behind our cabin. There's a stump back there, and no one's ever around."

One by one, the rest of the girls hiked away from the obstacle course, disappearing along the different paths that led into the trees.

"Where should I go?" I asked Charlene, suddenly feeling abandoned.

"Use your map. All the Kamama trails are marked in red."

"Which one do you recommend?"

"I can't recommend one," she told me. "You'll know it when you find it."

"How?"

"It'll be the place that calls to you."

Charlene started up the slight incline toward the cabins, looking over her shoulder one last time. "Whatever you do, Simone, don't miss lunch. A power bar and bottled water won't sustain you until dinner." She disappeared into the trees.

I stood on the edge of the empty obstacle course. Ms. Diggs was picking up cones and placing them back where they belonged. The monkey bars, the tires, even the tunnel seemed harmless without a bunch of panting girls attacking them. I turned to the sound of laughter as the next group rambled down the path. It was their turn now.

You won't be laughing for very long.

I wolfed down the fiber bar, guzzled some more water, and pulled the map out of my backpack. I unfolded it. In the map's middle was a big blue lake with *Camp Kamama* labeled in red ink beneath it. Within the trees on the map lay a spider web of bold red lines, each one representing a different path, each one going off in a different direction. There were so many choices. *Too* many.

Since I trusted fate more than myself, I would let fate decide, so if my choice turned out to be a mistake, I had something other than my own bad judgment to blame. I flattened the map as best I could against a tree trunk, closed my eyes, pointed a finger, and let it spiral toward the map. When I opened my eyes again, the tip of my finger lay against a spot to the west of the lake. Camp Kamama sat on the south side, so all I had to do was go left and then curve up a little. My legs were rubbery, like I'd just run the length of a dozen lacrosse fields, as I pulled my cumbersome backpack onto my back and headed in the direction that fate had chosen for me.

Chapter Ten

It took longer than I'd suspected. For fifteen minutes I made my way along the uneven path, passing the occasional camper either sitting in the lotus position beneath a tree, reading a book while sitting on a stump, or still wandering like I was. The trees were the same as the ones surrounding our cabins, pine and birch and fir, but the forest seemed thicker and less disturbed. The early afternoon sun was mostly blocked by the canopy, and I enjoyed the shade's coolness, the light breeze as it poured over my sweat like a giant fan.

Fate had chosen a spot on the map where the red line came to an abrupt stop, even though the path itself continued. There, in the middle of the trail, I stood face-to-face with an enormous tree, probably as old as the mountain itself, like a sentry protecting Kamama's border. I think the tree was a beech or maybe a basswood. Whatever it was, it stood out like a sore thumb, since most of the trees surrounding our cabins had skinny black trunks. This trunk had to be four, maybe five feet across. Its bark was dark gray, like elephant skin. Scores of tiny holes, small warts, and a collection of large goiters were scattered up and down the tree, and the twisted branches way up high seemed more like a fancy ceiling than a treetop.

I could barely make out the lake to my right as the sun's rays reflected like on the water like sparkling jewels. I heard the sound of a rabbit or other critter as it scurried through the underbrush somewhere nearby.

I stared up at the tree again. It wasn't only its size that attracted me to it, or the shade it offered. It was what lay on the ground at the base of the wide trunk: a solid four-foot log, perfect for sitting. I placed my hand against its bark a moment, dropped my pack onto the ground, and plopped down onto the log.

It wasn't until I sat that I realized how spent I was. My quads throbbed, and I had to rub my right calf to knock out the Charlie horse trying to invade. Twice around that freaking course. And this was only the first day, I silently whined.

My stomach gave a low grumble. To be sure I'd make it back to the cafeteria in time for lunch, I set the little timer on my watch. I readjusted my cap and shook out my shirt which was plastered with sweat to my stomach. I absently fanned the tiny no-see-ums away from my face.

For a moment I sat there, not doing anything, just breathing and listening to the woods around me. Catbirds called to one another and blue jays squawked like angry parrots. I listened to tiny paws as they skittered in the bushes alongside the path, and larger ones that roamed among the trees a little farther away.

I shut my eyes. Tight shoulder muscles started to relax. The pain in my legs subsided. The pulse in my neck slowed. I concentrated on my breathing, like Jake had demonstrated during yoga, and let myself melt into the rhythm. I no longer felt overheated or bothered by bugs, could no longer hear the birds or other animals, only the sound of my breathing. In and out. In and out.

Soon, a stream of thoughts poured into my head, as though they had been lodged behind a dam and were breaking through. The flood carried with it bits and pieces from the last few years, coming to me as clearly as if they'd occurred yesterday. There I was, playing lacrosse as the only freshman the high school lacrosse team had ever allowed on the varsity team. The stands were full of roaring fans, stomping their feet, calling my name: "Wheel-er! Wheel-er! Wheel-er!"

But I had no control over the fragments zipping through my memory, as the scene changed from a playing field to my father, sitting in the stands, his face large and close-up like he was underneath a magnifying glass. He was smiling and cheering, along with the other fans. I could feel my own smile form, and then fade, as his features went from Proud Daddy to Sad Daddy. His eyes stopped twinkling. How could I get the sparkle to come back to those eyes? I wondered. But before I thought of a way, his face disappeared, and I was suddenly flying in the air over my house, as light as a helium-filled balloon. My mother worked down below, planting herbs in the narrow garden on the side of the house. Bucky rode his skateboard in the empty field behind our back fence, where he and his friends had constructed ramps and railings to practice their jumps. And then I spotted my father again, only this time he was mowing the lawn, his Nascar cap covering his head. I called to him, "Hey, Dad!" to show him my new talent was flying, that I didn't need lacrosse to make me special. His face turned upward, and his eyes lit up—

A ringing sound entered my ears. A tinny bell, from somewhere close by: *ding-ding-ding…ding-ding-ding…*

My thumb instinctively pressed the timer button on my

watch. I shook my head and opened my eyes. All of the thoughts and memories were quickly drifting away, and I could only capture bits of them before they floated completely out of reach.

Had I reflected the right way? Were my thoughts the ones I was supposed to have?

I glanced at my watch, unbelieving how much time had gone by.

I winced as I stood, all of the pains coming back twofold. As I carefully bent down to pick up my backpack sitting between the tree's trunk and my log—*mine* because fate had chosen it for me—something caught my peripheral vision: a triangular piece of clear plastic poking up through the leaves in the tree's hollow.

I leaned over the log and tugged on the plastic. It had weight to it. Across the log I lay against tender ribs and pulled harder. The dark wet leaves fell away, exposing a plastic freezer bag, the once shiny skin now dull and spotty. As it came out of the hole and into the light, I saw that the baggie was protecting a small blue book, roughly five by eight inches, maybe a tad smaller, and not very thick. The thin binding held no title. The back was as plain as the front. Right away I knew the reason: this wasn't a novel, or a children's book, or a textbook. It was a diary.

I threw it back in the hole as though it were a snake.

Every diary has an owner.

I glanced around nervously, worried I wasn't alone. But the woods were silent. Not even the tweet of a bird. The sun had centered itself directly above where I stood next to the log, and even though I was covered by thick shade, I began to swelter.

Ignoring the dull pain in my lower back and the tight muscles in my calves, I again pulled the package out of the hole. I slid the plastic zipper across its track, slipped in my hand, and pulled out the book. The baggie dropped to the ground. I pressed my foot on top of it to keep the breeze from stealing it away. My fingers gently slid along each edge of the book. The diary's blue cover was a rubbery plastic, the cheap kind they sell at the Dollar Tree. I put the book to my face, let my fingers ruffle the pages under my nose, and took a whiff of stale air.

Again I looked around, scanning the trees that seemed to go on forever, the path that moved away from my reflection spot in either direction, one toward Camp Kamama, the other toward the lake.

Had someone lost it? Deliberately buried it? For what reason? To come back and write in privacy?

I didn't want to open it, but possession is nine-tenths of the law, or at least that's what we'd learned in my government class.

If that was true, then why did I feel like I was trespassing?

Because I had no right. This wasn't *my* book.

Who will know if I take a quick look?

Slowly, I opened it. The inside of the cover had a tiny daisy doodled in the top right-hand corner, and below that, an inscription. The cursive was delicate, like it was written by a professional scribe. I read the words under my breath, no different than a song laid out on paper:

You walk with your head first high, then low.
It bobbles sadly to and fro.
It moves with grace, it writhes in pain, its will is gone, there is no shame…
And yet you are the one to blame.

It was written simply, like the Haikus I'd read in English class, but more complex in the way the phrases contradicted each other. They gave me a chill, these words that did not belong to me; this personal beginning to a diary that shouldn't have found its way into my hands.

I closed the book, slid it back into the baggie, blew pieces of dirt out of the zipper track, then zipped it up and placed it back in the hollow. I made sure to bury it a little, piling a mound of leaves on top as though nature had done it instead of me.

As I pulled my arm back out of the hole, a girl's voice said, "That's *my* tree."

I was so startled, I think I actually jumped a few inches into the air, tired as my legs were. I looked around but saw no one.

"That's *my* tree," the voice said again.

The scenario reminded me of a children's story my father had read to me when I was little, about a tree fairy who begs a lumberjack not to chop down her tree, and when he abides, she gives him three wishes.

I stepped to the right and saw the voice's owner standing on the other side of the massive tree trunk, one flip-flopped foot on the path and one off. A thin pretty girl with silky smooth skin and polished pink nails, her long blond hair tied back in a high ponytail, sparkly earrings dangling from her tiny lobes. Her bottom lip stuck out in a perfect model's pout.

She wasn't a tree fairy. She was a Forest Barbie.

A Felina.

"What are *you* doing here?" she asked, moving closer to my log. A bottle of orange Gatorade dangled from her hand.

"This is my reflection spot," I told her, not meanly, but definitely with authority.

She wore tight skinny-leg jeans with a pair of Rainbows and a tan Old Navy hoodie with the zipper halfway up. Red and white striped material stuck out from the bottom of the jacket. I'd have fainted from the heat in a mound of clothes like that.

She looked me up and down, like her eyes were trying to adjust to my size.

"What's a *reflection spot*?" she asked, still pouting. I wanted to tell her to stop doing that. That she was naturally beautiful, and that pout sort of made her troll-like.

"A place to reflect…to think," I said. "It's mandatory."

"Mandatory?"

"You know, required by—"

"I know what mandatory means."

Her lips were perfect. As was her skin. I wondered what kind of cleanser she used.

"Who made it mandatory?" she asked, her eyes squeezing together.

"Our camp director."

She only stared at me, and I wasn't sure if she was tallying my weight, or if she didn't believe what I'd just told her.

"At Camp Kamama," I explained, holding out the bottom of my shirt to show her the figure on the front.

She made her way around the tree and gave a quick, but not subtle enough, sideways glance into the hole. I pretended like I didn't see her looking in there. That blue book was hers. Her diary.

"So, you're just reflecting," she said. "*Here*. Next to *this tree*. Well. I don't think that's a very good idea."

"Why not?"

"Because it's *my* spot." She placed her tiny hands with those long pink fingernails on her hips, and batted her long lashes.

"Puh-leeze," I said, feeling brave and somewhat territorial. I never was intimidated by tiny girls—or big ones, for that matter. I used to play lacrosse, after all. "You can't own a spot in the middle of a forest."

"I never said I *own* it," she said, her silver earrings vibrating with the movement of her head. We weren't allowed to wear earrings at Camp Kamama that were larger than tiny posts. "But neither do you," she added.

"Well…" I wanted to tell her that the tree had called to me, but decided to keep that little tidbit to myself. "This spot is within Camp Kamama's boundaries. It's on my map. Don't you belong to the camp on the other side of the lake?"

The girl looked toward Camp Felina but said nothing.

"Look," I told her. "We have to reflect once a day. It's part of our—" I stopped myself, embarrassed. Here I was, about to explain to Forest Barbie what Camp Kamama was really about. A camp for girls who were morbidly obese. Girls who needed to get to the root of things.

Charlene was right. Just by standing next to me, this pretty Felina made me feel like a bag of poop. But, I told myself, as long as I was stuck up here at this fat farm in the middle of nowhere, I at least deserved my own private spot.

I said, "You could find another place closer to your own camp."

"No, I can't," she said.

"Why not?"

"Because there's no privacy there. You know what I mean?"

I did know. My brother poked through my things at home so often, my mother had finally bought me a padlock for the outside of my door. Which by now was probably busted.

"I like it here," I told her. "This tree. It…called to me."

"Called to you?"

"Yes. It's a good place for me to—"

"Reflect?"

"Right."

She looked behind her. When she turned back to me, worry lines covered her forehead. Now that she was standing closer to me, I could see that her full lips were chapped, like she needed water.

"What do you think we ought to do?" she asked.

I shrugged. "How often do you plan to come here?"

"Maybe once a day."

I looked at my watch. It was already 11:53. Lunch would begin in seven minutes. I'd have to make a run for it.

"What time is good for you?" I asked, trying not to show my impatience.

"Around now," she said.

"Okay," I said. "So, I'll get here by eleven, stay until 11:45, and you can come right after me. Can you make that work? No one says we can't share a spot, as long as we don't show up at the same time."

"I don't know..."

Her right eye twitched and I knew she was thinking about her diary.

"I'm only coming here to think," I told her. "That's all I want to do. Though it's not as easy as it sounds. Today was my first time, and I'm pretty sure I fell asleep."

She laughed a little, and her pout disappeared, bringing back her pretty face.

"Let's share it," I said, sounding like my old kindergarten teacher. "Trees were meant to be shared by everyone."

She licked her lips. "Okay," she finally said. "But we need to make a pact."

I hadn't made a pact since I was twelve, when one of my friends shoplifted a pair of G-string underwear from Walmart, and I swore on my dog's life I wouldn't rat her out.

"What kind of pact?" I asked.

"Not to tell anyone else."

"Tell anyone else what?"

She whispered, "Our secrets."

I had no idea what she was talking about. It was getting hard to concentrate with my stomach grumbling. Rumor had it there was soup and bread for lunch. If I put the bread in the soup, and stirred it around, I could make it into more of a stew…

"Fine," I said, readjusting my heavy backpack straps on my shoulders. "I really gotta go."

She didn't say anything as I lumbered away up the path. I could feel her pretty kitty cat eyes peering out of her little blond head watching my fat whale body as it lunged forward to make it up the slight incline. As I rounded a curve in the path and glanced back toward the log, I could barely see her, still standing there, blending in with the skinny tree trunks that separated us.

Chapter Eleven

Lunch was fan-freaking-tastic! Vegetable soup with two slices of whole wheat bread. There wasn't any butter or salt, but who cared? I was just happy to have a little substance in my belly.

After lunch, the lead counselors brought cabins nine and ten to the garden.

"Before we enter as a group," Marion said, "I have to go over some specific rules."

I was getting sick of rules, to be honest. I was also in dire need of a nap. My lips pressed together to keep me from yawning.

Marion held her arm out like a game show hostess. "We need to respect the plants here. We eat this food, so we have to treat each and every living thing we grow with kindness. The nicer we are to the plants, the more they'll produce."

"Do we have to talk to them?" Diane asked. She had dribbled soup on the front of her shirt at lunch but I don't think she noticed. "My great-grandmother talks to plants. She pretty much talks to anything. But she's, like, as old as a fossil."

A few of the girls giggled.

Marion put that serious face on again, and her cohort, Karen, shushed us.

"It's like if ya'll have a pet," Marion said. "Or a kid. Treat it right, give it love, and you'll be amazed at the results."

I had a hard time believing these were Marion's own words. She sure didn't sound like a teenager. She was more like a parrot that imitated grownups.

Marion walked under the high wooden arch, and the rest of us followed. Once we were all inside, Karen closed the gate behind us.

Marion said, talking more quietly now, "Think of this garden as a place where y'all can get in touch with Mother Earth. Get your hands dirty. Take the time to smell things, touch things. But don't pick anything without permission."

I whispered to Charlene who stood beside me. "Do you like this sort of thing? Gardening?"

"I didn't used to, but after camp last year, my mom and I started a window garden in our kitchen. It produces year round."

Vanessa whispered, "I got my mom to grow sunflowers."

I couldn't picture my mother and me digging in the dirt together. She had her hobbies, like spin class, and I had mine, like finding new ways to make a sub. Plus, we had a gardener who did the yard work.

Marion said, "Today we're going to hang out by the blackberry bushes." She picked up a stack of small white buckets and started handing them out. "It'll be your job to pull off any dead leaves y'all see, fill up your buckets with them, then dump them in one of the wheelbarrows you see along the paths. By the end of the day, the wheelbarrows will be filled with compost material. Jake churns it and turns it into mulch to feed the garden with. He has an amazing green thumb."

A girl's whisper rose up from behind me. "I'm sure Jake has a *lot* of amazing parts."

I held back a chuckle.

"So," Marion continued, "go to it. There are a lot of berries, but don't pick them. I know you'll be tempted to pop a couple into your mouths, but it's forbidden. These berries are used to make jam for our breakfasts."

I stared at the dark purple clusters sitting among the leaves. These berries actually went into our breakfast jam? An odd notion to me, since I had never pictured where jam comes from, never pictured someone actually plucking the berries off the vine. I only thought about the way jam tasted when I blended it with peanut butter on bread and wolfed it down with a big glass of chocolate milk.

We followed Karen's and Marion's lead, and the other cabin followed its own leaders. Within seconds, twenty girls were stretched out in a long row on either side of the bushes.

Charlene stood on my right and Diane on my left. Somewhere down the row stood Vanessa. Together we girls picked dead leaves off the branches and dropped them into the white buckets.

The sun shone overhead. I pulled my baseball cap lower over my forehead to keep the sun from frying my nose. I was already perspiring, could feel the sweat as it poured down the center of my back and soaked the waistband of my shorts.

"How'd the reflecting go?" Charlene asked.

The girl from Camp Felina popped into my head, standing next to the massive tree wearing that mound of unflattering clothes, like she was ashamed to wear an outfit that complemented her pretty face.

"It went fine, I guess," I said.

"Anything strange happen?"

"Strange?"

"You know, like crazy thoughts coming to you without your say-so."

"Oh," I said. "Um, yeah, I guess so."

"Awesome. You can use that stuff during powwow."

"Use it?" Diane and I asked at the same time.

"At the powwows," Charlene explained, "some girls talk about what they learned during reflection."

"I didn't learn anything," I said, as I picked off a half-torn leaf with my fingers, then put down my arm for a rest. Sweat trickled down my temples. I wasn't cut out to be a gardener. Way too much sweating.

Diane said, "I found the sweetest spot behind the greenhouse. It's sort of damp back there. Perfect for a nap. You know what I learned? That our backpacks make awesome pillows."

Charlene and I laughed.

Marion came up behind us.

"Hey, you guys," she whispered. "We sort of need to keep it down in here. Y'all can chat during snack time."

"Snack time?" I asked, trying not to salivate.

"After swimming," Marion said. "Try to pick leaves in silence. The plants seem to respond to touch more than conversation. At least that's what Jake says."

She made her way up the path, found a spot not too far away from us, and began dropping leaves into her bucket.

Charlene whispered, "We wouldn't want to disappoint Jake, now would we?"

"I know, right?" I whispered back, and silently got into the rhythm of picking.

Chapter Twelve

"Get your suits from the window over there," Marion said as the group of us approached a rectangular hut next to the gymnasium.

All of the excuses I'd had for not packing a bathing suit would be of no use. I cringed as I stood in line.

"I still have my suit from last year," Charlene said. "But it doesn't fit me anymore."

Diane spoke to the girl behind the counter. "I'm allergic to chlorine," she said. "It's a genetic thing. Sad, really."

"You don't need to worry about that," said the girl. "Our pool is filled with salt water. All natural."

Diane grabbed her bathing suit. "Should have faked a doctor's note," she mumbled as she sulked away.

I stepped up to the window.

"Last name?" the girl—*two-sixty*—asked.

"Wheeler."

The girl roved through a box on the window sill and pulled out a large index card.

"Simone?"

I nodded.

She stepped away for a second and came back with a one-piece black bathing suit and a large white towel.

"Put your name on the tag," she said, handing me a Sharpie. I marked the tag on the inside of the suit and handed her back the marker. "The bathing suit you keep," she said. "The towel you put in a bin outside the showers when you're through. You can keep your clothes in one of the lockers." She looked past me. "Next."

Charlene and I went into the dressing room located between the hut and the pool building. A few girls, unaffected by others in the room, were already nude and stretching their suits over their extra belly rolls. I looked away and spotted a row of private stalls.

Once inside, I peeled off my sweaty shorts and T-shirt and socks and underwear, and held up the bathing suit. The material was stretchy and I managed to yank it over my sticky body, twisting and untwisting the straps as I pulled them over my shoulders. I turned around but found no mirror in the tiny room. I hung the towel around my neck, snagged a locker, and shoved my clothes inside, then twirled my thick hair into a bun and double wrapped the band around it.

Charlene waited for me by the bathroom stalls. Even though she weighed more than me, we looked like twins. I glanced around the room at the other girls. We all looked the same. I felt like part of a scientific cloning experiment.

"You look like a supermodel," Charlene said.

"Yeah, right," I said, laughing.

"You know, they do have supersized models. They interviewed one on TV. She makes over a hundred dollars an hour."

I wondered if Charlene thought she was pretty enough to be a supersized model, but I didn't pry. Instead, I asked, "Where are the mirrors?"

"Not around here, that's for sure. Just the small ones in the cabin bathrooms. I've heard that the doctor used to bring a full-length one. But not anymore."

"Doctor?"

"She comes up on Fridays for our weekly weigh-in," Charlene explained. "She works at a hospital somewhere down the mountain."

"Oh."

I pictured a prairie medicine woman, chugging up the mountain in an old pickup truck, and just before she leaves, I jump in the back and hide under a tarp. I sneak down the mountain and call a cab, or maybe a Greyhound bus, from the hospital lobby. Stick the bill on my father's credit card. He'd totally freak, maybe even disown me, but my mother would be so happy I was home, she'd make me a big fat celebratory burrito, with beans and rice and hot sauce and sour cream...

I followed Charlene and the other girls to an open shower before heading to the indoor pool, where we hung our towels on hooks. Even though I couldn't use the chlorine excuse, it was nice to have a pool that didn't reek of chemicals. Girls were lining up along the cement edge, a few of them sucking in their guts and standing in a three-quarter ballet stance like they were auditioning for *The Nutcracker*.

A barefooted Jake stood on the other side of the pool. He still wore his Camp Kamama T-shirt but had traded his hiking shorts for a pair of OP swim trunks. A whistle hung around his neck. He put it to his lips and tooted it twice.

When the echoing sound of cackling voices diminished, he

spoke. "Welcome to water aerobics, ladies. As you know, one of the prerequisites for this camp is knowing how to swim. And swim we will. But first, we're going to do a little disco."

I turned to Charlene. "Did he just say *disco*?"

"Uh-huh."

"What about the English Channel?"

"He only starts out with this," she said. "In a few weeks, you'll be wishing for disco."

Jake walked along the pool's edge across the pool from us, eyeing us. When his eyes skimmed over my face, I stared at the tips of my chubby toes.

He said, "Today, you're going to learn a little something about how to have fun in the water."

I already knew how to have fun in the water. Why would I have to prove it in front of everyone, including Jake?

He went on. "Being active is an important part of any weight-maintenance program. When you're active, your body uses more energy. This is commonly referred to as calories. You cut out only five hundred calories every day, like that Dairy Queen milkshake you crave at lunchtime, or that Dominoes double meat pizza you have on movie night, you will lose weight, period. Five-hundred calories a day, times seven days, equals 3,500 calories. A pound a week, without even trying."

"A pound a week?" Diane's loud voice boomed from somewhere down the line. All heads turned in her direction. "At that rate, it would take me ten years to lose this." She gripped a couple inches of belly fat and shook it.

Everyone laughed. Except for Jake.

He continued without missing a beat. "Naturally, *burning* calories will help as well. Let's say you cut just a tad more calories, like those candy bars you sneak into your bedroom at night.

Then, on top of that, you burn a few extra calories each day, say, a couple of extra laps around the pool, or a walk in the evenings. So, now you lose two or three pounds a week, times four weeks a month, that's eight to twelve pounds. The safest way to lose is to do it slowly and consistently. On the lower end, we have eight pounds a month times twelve months. Do the math."

A couple of the girls closed their eyes, doing the math problem in their heads.

"You getting the picture?" Jake said. "Ladies, I cannot say it enough: when you burn more calories than you consume, you lose weight. People have a misconception that they have to spend their days eating celery and running marathons. We are going to kick that rumor into the gutter. Now. There are dozens of ways to enjoy exercise. Just like there are dozens of ways to change your diet. We're here to show you creative ways to do both. A little creativity goes a long way. Nobody knows that better than I."

He paced along the far side of the pool, reached down and dipped his hand in the water, and stood again. "Water aerobics is one of the easiest ways to get in shape. Let's say you weigh one-sixty and do an hour of water aerobics. *Just one hour.* You can burn nearly three hundred calories in one session. You weigh two hundred? You burn three-sixty. Weigh two-forty? Well, lucky you. You can fry over four hundred. And that's without ever sweating."

"I like *that* idea," said the girl to my left.

"Okay," Jake said, walking around the top edge of the shallow end. "Everyone into the pool. Get to where the water is between waist and chest-high. I don't want to see anyone deeper than the three-foot mark, no exceptions."

As we lowered ourselves over the edge and into the tepid

water, Jake continued to give instructions. "No diving, no running, no pushing, or dunking. If I toot my whistle, it's either because someone is breaking a rule, or because you are getting too close to one another. Give yourself some personal space. You're going to be moving around. When the music starts, you will do exactly as I do. Even if you have two left feet, even if you hate disco, this activity will make you forget you're exercising."

Jake waited until all twenty of us had found a spot and had given ourselves space between.

"As soon as the music starts," he said, "follow my steps."

Before I knew it, the Bee Gees or some other old or maybe even dead disco group was blaring through the speakers in the corners of the gym. Jake remained up on the ledge in front of the pool. As he moved, his long braid swayed with him like a tail. First he stepped to the right, one leg over the other, then back to the left again, his right over his left. It was the Electric Slide. I only recognized it because my parents did it at their twentieth wedding anniversary party. And I would have never shared this with them, but it was pretty dang fun doing it with all those tipsy grownups. And it was fun now, though much different than doing it on a dance floor.

My legs felt like they were in an anti-gravity chamber. It was hard to move them quickly or gracefully through the water, and I had a hard time keeping up. I could tell that Jake had slowed the movements down to accommodate us, but it was still harder than I thought it would be.

We moved our arms into the air and brought them down again. While on our tippy toes, we shook our hips which were hidden beneath the tiny waves. We kicked forward and back and forward again. We squatted. We jumped into the air.

Laughter came from my right. I turned to see Vanessa with a

wide grin spread across her dark face. She was cackling so loud, I thought for sure she'd get into trouble. But Jake just kept on shaking his bootie, and we followed.

I glanced around me a few minutes later, comparing myself to the other girls, wondering how I measured up to them in stamina and style, when I noticed that nearly all the girls were laughing just like Vanessa. Laughing, cheeks bright red, heads nodding to the music, whale-like bodies moving with an odd sort of grace through the water.

And it wasn't until the class was nearly over, after I'd listened to everything from "Ladies Night" to "Stayin' Alive" that I felt a pain in my jaw, like I'd recently had a set of braces tightened or had chewed gum for hours. I brought my hand to my chin, then to my cheek, and realized with a thrill I hadn't felt since making Varsity lacrosse that the pain was caused by an hour's worth of grinning.

Chapter Thirteen

Some snack: a small cup of vanilla yogurt with granola on top. Barely enough to satisfy a hamster.

Luckily, I was still reveling in the whole water aerobics thing, still humming a KC tune I thought I'd hated.

Charlene said, as we walked our dirty trays and dishes to the back of the cafeteria, "I never knew I loved that disco crap until last summer. Now my mom and I listen to it all the time."

Charlene seemed to have a lot in common with her mother. About the only thing my mother and I had in common was food. I asked for it, and she gave it to me. It was a good, symbiotic relationship.

I licked my spoon one more time before dropping it into the tub, then followed Charlene and the other girls to the air conditioned building that housed the classrooms.

As we peeked into the first room, Charlene said to me, Vanessa, and Diane, "Best part about the art and music rooms: no chaperones."

The room had three long tables covered with white butcher

paper. Along the back wall stood a line of cabinets that reached from the floor to the ceiling. A different sign hung on each of the three sets of cabinets: PAINTING SUPPLIES; BEADING SUPPLIES; SCULPTING MATERIALS.

Across the hall from the art room was the music room. Already, some girls had chosen spots on mats or pillows. More than a dozen guitars stood propped up by wooden stands. Two electric keyboards and a set of electric drums sat across the room. A girl wearing earphones sat at the drums, and you could barely hear the tap-tap-tap of her sticks. A television in front of an old couch had the Wii going, and three girls were checking out Zumba, daring each other to go first.

"I'm gonna try playing guitar," Vanessa said, nodding her head for emphasis.

"I'm with Vanessa," said Charlene. "Maybe we could do a duet. What about you guys?"

Diane said, "I love music, but if you heard me sing or play anything, you might be tempted to pour cement in your ears. I guess it's fine arts for me."

"I think I'll make some jewelry," I said. With lacrosse practice taking up most of my previous life, creating art wasn't something I'd thought about, or had time for.

Diane and I went back into the art room.

"You ever painted before?" I asked Diane as we made our way to the cabinets.

A few girls had taken plastic containers from the shelves and were rooting through them on the tables.

"Not since I got a spanking for coloring my mom's bedroom wall with her lipstick," Diane said. "But I'm willing to try it, now that I have self-control." She reached into a cabinet for a large white poster board.

I opened the bead cabinet. Girls were swarming in now, the chatter growing, everyone excited to create something without a guardian looking over our shoulders.

I grabbed a large container of beads and headed to the table. I chose a seat at the end, and Diane sat across from me. She opened up a box filled with dozens of colored pencils and laid some out in a row next to her poster board. I opened the bead container, overwhelmed by the choices which were neatly divided into separate compartments.

"What are you going to draw?" I asked her.

She shrugged. "What are you going to make?"

I shrugged.

We both sat pondering as Diane rolled her pencils back and forth and I sorted through the multitude of beads.

Soon, we were both into what we were doing, and everyone else must have been as well, because the room was relatively quiet.

"I like not having a babysitter," I told her.

"Who needs a chaperone when you're discovering the Van Gogh within?" Diane asked.

I smiled as I continued to pick out beads. I didn't particularly like necklaces, as they always managed to get caught in the folds of my neck. Ankle bracelets were definitely out of the question, since I really didn't have ankles to speak of, even though I used to. Now I had cankles. That's when the calves seem to join with the feet without the interruption of those annoying ankles. I did like rings, but my hands swelled up so much before my periods that if I didn't remember to take them off, my fingers would turn blue. Earrings were cool, but since we weren't allowed to wear dangles at camp, what would be the point? A bracelet was the winner, if only by default.

"How do you like it here so far?" I asked Diane as I rounded up more beads.

She shrugged. "You?"

I shrugged back. "Same."

Diane twirled a black pencil between her fingers and asked, "Did you ever think you'd be in a place like this?"

"You mean Camp Kamama?"

"I mean in life. Did you ever picture yourself in a place as morbid as this?"

I looked at her, confused.

"Morbidly obese," she said. "Morbid means sinister. The word makes me think of witches or devils." She let out a deliberately creepy laugh as she swooshed her pencil across the board, making the first mark.

I thought back to when I was a little girl, with my long wavy hair and tiny nose and soft brown eyes. I was an obedient child, always wanting to please others, always the little helper. I didn't cause any trouble for my parents. I did what was asked of me, both at home and at school. I loved my family so much, even loved it when Bucky was born. I was never jealous of him. I hated to be away from any of them for any length of time, though I was sent away each summer to one sports camp or another. I was a good child with a good life. And then, almost overnight, everything changed. My father changed, my life changed, and here I was explaining to a girl like me if I thought I'd be here now.

"No," I told her, answering the question honestly. "I did not think I'd ever be in this place. Either at a fat camp *or* in life."

We remained mostly silent for the next forty-five minutes as I threaded together pretty gold and red and copper beads. From time to time, I glanced across the table to see what Diane was drawing, but it was hard to tell upside down. Her top teeth chewed on her bottom lip, like mine used to while picking out the perfect shot in lacrosse. Her dark pencil scratched across her poster board almost nonstop.

When she was finished, she held it up for me to see.

"Wow," I said. She had sketched Lake Kamama with trees behind and a full moon overhead. "You found your Van Gogh."

She smiled. "Thanks. I like it, too. And I like your bracelet."

I slid it onto my arm. It looked perfect against my orange watch band.

"Thanks."

Diane turned her picture face-down.

"I'm nervous about powwow," she whispered.

"Same," I whispered back.

The room grew noisy as girls started putting their supplies away. Some carried their pictures out of the room; others hung them on the wall with Scotch tape. A few donned their new bracelets, just like me.

Diane said, "Think it'd be okay to hang this up over my bed?"

"Sure," I told her. "Maybe we could get HGTV to film us. They can call it, *Revamping Camp Cabins*."

In the hallway, we met up with Vanessa and Charlene.

"Charlene and I are starting a band," Vanessa said. "We've already learned how to play two chords."

"We're going to call ourselves the Fat-tastics," Charlene said, laughing.

Diane said, "Maybe you should come up with a name that doesn't, you know, have the F-word in it."

Charlene put a flat hand against her chest. "And deceive our fans?"

"What if you lose weight?" Diane asked.

"You really are a funny girl," Charlene said, hooking her arm with Vanessa's. "The Fat-tastics. It has a nice ring to it."

They walked a few paces ahead of us up the crowded hallway as we headed toward our next adventure: powwow.

Chapter Fourteen

The last room on the right was larger than the art and music rooms, but it was less stimulating. Beige walls were void of other colors, except where someone had painted in large red letters, taking up one of the four walls:

O' Great Spirit, help me always to offer the truth,
to listen with an open mind when others speak,
and to remember the peace that may be found in silence.

Silence, I thought. *My middle name.*

The floor was ugly green linoleum. In the center of the room, tan metal folding chairs were arranged into a large circle. Even though the room was air conditioned, a ceiling fan suspended from a beam in the center spun around. Four rows of fluorescent lights ran the length of the room, like in the biology labs at school.

That's what this feels like, I thought as I stared up at the lights, *a lab.*

Charlene twiddled her fingers close to my face and said in a spooky voice, "Welcome to powwow." Then she laughed like a black and white movie vampire.

Her joking was not appreciated because I was nervous. It was bad enough talking to a therapist, which I did for two months during my freshman year at the request of my socially challenged guidance counselor. But to share my deepest thoughts, here, in front of all these strangers? *Ugh.* Twenty sweaty overweight girls sitting around airing their dirty laundry. My feelings were my own, and I liked it that way. Keeping things buried was how I worked best.

"Does everyone have to get up and speak?" Diane asked.

For the first time since I'd met Diane, her vibrant personality turned timid.

"Only speak if you want to," Vanessa said. "Some girls never say a word."

My tight shoulders relaxed.

"Besides," Charlene said, "plenty of girls end up venting without the help of powwow."

"What do you mean?" I asked.

But Charlene had no time to explain. The camp nurse walked into the room, clapping her hands to quiet us down.

"Please, ladies, when you come into this room, do it quietly. Put your backpacks against that wall and choose a seat, pronto. Time wasted is time taken away from your chance to speak. And you don't want to be cheated, do you?"

Um, yes, I do, actually, I thought as I dropped my bag and picked a seat in between Diane and Charlene. Vanessa sat on the other side of Diane.

"My name is Mary," she said, turning around slowly in the middle of the room. "For those of you who missed my introduction at the orientation yesterday, I'm the nurse-slash-counselor here at Camp Kamama. In this room, I am more counselor than nurse, more friend than counselor."

A girl across from me—*two-twenty*—asked, "What exactly is a powwow?"

Mary said, "A powwow was originally used by the Algonquin Tribe as a religious ceremony, and it later took on meaning as a social get-together. For us, it's a little of both. We're getting together in order to celebrate who we are in mind, body, and spirit. To celebrate who we are as humans. And while I'm not a shaman, I am here as your leader and confidante to help guide you. Any other questions before we begin?" When no one responded, Mary said, "Then I'll get right to it. My background is pretty cut and dry. I grew up in a family riddled with drug abuse. At the ripe old age of fourteen, I was sent into foster care after my mother died from a heroin overdose and my father fell off the planet."

She took an empty seat across the wide circle from me and made eye contact with each of us as she spoke.

"It's hard to come from a family that suffers from the disease of addiction without suffering some of the symptoms yourself. But I told myself from the time I was little that I would never do drugs. And technically, I didn't. Not illegal ones, that is. My addiction was and is perfectly legal. It's even supported by society. Chances are, though it may be for different reasons, you all have the same addiction as me: food."

Someone mumbled, "Food's not a drug."

"Anything is a drug if you use it for the wrong reasons," Mary said, "and if you can't stop using it even when you know you should. Addiction comes in many forms. You could be addicted to shopping. Or sex. Or television. Addiction is as addiction does. Trust me. My weight has yo-yoed from as high as three hundred to as low as ninety."

The room let out a collective gasp.

"Today is your first powwow," she continued, smiling kindly. "We are not only here to explore the way you feel about food, but the reasons behind those feelings. I don't like to call it therapy, even though I am a family therapist and nutritionist. We call it a powwow because we're here to talk, ask questions, offer advice, listen, examine, and show thanks. We'll explore the reasons why you are here at Camp Kamama. And FYI: you aren't here solely because of your weight."

"We're not?" a girl across from me asked.

Mary shook her head. "You're here because you need to gain insight into who you are. By searching within yourselves, you can discover *why* you do the things you do. Food addiction is not about the actual food. It's about the way food makes you feel. The way it overtakes your life. The way it controls you."

Food does not control me, I thought to myself. *I choose whether to eat it or not.*

"Starting today," Mary said, "all of you are going to start working toward getting back some power by looking deep within yourselves. Into the part of you that is too afraid, or perhaps too stubborn, to see the truth. Your weight is merely a symptom of a greater problem. Here, at Camp Kamama, you'll learn that nourishment for the body, the mind, and the soul comes from the same place. From love of self. But you must first learn to forgive."

"Forgive who?" another girl asked.

"Yourselves."

"For what?"

But Mary only smiled. "Let's start by bowing our heads in a moment of silence. And then we will begin our powwow."

I closed my eyes and thought about what Mary had said, that

food had control over me. But as soon as I started analyzing the theory, my father's big round face popped into my head, like it had earlier during reflection. I tried to shake it out, tried to get rid of those sullen, disappointed eyes but could not.

Thankfully, I was pulled away by Mary's voice.

"Okay, then," she said. "I started, so who wants to take the ball and run with it?"

"Me," said an eager beaver—*inching on three-hundred*—seated directly across the circle from me. Even though she was heavy, she was beautiful. Her long black hair was held back in a clip, opening up her tan pore-less face and narrow eyes. "My name's Patti."

Mary said, "Whenever you're ready, Patti."

She spoke confidently, like she was giving a TED Talk. "My mom has MS. That's multiple sclerosis. Basically, it's when the sheaths of nerve cells in your brain and spinal cord are messed up. For my mom, it got real bad over the last year, a lot of pain all the time, and now she's in a wheelchair. It was her idea for me to come here. We actually got into a huge fight because I didn't want to leave her."

Mary asked, "And your father?"

"He's a pilot in the Air Force. We used to move around a lot, you know, to different cities depending on what was going on in the world. But then Mom got sick and couldn't move around like before. Dad got stationed in Germany, and we stayed behind. I was sort of chunky when I was little. I have some Hawaiian genes from my mom that make me bottom-heavy, no matter what I do. And I was always okay with that."

"That's good," Mary said.

"But the extra pounds came on when my dad went to Europe. I mean, I totally knew that I was overeating. It was just, well, once I got started, I couldn't stop."

Mary prompted, "And you ate because…"

Patti said, "Oh, it's no great secret. It's because my dad left."

"And?"

"I'm my mother's caretaker. She used to be a dancer. She used to teach dance, too. Now she can barely walk on her own. And she's in so much pain all the time…"

"Some people need to be taken care of," Mary said to the group. "But we must first learn to take care of our own needs. Only then will we be healthy enough to take care of those around us. Think of an airplane, when the flight attendant tells the passengers that if the cabin pressure drops, and the oxygen mask falls, the parent is to put it on her own face first, then on the child. If the mask goes to the child first and something happens to the parent, then what?"

"I'm definitely the one giving my mom the oxygen mask," Patti said.

"Without breathing yourself," Mary said.

"I would take care of my mother for the rest of my life if I had to."

"That's admirable," Mary said. "Especially when you didn't choose this for yourself."

"Yeah," Patti said. "I didn't choose for her to get MS. I didn't choose to have a dad who—"

She stopped.

"A dad who what?" Mary asked.

"Who asked to be stationed in Germany." Patti looked at her hands. Her voice didn't sound so confident anymore. "I saw the letter. It was on his desk. It said that his request had been approved. His *request.*"

"So, then, you're angry with your father?"

"No. Not at all. I understand why he did what he did. He couldn't stand to see my mother in pain."

"But he left it all up to *you*. He left *you* in charge. How does that make you feel?"

"It makes me feel sorry for him," Patti said.

"For *him*?"

"I totally love my dad. It broke his heart to see my mother like that."

"Patti," Mary said.

Patti waited.

"This room, this powwow, is for opening up all the way. There is nothing wrong with not being ready yet. But if you're not, then perhaps we should move on to a different person, give someone else a chance, and get back to you when—"

"No," Patti said. "Don't. I want to talk about it. I really do. I'm ready. I have no one else to talk to. I have no friends."

"Why is that?" Mary asked.

"We've moved around so much. I go to a different school every two years. Now we live in a really small town. My dad moved us to this lame town, where I know no one, and then he left. He left me in charge. But I'm not a freaking nurse." Her voice began to rise. "I have to help her bathe, brush her teeth, I even have to wipe her. Some mornings I have to feed her breakfast, when her pain is really bad. I have to do everything. Pay the bills. Do the grocery shopping, the laundry, the housecleaning. I cut my junior year down to half-days. I dropped theater. And I still barely have time for homework. Every day it's the same. My whole life is about taking care of—" She stopped abruptly. When she spoke again, her voice was softer. "And I'm fine with that. I am. I love her. I'm just…tired. Really, really tired."

"Patti," Mary asked, "who's with your mother while you're at camp?"

"My grandmother came out from Hawaii for the summer. But she has her own stuff to deal with. She'll leave in August when I get home. And then it'll start all over again."

"Have you explained to your father how you feel?"

Patti shook her head.

"Why not?"

"He's counting on me. He said, 'Patti, I'm counting on you to take care of your mother.' I made him a promise."

"What about your father's promise?" Mary asked.

"What do you mean?"

"His promise to take care of your mother when he married her. His promise to take care of his daughter when he and his wife decided to have children."

Patti began to cry.

I thought about my own mother, the picture of health with her treadmill and free weights taking up the sun room, and the way she be-bopped around the house like she had more energy than she knew what to do with. I was suddenly feeling lucky.

"I don't want to let him down," Patti said after a moment. A girl handed her a tissue, and she wiped it across the bottom of her nose. "I don't want to let *anyone* down."

Charlene raised her hand and Mary nodded to her.

"Have you tried talking to your mom about it? About getting a caretaker?"

"A nurse can't take care of her the way I do," Patti said.

Mary said, "Your role in life right now is as a daughter. As a student. As a teenager. You deserve to have those opportunities."

"But what about my mother?" she asked. "She'll never have

the opportunity to walk again. To do the things other mothers do. It's totally not fair."

"You're right, Patti," Mary said. "It's not fair. You won't be able to give her back her health. But she certainly deserves to have a happy daughter. A kid who comes home from school and tells her mom about her day, about her life. What if she misses those mother-daughter moments? If you have someone else taking care of her physical needs, then you'll have the energy to take care of her emotional ones—the ones that represent her love for you as your mother, not as your patient. Did it occur to you that she might feel guilty?"

Patti shook her head. "I've never thought about it. I don't really have too much time to think back home."

"Well, then, think about it here," Mary said. "That's what we're her for. Figuring things out."

"Do you think you can help me do that?"

"You betcha," Mary said, smiling, fanning her arms out wide. "Me and all these other amazing young women in this room. We're all in this together. We are Kamama-mamas."

Chapter Fifteen

Tonight's Blue Plate Special: a thick slice of cooked turkey, a pile of steamed baby carrots, and a lonely red potato, *sans* cheese, sans butter, sans sour cream, sans salt. A poor little naked potato!

"Powwow was hardcore," Charlene said as we sat down to dinner. "I can't believe it was only the first one."

"Mmm-hmm," Vanessa said. "Usually it takes a week for anyone to share like that."

Charlene put a chunk of carrot into her mouth. "I'm always happy when I get to help."

"It made me sad," Diane said as she mashed all of her food together in one big pile.

I nodded in agreement, thinking about the girl and her mother with MS. After Patti had finished speaking, another girl talked about something to do with her stepfather, and still another talked about who-knew-what. I kept finding myself drifting away from powwow. I was thinking more about that morning's reflection, about the girl I had met in the woods, how she didn't have to sit around and cry in front of strangers, or listen to others whine. While we were sitting on those hard metal chairs under that old fan, Miss Felina was probably painting her toenails a summery shade of pink, or taking a nap in a hammock beneath the trees. I pictured their camp like a spa, with a hot tub and a steam room, and smoothies with a pineapple chunk jabbed on the edge of the glass. I wondered if it was too late for me to sign up for Camp Felina? Maybe they would take me on as a mascot or something. I could dress up as a giant cat. Go to their pep rallies. Cheer them on during Color Wars.

Charlene took a small bite of turkey and chewed it thoughtfully. "Why are you here, Simone?"

"Because my father wanted to get rid of me for the summer," I told her.

I held up my meat and snagged a piece. I would try to nibble my measly portions the same way Charlene did.

"I totally doubt that," she said. "Everyone was interviewed, remember? We're all here for specific reasons. Once you figure out the whys, the rest gets pretty easy."

Diane said to Charlene, "If it gets easier, then why are you here a second time?"

Charlene shrugged. "I like it here."

I said, "But you weigh *more* than you did last—" I looked down at my plate, embarrassed that the words had just popped out of my mouth.

"Hey," Charlene said, "it's not a secret that I've gained twenty pounds since last summer. That's the best part about this camp. Nobody here judges me, except for me."

Vanessa quipped, "Agreed."

"So you *chose* to come here again?" I asked.

Charlene and Vanessa said at the same time, "Yup."

"And you still don't know why you're here?" I asked.

"I know why I'm here," Vanessa said.

"If you already know," I asked Vanessa, "then why did you come back?"

"Where else am I gonna go during the summer? Miami Beach?"

Diane laughed. "Why not make it Rio? The bikinis are skimpier there."

A tiny cloud of laughter rose up to the wooden beams.

"What about you, Charlene?" I said. "Do you know why you're here, besides the obvious reason?"

"We all know why we're here," Charlene said. "But knowing *why* isn't enough. You have to figure out what to do with the information."

"So you haven't figured that out yet?"

"I'm a work-in-progress," she said.

I ate the last of my plain potato, pretending it was a loaded number four from Wendy's instead of kindergarten paste.

After a moment, I said, "I'm here because my doctor convinced my parents I should be here."

"Right," Charlene said, giving Vanessa a quick glance. "Not for any other reason. I can't wait to hear about the skeletons in *your* closet."

A few of the girls at the table giggled. I noticed that Diane did not.

"I don't have any skeletons," I said defensively.

Charlene said, "That's what they all say the first week of camp."

***

I hid from Charlene during the after-dinner movie, *Finding Nemo*, which I'd seen a thousand times as a kid. I grabbed a boring rice cake, filled my thermos with green tea, and sat in a back corner of the gym next to Diane. I devoured the crumbly brick and drank half my tea before the opening credits were done.

The word *skeletons* rang through my mind.

In the dark, the little funny fish swam around on the pull-down screen. I listened to the laughter around me while picking pieces of rice cake out of my teeth.

I missed dessert even more than center-cut bacon or sweet potato fries. If I were home right now, my mother would be cleaning up the dishes from lasagna or fried chicken. Bucky would be hiding out in his room, listening to Pandora or creeping around on the Internet. My father would be in the living room, dozing in his recliner in front of a baseball game. And I would be…what would I be doing? Well, since dinner had just ended, I'd be planning what to have for dessert, of course. Maybe some ice cream with chocolate sauce on top, or a couple of chocolate chip cookies with a fat glass of milk. I never discriminated when it came to sweets.

While Nemo and Dory were busy acting like stupid old fish, I pictured myself walking with my dessert—now it was clearly a chocolate on chocolate cake, the glossy icing dribbling down the sides—past my father, who suddenly sits up in the recliner, his beefy legs forcing back the footrest, making a loud *woomp*! He stands up and reaches out to grab the plate from my hands, but I yank it away before he can get it. I run up the steps two at a time with the cake still intact, and look behind me to see him standing at the bottom of the staircase. He doesn't follow me. He only shakes his head. What does that head shake mean? Is he saying, *I give up*? Is he telling me, *You are nothing more than a fat slob?* I don't know, because his lips never move, and everything he is thinking I have to guess. I *always* have to guess. And the guessing isn't ever any good, because the very second I start trying to guess what he's thinking, my brain turns off and switches to something else, like what I'm going to have for my midnight snack.

All the girls in the warm gym were laughing. After a few minutes, I started to watch the movie, and soon I was laughing along with them. After all, it was much easier to laugh at dumb Dory and silly Nemo and those cute baby turtles than think about all the other junk buried deep in my brain.

Chapter Sixteen

The moment that shock of music shook me out of bed, my sore muscles cried out in pain. My calves, my thighs, my hips, my shoulders. While inching down the path toward the beach with my backpack slapping against my spine, I thought I would scream. In yoga, I could barely bend over, let alone touch my toes. It hurt almost too much to drag the spoon to my mouth at breakfast, which was a smidgeon of oatmeal and one slice of crumbly whole wheat toast, barely improved by blackberry jam. Some of us girls took turns rubbing each others' necks before crawling with our trays to the trash cans.

Café Kamama was a bit better than breakfast. Willie diced up cucumbers and tomatoes into penny-sized chunks with a really sharp knife, and we girls created an olive oil with lemon dressing that was even better than Pizza Hut Italian. Cooking was easy because we could move like sloths as we pulled pans down from the rack or wiped up a drip on the floor. Playing around in the kitchen temporarily pushed out of my mind the next activity: obstacle course. But then it was time.

Charlene caught up with me and together we made our way along the path with the others. Constant groans of agony and jagged breaths sputtered into the summer air.

"Now you know why I hate that course," Charlene said, holding her side.

At the bottom of the hill, we dropped our backpacks to the ground, put on our ankle weights, fell into line from shortest to tallest, and headed to the front of the course. We moved in slow motion, all of us, like a herd of manatees.

Ms. Diggs had so much energy, screaming through her megaphone like someone was caught in a rip tide, "You can do it! You can do it!"

One girl tried to climb under the first fence instead of over it then realized she was too weak. She finally gave up and limped her way around it. Another camper stood looking at the foam blocks like they were pillows. Some girls actually crawled across the tires. Sabrina from South Carolina fainted, and I ran to her side, rolled her over, checked her pulse, and screamed for Ms. Diggs, who spoke into a small radio which had been hidden somewhere on her tiny body. Within minutes, Sabrina was carried up the hill on a stretcher, her tie-dyed bandana wadded up on her chest.

I thought, *I could faint. Or, at least pretend to.*

But Charlene kicked that idea to the curb. "She'll have to miss another activity in order to redo the course by the end of the day."

"Even after she fainted?"

Charlene only shrugged, took a deep breath, and headed across the monkey bars, her grunts coming back to me like a gorilla's.

It took us a lot longer than the first day to make it through the course. My whole body ached. My neck, my wrists, even the bottoms of my feet.

But I did it. And that's what I kept telling myself an hour later as I hobbled alone down the path to my reflection spot: *I did it.* It had been a long time since I'd felt any kind of pride, and now it was oozing out of my pores along with my sweat.

After trudging over roots and trying not to fall in a rut, I made it to my log.

As I dropped my backpack to the ground, I thought, *I don't want to share my spot with a Felina girl or with anyone.* I knew I could look for a new spot, but I didn't have the stamina to wander aimlessly, and the log was looking as good as my family room couch. I plopped down on my rear end, took a couple swigs from my water bottle, slipped off my baseball cap, and put it beside me on the log. I slid the tie from my ponytail, shook out my damp hair, and tilted my head back letting the slight breeze rub its fingers over my face.

Then I closed my eyes and waited. And waited some more. I shifted my weight from one buttock to the other. I opened my eyes and closed them again. I stretched out my legs. Took in a deep breath and let it out. Felt my chest rise with air then collapse again. All that came to me were scenes from *Finding Nemo.* I couldn't get my mind to let go, to think about important stuff like self-forgiveness and love and peace for all mankind.

Sighing, I opened my eyes again, and my peripheral vision caught that triangle of plastic poking up through the leaves in the hole. Sitting there, tempting me. Begging to be held. To be read.

A woodpecker tapped his beak against a nearby tree, sounding through the woods like a jackhammer. The tapping stopped after a moment, and again I sat in silence.

Now my neck forced me to look directly toward the hole.

You can not read it...you made a pact...

I made a pact not to share secrets, whatever that means. I said nothing about reading a random book I found in a tree stump buried about as well as a two-year-old buries a shovel in a sandbox.

I wondered then why Forest Barbie hadn't found a different place to hide the diary, since she knew I'd be spending time here. It wasn't as if there weren't any other hiding places. The forest just about went on forever. Maybe the diary wasn't hers after all.

No. I knew it was hers, the same way I knew she had a perfect body under those layers of clothes. So, either she was dense, or she didn't really care.

Or she *wanted* someone to read it.

I sunk my hand into the moldy leaves, pulled the plastic baggie out of its hole and the diary out of the baggie, then placed the book on my lap. I opened it.

Then I closed it again.

Forest Barbie already considered us friends—at least enough to make a pact with me.

But that wasn't *my* fault.

One more time, I opened the book.

I'd had a few friends back home, girls who used to come to my slumber parties, who would brag about reading an older sister's journal. Most of the stuff they shared was pretty boring, but every once in a while something happened that they couldn't wait to tell. Like Tamara, my best friend back in middle school, whose sixteen-year-old sister wrote about a fling she was having with her clarinet teacher. Or my other friend from freshman year, Marissa, whose sister, a senior, was paying a college boy in her neighborhood to get her and her friends booze on the weekends. Stuff that made our eyes grow big. Stuff that made our own pre-pubescent minds expand in so many different directions.

But this wasn't the same thing, and I knew it. It wasn't the same, because this Felina wasn't my sister. She wasn't someone I went to school with. I didn't know anything about her. Hadn't I already had enough stimulation during that first powwow? Didn't I realize that seeing into another person's life isn't always what we think it is, and sometimes it's downright depressing?

Maybe I was one of those types who needed to hear smut. Maybe I was hoping to read that this gorgeous Size One had secrets that would make my mother blush. Like reading the cover of *US* or *The National Inquirer*, showing famous stars at their worst moments. Maybe I was hoping that by peeking into someone else's life, my messed-up summer at this camp would become more interesting, maybe even fly by faster. Or, if I discovered her life wasn't so perfect, my own might seem a little bit better.

I flipped to that weird poem on the first page, the Felina's handwriting as flawless as her skin. Silently, I re-read the words:

You walk with your head first high, then low.
It bobbles sadly to and fro.
It moves with grace, it writhes in pain,
Its will is gone, there is no shame…
And yet you are the one to blame.

Then I made my way to the first entry:

You don't want to be here. You want to be home, sleeping in your own room, not sharing your space with a bunch of girls you don't know. You miss your posters, your laptop, your bathroom. You even miss your kitchen…

I understood the poem being written in second person, but who would write a diary that way? I tried doing that once in a paper for Honors English, thinking I was being oh-so-clever. But Mr. Thompson made me rewrite it in third-person, claiming that no one wants to read an entire book in second. I didn't tell him that I was writing a freaking *paper*, not a *book*. And I also didn't bother to remind him there were plenty of books that had been written in second person, like *As I Lay Dying* and those little kid adventure books.

I peeked around the tree, heard and saw nothing, then turned to the next page:

You are not who they think you are. Does it show on your face? What you know? What others don't know? Do you remember how life used to be before everything changed?

This wasn't a diary, at least not by definition. It was a sort of self-help book, the kind my therapist had on his shelf in between *Reviving Ophelia* and *A Girl's Guide to Growing Up*. A book to help a girl find her way.

Your parents sent you to this camp for a reason. You have to trust others. Trust that they will not take what happened to you and throw it in your face. Trust that they will be there for you, without judgment. They will not blame you. You will be forgiven. You can do this.

Sweat poured along the backs of my knees, down my calves, and into my ankle socks. Suddenly I was nervous, not only because I might get caught reading the book, but because the words sounded like something I would write. If I kept a diary. Which I did not. I knew better. Bucky would probably find it and share it on social media before I had a chance to kill him.

You will be forgiven. You can do this.

Forgiven for what? Had this Felina girl done something so awful she could only write about it in a diary?

Feeling a little overheated, I closed my eyes and fanned my

face, and that was when I heard a twig snap. Fear and instinct took over as I jammed the book back into the plastic baggie, tossed it back into the hole, and quickly buried it.

I stood up and turned to see the pretty Felina, standing a few feet away on the other side of my tree, in the middle of the path off to the right. She looked like a seedling, a new dogwood that had sprouted a few months ago and was growing wild. Her blond wavy hair was down, tucked behind her ears, cascading down her back, almost to her hips. She wore a different pair of expensive jeans, but still wore her Rainbow flip-flops. Her sweatshirt was tied around her waist, and she had traded in her long-sleeved red and white top for a solid blue one. The colorful fabric stood out like a lost kite among the tan trunks and green leaves.

"I thought we made a deal," I said, holding up my watch for emphasis. My homemade bracelet reflected tiny strands of sunshine slipping through the canopy. Dirt covered my palm, and I casually wiped it on the back of my shirt.

"Deal?" she asked. She carried another bottle of Gatorade, this one filled with purple liquid.

I began to salivate, thinking about how sweet that fake juice would taste going down. I worked hard to stay on track.

"I come here first, and you come after I leave," I reminded her.

"Oh, I forgot," she said. "Sometimes I'm just a dummy."

Why wasn't this Felina hanging out with her bunkmates, giving one another mani-pedis or coloring each others' hair? I wondered if maybe she wanted to talk about that stuff in her diary.

Or, more likely, if she was hoping to catch me reading it.

As we stood there, the gentle breeze grew stronger. Loose strands of hair flew around my face like cotton candy. I gathered up the wisps and pulled my thick hair into a tight bun at my neck.

"So…" I said, giving her a gentle hint to leave. I promised myself that if she left now, I wouldn't read the diary anymore. I'd do what I came here to do: reflect.

"That's fine," she said. "I'll come back."

She said the words, yet she didn't move. Maybe she was hoping I'd invite her to sit. After all, she had trekked farther than me to get to this spot.

But I didn't ask her to sit. Far or not, I was protective of my log. And, ironically, part of me was protective of the diary, which made no sense since it was probably hers.

"I like your bracelet," she said.

"Oh. Thanks. I made it."

"Cool."

She still stood there, two feet from the log. If she wasn't going to leave, I would try to find out what her deal was.

"Are you, like, free-range over there at Camp Felina?" I asked.

"What do you mean?" she asked.

"Well, it seems like you can come and go anytime you want. Don't you all have activities? You know, stuff to do together?"

"Trust me," she said. "We do plenty together. It's just that, in the mornings, I choose to bail out of the activities. My parents pay a lot for me to be there. So the camp sort of has to let me choose."

"We don't have a choice at Camp Kamama."

"Oh."

"They make us check in at mealtimes, too."

She took a step forward. "They do?"

Why had I shared so much? She didn't need to know anything about me, did she?

"What kinds of things do you do at your camp?" she asked.

"Regular old camp stuff," I said. "Like swimming." I didn't tell her about the disco. "And we saw a movie last night." I didn't share that it was a kid's cartoon. "And we had a bonfire the night before." I left out the rice cakes and green tea.

"I saw the fire," she said. "We had one, too."

"Don't you guys ever see movies? Or do crafts or anything?"

"This is Acclimation Week," she said. "Socials and stuff. You know, getting used to being here. Up in the mountains. Away from city stuff. Peer pressure and all..." She looked past me toward Camp Kamama. "Do you have a lot of friends at your camp?"

"Some," I said, though I hadn't really thought about them as friends until now.

"Do you have boys over there?"

"No. Only girls."

"Oh," she said, letting out a loud stream of air. "That's good. Ours is all-girls, too."

"We do have a really hot yoga instructor. But he's the only male."

"As good looking as Keith Urban?" She smiled but only used her lips instead of one of those bright pearly white smiles most lucky girls flash. It was a timid smile. "He's my favorite country singer of all time. Do you like him?"

Of course I liked him. What Southern high school girl didn't? "I guess so," I said, not wanting to admit out loud that we had something in common.

Her eyes quickly glanced at the hole again. "I'm sorry I interrupted your reflecting...again."

"That's okay."

"I like to reflect by writing," she went on. "Sometimes I write poetry. Other times I write junk. Nonsense. Like it just streams out of me. One of my old English teachers told me I should study journalism." She licked her lips and tucked her hands inside the front pockets of her jeans. "What about you? What are you going to do when you go to college?"

I hadn't thought about college much since my hope for a lacrosse scholarship had been nixed, so I didn't have a solid answer. Besides, this Felina was talking to me like we were suddenly BFF's.

"Not sure yet," I told her. "I'm going to be a junior, so I still have some time to think about it."

"I'm a rising junior, too. I plan to go to Vassar. That's an all-girls college. I think that's a safer bet, don't you? It's up in New York. So I'll be going out of state. I live in Raleigh."

"New Bern," I said.

"Practically neighbors."

She inched closer to where I stood. She smelled like honeysuckle.

"I'm Phoebe," she said. "Like Holden's little sister in *Catcher in the Rye*. You ever read that?"

"Last year. In Honors English."

"Oh, isn't that funny?"

"What?"

"That we both took Honors English."

I nodded, even though plenty of people took the class.

Phoebe went on. "My favorite book of all time is *The Bell Jar* by Sylvia Plath. You ever read that one?"

I shook my head.

"It's about this girl, just a little older than us, who is trying to make it in the fashion world, but then her whole life falls apart, and she ends up in a mental institution. It's an amazing story.

Did you know that Sylvia Plath killed herself?"

I shook my head again, agitated. I had twenty minutes until lunch, I hadn't reflected, and my legs were throbbing from my hips to my ankles.

"If I ever have a daughter," Phoebe said, "I might name her Sylvia. So, what's your name?"

I thought about making one up, but nothing came to me.

"Simone," I said.

"Do you think you'll ever get married, Simone?" she asked.

"I don't really think about it," I said, but of course I'd thought about it. What lonely girl, fat or otherwise, doesn't? Maybe Phoebe was messing with me, since it was obvious by comparing the two of us that *one* of us might never get a proposal.

"Sometimes I worry that the right boy won't come along," she said. "Or that when he does, he won't want me."

She unscrewed the cap from her Gatorade and took a swig.

I studied Phoebe, even though I didn't want to, but her face drew me to her. She really was beautiful. *Striking*, a word my mother used every now and then. She was petite, like a pixie. Her large blue eyes took up most of her face, and her blond hair wasn't the yellow that came from a bottle. Her face was round like the sun. She didn't smile like a girl who has all those qualities, but her shyness made her even more beautiful. How could she possibly think she'd never meet the right guy? I could name ten boys from my high school who would drool over themselves for someone like Phoebe.

Was she putting herself down to hear me tell her the opposite, fishing for compliments?

I turned the tables.

"At the rate I'm going," I told her, "I'll end up with some guy who weighs twice as much as me, and thinks the perfect date is dressing up for a *Star Trek* convention."

Phoebe snickered through her nearly closed lips. But she didn't disagree.

I chugged from my water bottle. I was suddenly feeling bold. Where it came from, I have no idea. Maybe it was because Phoebe was sucking down that delicious purple drink and probably had S'mores and hot dogs and fried chicken at Camp Felina, and I was stuck with a surplus of green tea and rice cakes. Maybe it was because this gorgeous tree fairy was fluttering in my space. She had interrupted my reflection twice. And now she was telling me about herself, when all I really cared about was getting back to the cafeteria before the vultures at my table thought I was dead and divvied up my paltry lunch.

"Camp Kamama is a fat camp," I told her.

"I'm sorry?"

"You know, for super fat girls. The fatter the better. The more you weigh, the better the chance you get to come here. What's really cool is, I'm not even the fattest one here. There are other girls who make me look like a twig. Can you imagine that? A girl who could make me look thin? Oh, and did you know that Kamama means *elephant*? How messed up is that? Naming a fat camp after one of the fattest creatures on the planet."

"I don't think elephants are fat," Phoebe said. "I think they're…you know…big. But they're beautiful creatures."

"Haven't you ever heard the phrase *fat as an elephant*?"

"Well, yes, but—"

"So, there you have it. I'm supposed to come here every day to reflect on why I'm fat. You see, it's not about the food. It has nothing to do with the fact that I shove Krispy Kremes and Twinkies and anything fried down my throat at the rate of a bullet train. It has nothing to do with the candy I eat in the middle of the night, or the way the smell of gravy gives me goosebumps. Nope. It has to do with other things."

"What kinds of things?"

"I don't know. I haven't discovered them yet. Because I haven't had a chance to reflect!"

My loud voice didn't seem to bother her.

"Well then," she said, "you should reflect if that will help you feel better. I'll come back a little later, after you're gone."

From the direction of Camp Felina, the sound of skinny laughter wrapped its way around the trees like a snake. Phoebe turned her head as though her name was hidden in the folds of that laughter, but she still didn't move from her spot.

What are you waiting for? I thought. *Go on back to your entourage of kitty cats. They must be missing you by now.*

I looked at my watch. I had ten minutes until lunch. I let my eyes travel along the long path leading back to Kamama, the worn trail disappearing at the first bend. I'd have to run. Crap.

I picked up my backpack and turned back to Phoebe. "Just so you know, I don't have anymore time to re—" But I stopped myself. Phoebe was already heading into the brush, off to join her pride of cats.

Chapter Seventeen

We stood in the garden after a meager lunch of fruit salad and a wafer-thin biscuit that looked and tasted like cardboard. Today we had to kneel down in the soil, my joints screaming in pain as I crouched into position, pulling green spiky plants from a row of sunflowers which stood two heads taller than me. I tossed a handful of weeds into my white bucket.

"What's up, buttercup?" Charlene whispered. "You barely said a word at lunch."

"I didn't reflect," I whispered back.

"Why not?"

Charlene had warned me not to talk to any of the Felinas, but I hadn't promised I wouldn't. Anyway, it was only a piece of advice, and I'd been given gobs of advice for two years from doctors, guidance counselors, coaches. I wanted to dislike Phoebe. To find something about her that made her match the words Charlene had used. But I could not. And the harder I tried to find something, anything, the more I realized I should keep our second—and our first—meeting a secret.

"Couldn't get my mind to chill," I told Charlene, watching a lady bug as it jumped from one sunflower's leaf to another.

Spread out among the two cabins of campers under the baking sun, I continued to weed in silence.

I pictured Phoebe in her long-sleeved shirt and skinny-leg jeans. Her pretty hair and newly manicured nails. She should have been out in the real world shopping for a new cotillion dress or a pair of Jimmy Choo shoes. How out of place she seemed up here among the trees in the middle of nature. Like a colorful flower that doesn't know any better than to grow in a densely shaded forest.

After a long hot hour in the garden, dipping into the pool felt divine. Anything to get out of the sweltering heat. And the disco music was actually growing on me. I wondered if I would ever share that with my mother, the fact that I sort of didn't hate her music. We moved to the beat, creating waves as our legs kicked and our arms flailed up and down, and by the time the class was over, my muscles actually hurt a little less.

But it really wasn't my muscles that I was thinking about. It was that stupid powwow, hovering over me like a blade in a guillotine.

It felt like only seconds passed between working on jewelry and sitting in the tan brick room, where chattering girls filled up the circle.

"Welcome, ladies," Mary said, taking a seat. "Please bow your heads in a moment of silence." When we were through, she asked, "Does anyone have anything to say about our last meeting?"

A girl from our bunk—Hannah from Virginia—raised her hand. Her tennis shoes were the top-of-the-line Nikes. She wore a pair of diamond studs in her ears which glistened, even under the fluorescent lights. They looked odd with her T-shirt and shorts. Like carrying a Michael Kors purse while wearing a dirty pair of sweats.

Mary nodded to Hannah.

"I don't think that everyone works the same way," Hannah said. "Back home I have a therapist. And it obviously isn't working, because, ta-da!" She patted her belly.

Some of the girls giggled.

Mary said, "You're convinced that speaking to another person about your feelings is pointless?"

"Well, maybe not for everyone," Hannah said.

"But for you."

"Yes, ma'am."

Mary asked the group, "Does anyone else feel this way?"

At first no one raised a hand. But then, one by one, girls started putting their arms into the air. I waited until there were four or five, and then I joined them. If enough of us decided this wasn't for us, would Mary cancel powwow? Let us roam around for an hour like the Felina girls? Maybe without a powwow, hanging out at Kamama would become bearable.

Charlene, who sat next to me with her hands in her lap, gave a surprised look when she saw my arm in the air.

"That's not what I mean," Hannah said, sounding frustrated. "I don't fit in with these girls." She looked around the circle. "I'm sorry, but I'm okay with who I am. I'm okay with my weight. I look in the mirror, and I feel beautiful. I don't think every person has to lose weight to be happy."

"You're absolutely right," Mary said.

"I am?"

Marry nodded. "And there isn't a person at this camp who doesn't want you to be okay with who you are, inside *and* out. Luckily, there are many people out in the world who fall into that category. But you all are here right now because something else is going on. You were interviewed and subsequently *chosen* with that in mind. You are part of a very elite group of young women."

"Maybe someone made a mistake," Hannah said. "Maybe what I have is physical. You know, slow metabolism, or whatever."

"Each one of you was tested," Mary said softly. "No one at this camp has a metabolic issue, or anything physical to prevent them from becoming healthy."

"There is nothing wrong with me or my life," Hannah said. Light red blotches had spread across her cheeks and her lips were pulled tightly together. "Everything is perfect."

Charlene, who was sitting beside me, moved to the edge of her seat. She leaned her body forward. She seemed excited, like she was in the front row at a concert and wanted to get close to the lead singer. She asked Hannah, "What makes it so perfect?"

Hannah tilted up her chin. "Lots of things. For starters, my parents are still together. They love each other a lot, as a matter of fact. I don't think I've ever seen them fight. My dad owns his own business and makes bank. My mom is a stay-at-home. She treats me and my little sister like princesses. I have a closet full of dresses I have yet to wear, and it's not even back-to-school. My mom loves to buy us things. Things that make us pretty. And our house. It's huge." She fanned her arms out like a television hostess. "There's a white fence that goes all the way around the property, and all kinds of roses that grow on vines. Our lawn wins awards all the time. We have a built-in swimming pool. All my friends love it. We have a maid who comes every day and helps my mom 'cause our house is so big. The maid does the hard stuff, like cleans the toilets and the floors and the oven, while my mom vacuums and Windex's the plastic on the furniture. My mom loves to keep the house ready in case anyone ever stops by. You know, like the neighbors or a delivery man or whatever. You can even see the vacuum lines on the living room rug." She laughed a little, like the giggle popped out accidentally.

Someone whispered, "Plastic on the furniture?"

Hannah paused, ran her fingers through the ends of her hair, and looked around at the dozens of eyes watching her. "You know what? This is bull. All of this. There is nothing wrong with me. And there is nothing wrong with being fat!"

Hannah stood up, pulled her backpack onto a shoulder, and stormed out of the room, slamming the door behind her.

One of the girls got up to go after her, but Mary told her, "No! Let her go."

It took a while to get the room to settle. No one seemed to want to share anything deep, so for the rest of the hour, we chatted about surface stuff. A couple of girls talked about how proud they were of themselves on the obstacle course, others bragged about how their pants were already becoming loose, which I didn't believe for one second could happen after two days. A few mentioned what they did in music class, or during art expression. It was like a verbal show-and-tell. I was dying to show off my new friend, Forest Barbie Phoebe, live from Camp Felina, but then I thought, that's something I should probably keep to myself.

***

After dinner—a fat green bell pepper grown in the Kamama greenhouse, stuffed halfway with ground turkey meat—Ms. Diggs made an announcement over the loud speaker.

"Kamama-mamas, please stop by your cabins on the way to

the bonfire to grab your sweatshirts or windbreakers. There is a chance of rain tonight, and the wind will be picking up. We'll stay at the bonfire as long as weather permits."

When the microphone clicked off, everyone in the cafeteria began chattering excitedly. Mountain thunderstorms are awesome.

When Diane and I arrived at the cabin, Hannah was standing in the center of the room with Charlene. A few campers were standing around them in a small circle. They looked like characters in a play.

"I have no trash anywhere in my family," Hannah was saying. "My life is as close to perfect as anything you could ever ask for. I swear."

"Wow," Charlene said in a loud voice.

Hannah glared at her. "What, Charlene?"

"Well, that would drive me insane, having to be perfect."

"I never said *I* was perfect," Hannah said. "Open your ears. I said *my life* is perfect."

"Says who?" Sabrina from South Carolina asked as she pushed her tie-dyed bandana back from her forehead, exposing a tiny lump from her earlier fainting spell.

"Says everyone," Hannah said.

"Everyone *who*?" Charlene asked.

I could feel the room stiffen. My stomach felt sick. I hated seeing people argue, especially over something petty. Diane moved closer to me.

"Are you calling me a snob?" Hannah asked Charlene. "Or a liar?"

"Neither," Charlene said. "We just want to help you."

A few of the girls nodded in agreement.

Charlene continued. "I'd lose my mind if I thought I *had* to be perfect. Way too much pressure."

Vanessa piped in, "I agree."

"I never said I was perfect!" Hannah shouted. "Stop putting words in my mouth!"

"Okay, okay," Charlene said. "Calm down. If you don't say you're perfect, then who does?"

"My mother!" Hannah shouted. "She thinks we're perfect! Fine! There it is! You happy, Charlene?"

The room was a tomb.

Hannah opened her mouth to say something but shut it again. Those red splotches had invaded her cheeks again. A line of sweat glistened above her lip like an oily mustache.

When Charlene spoke again, the tone of her voice sounded like Mary's trained one, low and methodical. Hearing it come from a sixteen-year-old was creepy.

"Why does your mother want you to be perfect?" she asked. "And what would she do if you weren't?"

"My mother is wonderful," Hannah said as if she were suddenly tired. "She's kind. And happy. Always singing. She's beautiful. Her hair, her makeup, the clothes she wears. Like a model. She keeps a beautiful home, makes sure we have the right clothes to wear, that we get good grades, become pillars of the community. These things make her happy. Just because she wants us to be as perfect as her…just because she tries to keep everything under control…is that so wrong? Is that…"

Her words drifted away. A quizzical look covered her face like someone had asked her a difficult math question. "Oh," she said. She looked directly at Charlene then down at her tennis shoes. "Oh, crap."

Charlene looked at the group as if to say, *Girls, we have a break-through!*

The cabin door opened and Mary entered. Marion and Karen trailed behind.

"What's going on?" Mary asked. When no one answered, she said, "Hannah, come take a walk with me."

Tears were streaming down Hannah's face. She whispered so quietly I could barely hear her. "I don't want to be perfect. I just want to be normal, like everyone else. With dog hair and popcorn on the couch. Homework spread out all over the kitchen table. Get a B now and then. Fight with my sister sometimes…" Her face fell into her hands as she sobbed.

I couldn't look at her. Instead, I stared past her at the picture Diane had drawn of Lake Kamama, taped to the wall above her bed.

Mary took Hannah's hand and led her through the cabin door. Charlene started to follow.

"Stay with your bunk, Charlene," Mary told her.

The door slammed behind Mary and Hannah. We listened to their footsteps as they disappeared up the path.

"What happened?" Marion asked our group. "Y'all were only here for five minutes."

Vanessa spoke up. "Hannah had a meltdown."

Marion didn't say anything as the girls turned away from her and grabbed their jackets and hoodies for the bonfire.

Charlene stared at the screened door. Her head was cocked to the side, and for a second she looked like half toddler, half psychologist.

I decided right then I didn't want Charlene on my side if I was ever bold enough to share anything personal, whether in our cabin or in powwow.

Chapter Eighteen

We headed down to the beach, dozens of flashlights lighting the way. Rice cakes were passed around to all the girls, and bottles were filled with green tea. But this bonfire was different than the first night. Tonight was story-telling. After Hannah's earlier meltdown, I thought telling stories was a good idea.

"I hope they're scary stories," I told Diane. "Like the one about the werewolf that—"

"These aren't those kinds of stories," Charlene interrupted, taking a spot on the sand next to Vanessa, a few feet from the huge fire, her back to the lake.

Diane and I meandered away from Charlene and Vanessa and plunked down on the opposite side of the circle, the fire between us.

While we waited for everyone to get settled, I looked up at the sky. Clouds thickened above us, wiping out the stars like a giant eraser. A tiny flash of light appeared in the distance, momentarily turning the distant sky a deep purple. A roll of thunder caused excitement to ripple through the group.

"Sounds like they're having a party," Diane said, nodding toward the other side of the lake. I could barely make out the bonfire across the way. Loud voices rolled across the dark lake, a song filled with equal parts of harmony and melody, but with no actual music to guide them. It sounded more like a chant. For a moment I pictured the Felinas, prancing around a cauldron like the girls in *The Crucible*, casting spells to keep themselves thin and rich and beautiful.

Diane said, "I heard we're not supposed to go anywhere near them."

"Charlene tell you that?"

Diane nodded.

I wanted to tell Diane about Phoebe; tell someone I had been talking to a Felina. In an odd and fascinating way, I liked Phoebe. It was like wanting to hang out with the weirdest Goth in school simply for the novelty of it.

Girlish laughter from across the lake rose and then disappeared again. I thought of *Horton Hears a Who*, the Doctor Seuss book where those sweet microscopic characters live on top of a fuzz ball, trying to communicate with the outside universe.

Ms. Diggs and Jake, with help from other staff and counselors, brought us under control, and within seconds all that could be heard was the sound of popping wood as the fire steadily grew.

Jake made his way around the flames as he spoke.

"Many of you have been asking questions about Camp Kamama, mainly regarding its Cherokee name. Why not call it Camp *Mini-ha-ha*, or Camp *Wiggle-miggle*?"

Or Camp Fatty-Watty? I thought to myself.

"This land used to be a place where many Cherokee people lived and flourished," Jake said, opening his arms wide. "Where they hunted, and fished, and prayed. And many still do, despite what happened to them. The Cherokee, back then and now, believe that when a story is told to others, and they in turn pass the story on, their spirits will continue to live in our hearts indefinitely."

Another flash of light zigzagged through the faraway sky, and then another rumble, this one louder than the first.

"This is the story of the Cherokee rose," Jake said. "As some of you may already know from your history classes in school, the Cherokee were driven from their homelands in North Carolina, Tennessee, Alabama, and Georgia in the 1800's by men who came to the Americas from Europe. Gold and other riches were discovered in these lands, and the men wanted to reap the rewards. But the only way to reap them was to rid the land of its indigenous peoples. This nearly thousand-mile journey is known as the Trail of Tears. It was a terrible time for the Cherokee, leaving their homes and possessions behind. Countless died from the hardships, most of them forced to walk overland all the way to Oklahoma."

Jake moved slowly from one side of the fire to the other, each pair of eyes following him. Watching. Listening. The fire made his tan skin look orange, his eyes red. His voice was smooth, almost motherly, like a piece of velvet rubbing against my cheek.

"While this journey was taking place, the Cherokee women wept enough to fill a river. The old men knew the women must stay strong to help the children survive. So they called upon the Great One to help their people and to give the mothers strength."

Jake looked up into the sky for a moment.

"Hearing their pleas, the Great One caused an extraordinary plant to grow every place a Mother's tear fell upon the ground on their way along the trail. The plant would have white blossoms, a beautiful rose with five petals and gold in the center. The gold stands for greed. The leaves of this flowering plant would have seven green leaflets, one for each Cherokee clan. The plant would be strong and grow quickly along the Trail of Tears. The stickers on the stem would protect it from those who might try to move it, as it spread to reclaim some of the lost Cherokee homeland.

"Only hours after the first tear hit the earth, the women saw the beautiful white blossom on the trail. When they heard what the Great One had said, they knew they would survive, knew they would stay strong as a community, and the children would grow and the people would flourish in the new Cherokee Nation. In the end, the Cherokee's life was not in vain." After we were through clapping, Jake took a seat on the sand in between Ms. Diggs and Mary.

Ms. Diggs stood up. "Thank you, Jake. You always tell that story like you lived it. My story is a bit more on the girly side, so I—" She was cut off by a wide shot of lightning, followed by a crack of thunder, this one close enough to make some girls scream. The sky opened up, and dime-sized drops of rain began to fall.

"To your bunks for indoor merriment!" Ms. Diggs shouted.

But we were already running. The fire sizzled as we ran away from the beach.

"Watch your step!" Jake called out, as we tore laughing through the woods, our jackets and sweatshirts barely covering our heads.

Chapter Nineteen

I was the last one in the stampede to reach cabin ten. The girls were probably opening a box of puzzle pieces, throwing its contents onto the floor. Or maybe breaking out a couple of board games. Or, as I expressed to my mother on rainy days, "*Bored* games."

Inside the cabin, eight girls were sitting around in a large circle on the floor. Including me, that was nine. I noticed that Marion was missing.

I wiped my wet face with the bottom of my shirt as the door slammed behind me. "What are you guys doing?"

"Truth or Dare," Sabrina said, her voice low and mysterious like a spy.

"*Kamama* Truth or Dare," Karen corrected.

The last time I'd played Truth or Dare was at an eighth grade slumber party. I had to sneak up to the birthday girl's brother's bedroom and kiss his cheek while he slept. He was a year older than me, and had pimples on his chin and greasy hair. But I did the dare, because that's what you do in Truth or Dare. Even if it's something repulsive, you do what you're told to do. I felt a little old to be playing the game now, but there wasn't much else to do with all that rain coming down.

"Where's Marion?" I asked, squeezing in between Diane and Charlene on the floor.

"Talking to Ms. Diggs about what happened to Hannah," Karen said. "She'll be back in a little while. In the meantime, the game rules are simple: you can change from a truth to a dare, but you can never change from a dare to a truth. There's no lying, no exaggerating unless it's something hot, and most importantly, no bullying." She looked directly at Charlene. "Got it?"

"What? I'm not a bully," Charlene said. "Hannah *needed* to let it out. I was just there to help her do it."

"Think she'll go home?" Sabrina asked.

"Her suitcase is gone," Karen said.

We all turned toward Hannah's bed. The space underneath was empty. Her pillow was gone, too.

"That's messed up," Diane said. "I thought she was really nice."

I nodded.

"Camp Kamama isn't for everyone," Karen said, sighing. "By the end of the summer, we could end up with half as many girls. Like ten little Indians, chop, chop, chop…" Her hand imitated an ax as it chopped her neck three times.

"That is the truth," Vanessa said. She had twisted her thick black hair into a pair of braids, and with her smooth skin, she looked like a twelve-year-old.

Thunder shook the cabin, and everyone laughed nervously.

"Okay," Karen said. "You ready?"

"I'll go first, if that's okay with everyone," Charlene said. No one argued. "I'll start with the person on my left, and then we'll go around the circle." She turned toward Karen. "Karen," she said, "truth or dare?"

Karen said, without hesitation, "Truth."

"Make it a good one," Vanessa said.

Charlene thought for a moment, then finally asked, "Have you ever had a lesbian dream?"

"Seriously?" Karen said.

Diane puckered up her lips and sang a line from an old Katy Perry song, "I kissed a girl and I liked it, the taste of her cherry Chapstick…" and everyone laughed.

"Damn," Karen said. "If I switch to a dare, then you'll think I did. Oh, gawd, ugh. Yes. I did. One time. When I was ten. About my babysitter. But all we did was kiss. She let me have cotton candy afterwards. In the dream, not in real life."

The group snickered.

"My little brother probably had dreams about her, too," Karen added, laughing, her chubby cheeks like pink balloons. "She was really pretty."

Diane whispered in my ear, "Why didn't she just lie?"

I shook my head.

"Okay," Karen said. "My turn." She turned toward Trish. "Truth or dare?"

"Um…truth," Trish said.

"How much candy did you sneak in?"

Trish's mouth turned into an oval as her jaw dropped. "How did you know?"

"I have my ways," Karen told her. "All's fair in the game of Truth or Dare. And if you change it to dare, I am going to give you the meanest, grossest—"

"Okay," Trish said. "Leftover Easter candy. A bagful."

I was blown away. Here was Karen, a co-counselor, privy to

the fact that one of our bunkmates had snuck in contraband. Even if it was almost three months old.

"Does Marion know?" Sabrina asked.

"No way," Karen said. "She wants to be a hall monitor when she grows up." She turned to Trish. "Where do you keep it?"

"I made a fake bottom in my suitcase." The whole circle turned toward the big black bag under her bed. "None of you snuck in anything?" she asked.

We all shook our heads.

"Aren't you afraid of getting caught?" I asked.

"Are you kidding?" Trish said. "I'd be happy to get thrown out."

"Having candy won't get you thrown out," Karen told her.

"It won't?"

"Nuh-uh. You'll end up getting extra duty somewhere. Cleaning toilets, or working extra in the garden. Some girls try hard to get sent home, but it takes a lot to actually get kicked out."

My stomach sank. Even though the thought of escape had stayed in the back of my mind since arriving at camp, I probably didn't have what it took to get thrown out.

"Show us what you have," Karen ordered Trish.

"That's not part of the game," Trish said.

"She's right," Charlene said. "You would have had to give her a dare."

We all looked toward Trish's suitcase, lying innocently under her cot. I touched my lower lip to make sure I wasn't drooling.

"Okay then," Trish said. "Now you all know. Big deal. It's my turn. Sue, do you want a truth or dare?"

"Truth," Sue said. She was the quietest and heaviest one in our bunk, yet it wasn't until that moment that I noticed a red birth mark on the side of her cheek, and the tattoo of a teddy bear on the outside of her ankle. I wondered how she'd managed to remain nearly invisible until now.

"How come nobody's picking dares?" Vanessa asked.

Trish ignored her question. She asked Sue, "Have you ever done it anywhere other than a bed or a car, and if so, where?"

"Done what?" Sue asked.

"*It.*"

Sue shook her head. "No," she said quietly. "Not anywhere or anytime. I don't plan to until I'm married."

"Ditto," Karen said.

"Karen's holding out for her babysitter," Trish said, laughing.

"Ha-ha," Karen said.

Sue held up her left hand, showing us a tiny silver band around her ring finger. "This is my commitment to abstinence," she said. When no one responded, she turned to Vanessa and quietly asked, "Truth or dare?"

"Dare," Vanessa said. "I can't take any more truth."

"Oh," Sue said. "I was gonna ask you if you like kissing."

Vanessa laughed. "Kissing who?"

Sue said, "Just kissing. In general."

"Give her the dare," Charlene said. "No going back to truth after they choose dare."

Sue told Vanessa, "Um...stand in the middle of the circle and dance around for one minute."

Vanessa jumped up without hesitation and started moving to a song that must have already been in her head. She was an amazing dancer. We clapped in time until one minute was up.

"That was fun," she said, panting as she plopped back down on the floor. She turned to Sabrina. "Truth or dare? And please tell me a dare, 'cause I have a really good one."

Sabrina pushed her little round glasses up on her tiny nose. "Truth," she said. Her cheeks turned spotted orange as she retied her bandana behind her neck."

Vanessa looked up at the ceiling, thinking, as if the question would magically appear in the rafters. "Okay. I got it. Have you ever deliberately watched a boy get undressed? Or dressed? You know, depending on the situation."

"Yes," Sabrina said, blushing. "Once. At camp last summer. That was a fat camp, too, but it was co-ed. Girls on one side, boys on the other, separated by an invisible boundary line the counselors thought we wouldn't cross."

"Now, this is getting juicy," Vanessa said.

All of the girls, including me, leaned in, but no one as far as Charlene.

Sabrina said, "A couple of girls and me knew that some of the boys had spied on us getting undressed in our bunks, so we decided to get back at them and sneak over to their side of the camp, you know, to check them out."

"Did you?" Charlene asked.

"She already said she did," Karen said.

"It was after dinner," Sabrina said. "The counselors took their showers after everyone else."

"You were creeping the *counselors*?" Charlene asked. "I thought you were getting even with the campers."

"We thought so, too," Sabrina said. "But it turned out to be the counselors in the locker room, most of them in college. I guess the younger boys had already taken their showers. Anyway, it was no big deal. We looked through the window, we saw what we wanted to see, and we went back to our cabin."

"What did you see?" Diane asked.

"What do you think we saw?"

"Any of 'em black?" Vanessa asked.

"I think so," Sabrina said. "I was so nervous, you know, seeing them naked and all, I hardly remember it."

"You never got caught?" I asked, impressed and horrified at the same time.

"Nope."

"No one could ever get away with anything like that around here," Karen said.

"One time," Charlene said, "when I was in the ninth grade, we had this huge history test I was totally unprepared for. That morning, I went out the front door and back in through the garage after my mom left for work. But right *before* she left I nabbed her cell phone so the school couldn't call her. I stayed up in my room and watched television for about two hours. Then I started getting bored. We didn't own an X-box, and there wasn't anything on television but lame soap operas and court TV. So you know what I did?"

"What?" we asked in unison.

"I studied for the history test. I knew I'd have to make it up the next day, so I spent, like, three or four hours putting facts on index cards. My mother never found out I'd cut school, and I got a ninety-eight on the test." She smiled. "I like getting A's, but I also like getting away with stuff."

"That's hardly the same as stalking a locker room filled with naked guys," I said.

Karen told her, "If you got caught sneaking off camp property, you'd probably get kicked out."

"Where would you sneak to anyway?" Sue asked. "There's nothing but a dark road out there."

"There are other places," Charlene said.

"Like where?" Diane asked. "The swimming pool in the

middle of the night? Or maybe you'd like to visit the compost heap?"

"Like the Felinas' camp," Charlene said.

I deliberately changed the subject. "Without boys," I said, "it's not worth creeping anywhere."

"Come on, guys," Diane said. "We only have a few minutes before lights-out and I want my turn."

Sabrina turned to Diane. "Truth or dare?"

Diane said, "I'll happily take the dare, thank you very much. And make it a good one."

Everyone hooted.

Sabrina said, "Okay, Diane. You have to…" She looked around the cabin. "Close your eyes and let everyone in the room whisper something in your ear. You can't know who says what. So everyone, change your voices. I'll blindfold her with my bandana."

"That's the weirdest dare I've ever heard," I said.

But everyone was laughing, and Diane closed her eyes as Sabrina tied her bandana around Diane's head, and each girl whispered in her ear. I don't know what anyone else said, but I told her, in my cartoon British voice, "I'm glad you're in me bunk, I am."

When the dare was over, Diane slipped the covering from her eyes and handed back the bandana. She turned to me. "Okay, Miss Simone. Truth or dare?"

"Truth."

She asked, "Hilary Clinton or Donald Trump?"

"You mean, who would I have voted for?"

"That's lame," Vanessa said.

"No," Diane said. "Duh. Which one would you *do it* with?"

"That's disgusting," Sabrina said.

"I've heard about this before," Karen said. "Where you ask someone to choose between two people, but they're always two gross people, so no matter who you choose, you can't win."

"Come one, Simone," Diane said. "Ante up."

"Well," I said, "Trump is richer than God, but that hair…and Hilary…well…what can I say about Hilary? Those pants suits are pretty sexy. But really, the problem is, I don't think either one of them is ready for *me*…" I pretended to sweep dirt off my shoulder. Everyone laughed. I think Diane brought out the funny in me. "I'll take the dare instead."

I trusted that Diane would give me something pretty chill. Something I could easily live down in a day or two.

"Take off your shorts and run around the bunk," she said.

"We already walk around in our underwear," Vanessa said.

"I don't mean *inside*," Diane said, pointing toward the cabin door with her chubby finger.

"Outside?" I said. The thunder rolled just as I asked the question, as if for emphasis.

Diane said, "Pretend you're in the Bahamas and a lifeguard is chasing you."

"No going back in Truth or Dare," Karen added.

The girls started chanting, like creepy men in a strip club.

"Take it off, take it off, take it off, take it off…"

I slipped out of my cargo shorts and threw them on the bed, took my hair out of the pony tail, and tossed it over a shoulder jokingly, trying to be Miss Sexy Stripper. Then I looked down. I sighed with relief when I realized my granny panties were mostly covered by my long T-shirt. Who cared if I ran around outside? No one would see me on a rainy night like tonight. I slipped on my Crocs and went to the door.

I looked out through the screen at the buckets of rain

cascading over the gutter-less roof. The girls giggled behind me.

"It's raining," I said, as if they didn't know it.

A few whined sarcastically.

"Suck it up," someone said.

The cabin door slammed behind me as I stepped onto the porch. For a moment, I stopped at the top of the stairs, then counted down from five and headed into the pouring rain.

In the dark downpour, I could barely see in front of me, but I slowly made my way around the cabin, working hard not to break my neck by sliding through the mud. Even though I was running through the rain in my undies, with my bunkmates warm and cozy while they laughed at me, it was the least lonely I'd felt since coming to Camp Kamama.

I had just finished my trek and was making my way to the porch steps when a figure standing a little off the path startled me. I froze. I wiped my eyes and squinted. It was Phoebe. Her earrings dangled like silver icicles. It was unnerving to see her standing there in the dark as rain fell like tiny pebbles all around me.

She stood ten yards from the cabin, her body half blocked by a tree, a black umbrella wide and protective over her head, like Madeline from the children's books. I found myself excited to see her, but the excitement came mostly from knowing she wasn't supposed to be there, that we were doing something we weren't supposed to.

"Phoebe?" I whispered. "What are you doing here?"

She didn't answer my question. Instead she asked, "Why are you in your underwear, Simone?"

"Truth or Dare. I took the dare."

It was teeming, but Phoebe had chosen a spot under a canopy of summer branches.

I stepped closer to her to gain some protection from the trees. "What are you doing here?" I asked again, dragging my wet hair away from my face.

"I was bored."

"Bored or not, I don't think you should be coming over here. If any of the girls see you, they might—don't y'all have fun stuff to do at your own camp?"

She looked past me as a rise of laughter rose from the depths of cabin ten. She brought her eyes back to me. In the dark, with the dim light from the cabins reflecting in them, they looked more green than blue.

"No," she said, sighing.

"Come on, Phoebe," I said. "I've been going to camps since I was, like, in the third grade. Every camp has fun stuff to do."

"All we do all day long is what you do at your tree once a day."

"You mean, reflect?"

"More or less."

"Won't they notice you're missing?" I asked.

"Probably. But whatever."

Even though it was summer, my arms rubbed one another to keep away the chill. "Look," I told her. "I'm sorry you don't like your camp, but you can't hang out here. You especially can't come over and stand out here in the rain, in the dark, like you're stalking us or something."

"I'm not doing that," Phoebe said.

"The girls might think you are."

"Then you can tell them I'm not."

"No, I can't."

"Why not?"

"Because they sort of expect us to keep apart. You know. Your camp over there, ours over here. We're not supposed to be talking to one another."

"Why not?" she asked again.

"Because you're a Felina. I'm a Kamama."

She scrunched up her nose. "I'm a cat and you're an elephant?"

"I have to go, Phoebe. Everyone will be wondering where I am…"

The cabin door slammed behind me.

"Simone?" a voice whispered through the rain.

Another rumble of thunder caused the ground to vibrate beneath my feet.

"Will you meet me at the tree tomorrow?" Phoebe asked. "I promise to give you time to reflect before I show up."

The voice from the porch whispered my name again.

Without answering Phoebe, I left her standing there in the dark and headed to the steps without turning around. I was afraid if I did, she would take it as an invitation. And I couldn't imagine the looks on the girls' faces if a Felina followed me into our bunk.

Chapter Twenty

After waking up feeling refreshed—the rain from the night before made my hair smell summery—Phoebe's face came to me in a blur of white skin beneath a black umbrella. Had it been a dream, the way she'd stood there in the rain, wanting to chat like best friends?

No. It was not a dream. Phoebe had come all the way to Camp Kamama along a dark winding path with the hope of finding me.

But why? Was she crazy? Lonely? Had she needed something from me? Something I was too busy to help her with?

Guilt tried to settle within my bones, but I refused to let it. No one in her right mind would just appear at someone else's camp, especially on a stormy night, and expect to have a normal girlfriend moment.

With Phoebe's image skillfully tucked between the folds in my brain, I did my best to enjoy our breakfast of one thin pancake with blueberries on top. In yoga, I bent some of the right ways without breaking a femur or pulling a hammy. At Café

Kamama, I learned how to make a very-berry-smashin'-bashin' smoothie, complete with berries from the garden. I ran hard through the obstacle course, proud to keep my smoothie from ejecting from my stomach onto the girl in front of me.

After the course, I grabbed my bag, threw my whistle around my neck, then barely said goodbye to the girls as the path led me to my reflection spot. Phoebe's image, having crawled out of the creases in my brain, followed me there. The closer I got to the tree, the more I needed to see her; the more I needed to know.

My tired legs shook, my backpack slammed against my back, sweat ran down my temples. At the tree, I dropped my backpack beside the log and waited. Birds chirped and trees rustled in the breeze above my head. The path leading away toward the lake was empty, except for a squirrel chasing its buddy from one side to the other.

Maybe Phoebe had been caught prowling around the night before. Maybe she'd decided that taking a chance being friends was too risky after all.

I sat down on the log, readjusted my ponytail, placed my cap on my lap, and closed my eyes. Every little forest sound seemed louder with my eyes closed, and I couldn't concentrate on anything other than the fact that Phoebe hadn't shown up yet. I opened my eyes. They gravitated to the hollow. There sat that worn piece of plastic, like a puppy dog's ear, sticking up through the wet leaves. I glanced again down the empty path, then leaned back and gripped my fingers around the baggie's tip. The book slid easily from its hiding place.

Too easily, I thought.

As I pulled the baggie out, something else appeared in the hole, just to the right of the diary. It was another baggie. As I slid it out, my eyes couldn't believe what they were seeing, and I actually wondered if I was having some sort of hallucination: an entire baggie filled with little aluminum squares, thinner than the Dove chocolates I snuck into the movie theater, but maybe just as delicious. I opened the baggie, stuck my nose inside, and took a deep whiff, nearly passing out from ecstasy. My hungry fingers took one out. The aluminum felt cool from being buried in the earth. I unwrapped it, and just like the perfect shot in lacrosse, when the ball enters the pocket and you know you've caught it, and you run with it, and your heart races as you soar across the field, that tiny piece of chocolate had a mind of its own. In lacrosse, my hands and feet often knew what to do before I even gave them direction. And this was the same sensation, only my feet weren't involved.

I felt like Charlie in *Willy Wonka and the Chocolate Factory*, when he finds a chocolate bar with the golden ticket. But this was way better, because this chocolate *was* the golden ticket.

My hand stopped mid-air. Phoebe might know that one of them was missing. And if she knew one was missing, she'd put two and two together: missing candy equals a peek in the hole equals a peek at her diary.

Maybe she already knows you're reading it.

This thought rang through my mind as I again scoped out the empty path. But that wouldn't make any sense. If she knew I was snooping, she wouldn't want to be my friend. And then, the bigger question gnawed at me: *Why would a Felina want to hang out with a Kamama to begin with*?

Maybe somewhere in that thin blue book would be the answer to that question. Maybe not…but *maybe…*

With the book on my lap, my fingers by rote opened the foil and placed a chocolate on my tongue. It tasted expensive, like the chocolates sold at boutique shops at the beach. Move over,

Nestle Crunch! Take a dive, you dumb old Snickers!

As the candy became one with my tongue, I cocked my head to the side. Except for the birds, all was silent. Trish had been pretty careless, I thought smugly, sneaking candy into our bunk. I would only take the risk way out here, next to my protective tree, where I wouldn't get caught by a roving counselor or a rogue camper.

Shoving the balled-up foil into my pocket and skipping the pages I'd previously read, I started:

Sometimes you wonder, is it written on your forehead like a scarlet letter? How is it you've managed to keep this inside you for so long without it exploding out of you, like a bomb or an erupting volcano? Maybe that's what you are. A volcano, ready to let loose but somehow not able to. There are ways around this, as you—

A twig snapped behind me. I stuck the book back in the baggie and back in the hole, then shoved the baggie with the chocolates behind it, careful to cover them both the way I'd found them, with a sliver of plastic sticking up through the leaves. I jumped up from the log, and just as I was brushing my dirty hands against my shorts, a voice spoke up from the other side of the tree.

"Hey," Phoebe said, walking toward me on the path.

My stomach soured. My spit dried up. Had she seen me?

"Sorry about last night," she said quietly. "Sometimes I get to wandering and then forget how far I've gone."

Her apology filled me with instant relief.

Phoebe wore a pair of hip baggy jeans with a gray hoodie and her Rainbows, like a blond white rapper. Small pink dangles hung from her ears. She held another bottle of Gatorade in her hand, this one half-filled with yellow liquid. Her face looked drawn and pale, like she hadn't seen the sun in a while. Even though we were surrounded by forest, it was very sunny up in the mountains, especially down by the lake, or out in the Kamama garden. I was growing a nice bronzy tan, even though I didn't spend any time sunbathing.

"No worries," I told her, trying to keep my voice even and casual. "So, how's it going?"

"Mornings are sort of a drag for me," Phoebe said. "Are you done yet?"

"What?"

"Reflecting. Aren't you supposed to be—?"

"Oh. Yeah. It's way harder than it sounds. You know. Reflecting."

"Like writing," Phoebe said.

"Writing?"

She nodded. "When I first started, it was really hard. Now the words just pour out of me. Maybe I'm inspired up here. You know. Like Thoreau."

Changing the subject, I asked, "Why do you hate your camp so much? I mean, it seems like you do. Coming all the way over to Kamama in the rain like that."

She sat on the log and stretched out her legs. "It's not that I hate it. I'm just not into it. Do you like yours?"

"So-so," I said, sitting next to her, trying to play it extra cool. "Some of the girls are nice enough."

I thought of Diane and how she made everyone laugh.

"Do you have friends back at school?" Phoebe asked.

At first, I wasn't sure whether to be honest or not, but then I thought about this movie I saw one time, where a really sad guy sits at a bar and tells the bartender everything bad about his life, things he can't share with people he loves. He has to dump it somewhere, but he doesn't know where to do it, so he tells the man behind the bar, a total stranger, who listens to every word.

"I'm sort of a loner at school these days," I told Phoebe. "I've made a few friends at camp. More than I thought I would, anyway. You?"

"Most of the girls complain about the dumbest things," Phoebe said. "Like how they didn't get the horse they wanted for their birthday, or how the recession took away their chances of going back to boarding school. I have nothing in common with them. Mostly anyway."

"How many girls are in your bunk?" I asked.

"Twenty. Yours?"

"Only ten, thank God."

I couldn't imagine sharing a room with nineteen other fat, sweaty girls, all stretched out on their beds at the same time while trying to get their shorts pulled up. No wonder so many of my bunkmates didn't change their clothes before bed. Too much work.

Phoebe said, "Sometimes I write about it."

The diary warmed my back. I swallowed from my water bottle.

"About what?" I asked.

"All the junk in my head. Stuff I can't say to anyone else."

She grew silent for a moment, staring up into the branches of brown and green suspended over our heads like an awning. Her long blond hair reached down to the log as her head tilted back. Tiny blue veins in her neck lay in contrast to her milky white skin.

"If you don't like camp," Phoebe said, looking at me again, "then why did you come here?"

"My parents thought it would be a good idea."

"Huh," she said. "Mine too. And my mom and dad hardly ever agree on anything."

"Same here," I said. "My mom thinks this place is like heaven. She'd probably sign up if she could. My dad—well, he nearly had a conniption when he found out how expensive it is."

"Yeah," Phoebe said. "Dads can be pretty brutal." She grew quiet again and looked at her pink nails.

"You wanna take a walk?" she asked after a long moment. "I saw this really cool grove down the path a little ways. There are like a dozen woodpeckers jumping around in the trees. They sound like a team of jackhammers."

Listening to birds that sounded like jackhammers seemed way more fun than trying to reflect, or worrying about the diary breathing on my neck.

"How far away is it?" I asked.

"Just around the bend," she said. "Not even five minutes from here."

I looked at my watch. I had a little more than thirty minutes.

"Sure," I said. I picked up my backpack and paused.

"What's the matter?" she asked.

"This backpack weighs a kazillion pounds."

"Just leave it in that hole till you come back this way."

She waited as I bent over the log and shoved my backpack into the tiny cave. Even though I was squashing the contents buried there, she didn't react.

I walked beside her along the path, slipping behind her when it got too narrow for both of us. Less than five minutes later, I heard the hammering.

I had grown up with woodpeckers in my own yard and the occasional one in the grove behind my school. But this was insane. There had to be at least ten of the red and white birds, hopping from trunk to trunk, pecking at the bark, burying bugs for later or digging out others for lunch.

"It's funny how they walk on the sides of the trees," I said.

"And upside down," Phoebe added.

We stood silent for a few minutes watching the loud birds as they moved from branch to branch. They made a high–pitched cry, like babies on helium, and then hammered away with their sharp beaks.

"I love it out here," Phoebe whispered, "where there aren't any freaks or weirdos or parents or teachers. Where there's nothing but peacefulness."

I didn't think that woodpeckers were especially peaceful, but I was happy to nod in agreement.

She went on. "If I died and came back, like through reincarnation or something, and I got to choose, I'd come back as a bird. You can fly everywhere; you can live up high in the treetops, safe from all the human craziness below. What about you? What would you come back as?"

It was an odd but interesting question.

"I think I'd come back as a girl again," I said. "You know, so I could get it right the second time around."

"Get what right?"

"Everything," I said, smiling sadly.

"I don't think you can do everything right, no matter how many times you come back."

The sound of the woodpeckers was drowned out by the sound of laughter as it rolled up the path from the direction of the lake, swirling around our legs like a cool fog.

"I guess I should go," Phoebe said. "I was supposed to stay with my group today. They're probably wondering where I am. I'll see you tomorrow, Simone. And I promise to give you time to reflect."

"Thanks," I told her, even though reflecting seemed about as remote a possibility as learning to like cauliflower.

Phoebe started walking on the path, but stopped about four yards down. "Promise you'll meet afterward?" she asked in a hopeful voice. "You won't bail on me?"

I nodded. "Promise."

"Okay. Good. See ya tomorrow."

She went in one direction, and I went in the other. A few minutes later, as I was pulling my backpack out of the hollow in the tree, a voice said, "Hey, Simone."

I twirled around. "Crimony, Charlene. You nearly gave me a heart attack."

Charlene stood a few yards away. She didn't have her backpack with her. Her cap wasn't on her head. She looked summery and pretty standing there, slices of sunlight sneaking past the branches and lighting up strands of wheat-colored bangs that lay across her forehead.

"I didn't mean to scare you," she said. "I wanted to see where your reflection place was."

"Why?"

"Just curious. Sorry I freaked you out."

With my heavy backpack in my arms, I deliberately stood directly in front of my log, feeling protective of the tree for more than one reason.

"This place is cool," she said, coming closer, looking up into the old tree, its twisted branches going every which way as they grew toward the sky. "I like it way out here."

I leaned awkwardly to the right as Charlene looked around.

"I thought you went into a trance during reflection," I said, trying to keep my voice light, not letting her hear the thumping of my heart against my chest.

"Mary says that sometimes the body needs to wander like the brain does."

"Oh."

"It's almost time for lunch. Wanna walk back together?"

"Sure," I said, my stomach grumbling loudly for emphasis. I pulled the backpack straps onto my shoulders, sneaking a glance around the other side of the tree even though I knew Phoebe was already down by the lake by now. All was still. Nothing pink or blond as far as the eye could see.

"What's that?" Charlene suddenly asked, looking past me.

I had moved too far to the side, away from the hole. The plastic was poking up through the dirt, and one thin beam of sunshine had found its way to the little dog ear.

"What?" I asked.

"*That*," Charlene said. She knelt down on the log and peered into the tiny cave. "Is that yours?"

"Uh, yeah," I said. "Part of the whole reflection thing."

"I thought you didn't have anything to share in powwow," Charlene said, scooting off the log and brushing off her knees. She pointed a thumb toward the hole. "Can't you use the stuff you're writing in there?"

Her pointing thumb made me want to slap her arm, to tell her she had no right looking in there and no right entering my space.

"Most of it's garbage," I said. "You know. Nonsense."

Nonsense. I had stolen Phoebe's word.

"Well," Charlene said, "you might wanna hide it better."

I repositioned the baggie without letting her see my shaking hands, then reached into a pile of decaying leaves and grabbed a handful.

"Why don't you bring it back to camp?" she asked.

"I like writing out here," I said, smearing the damp leaves all over it. "It's easier when no one's around."

I situated the backpack on my back, trying hard not to glance at the hole.

"Let's go eat," Charlene said. "We're getting a real sandwich today. With two slices of bread and everything."

"Cool," I said in an extra smooth voice.

Together, we walked away from the tree, up the path, and back toward Camp Kamama.

Chapter Twenty-one

The hotter the temperature became, the slower the day went. Work in the garden was tedious, but at least we got a bit of a cool down in the pool after. During expression time, Diane showed me how to make *op art*, an abstract style of painting that makes the eye go bonkers. I created wild lines of red and blue, and even though the painting looked like a monkey could have done it, I planned to hang it up over my cot. Expression time was followed by a particularly boring powwow. After what had happened to Hannah, no one was in the mood—or brave enough—to share, so most of the conversation was about school and critical thinking classes we should all take before college. Of course, Charlene was disappointed she wouldn't witness a catharsis, but personally, I was relieved.

After powwow, we marched to the cafeteria for a not-so-awful dinner of whole wheat pasta with garden-grown tomatoes and parsley mixed in. During the after-dinner movie, I noticed some of the girls had their eyes closed as Jackie Chan jumped a couple of fast-moving trains and Karate-chopped his way through enemy lines. My eyes were threatening to close as well, but I fought off the sleepiness. I didn't watch the movie though. All I could think about was Phoebe's diary—and diaries in general.

I had read Anne Frank's *The Diary of a Young Girl* three times in one summer, wishing each time that the ending would change even though I knew it never would. *Go Ask Alice* was another one, totally different from Anne Frank's life, drug abuse instead of the Holocaust. But as different as they are, both are true, and both main characters die in the end.

Anne Frank and the Anonymous writer of *Go Ask Alice* wanted to be read. They wanted to be heard. Is that what Phoebe wanted? To be heard? Maybe there was something she wanted me to know that she couldn't say out loud. Something that was easier to write in a diary.

But then, I thought, writing in a diary didn't help that *Go Ask Alice* girl and her drug habit. And it obviously didn't help Anne Frank, who ended up dying in a concentration camp.

***

When I got back to the bunk, most girls were already in lights-out prep mode, showering, using the toilet, brushing teeth, putting in retainers. I liked taking my shower last so I could crawl into bed with the least amount of sweat possible.

Next to my bed, I kicked off my Crocs. One bed over, Charlene rubbed her freshly washed hair with a towel as she spoke to Trish.

"I can't wait to study it in college," Charlene was saying.

Trish, who was sitting on the edge of her own bed filing her fingernails, nodded.

"Study what?" I asked. If the conversation had to do with Charlene's career choice, it probably involved interrogations.

"Psychology," Charlene said.

I didn't respond as I placed my sweaty Crocs under my bed. I expertly slipped off my bra without taking off my T-shirt and tossed it onto the cot.

"What about you, Simone?" Charlene asked me.

"What about me?"

"What do you want to be?"

She was the second person in as many days to ask me that question. The other was Phoebe.

"I used to want to be a coach, or maybe a physical therapist." I pulled out my pony tail holder and worked on yanking out tangles.

Charlene folded her wet towel, draped it over a shoulder, and started brushing her thick hair. "And now?"

I shrugged. "Not sure anymore."

I pictured myself running on the field, scooping the ball, passing it through the air into the pocket of a teammate. The memory was surreal.

"Why not?" Charlene asked.

I scooped up my folded SpongeBob pajamas from the foot of my bed. "Doesn't seem as important as it used to."

"How long did you play lacrosse?" she asked.

"How did you know I played lacrosse?"

"Your hat," she said, pointing to my denim cap with the lacrosse sticks across the front, hanging from a peg on the wall. It was the only thing I still held onto that reminded me of what I used to be besides the trophies I had hiding in my bedroom closet.

"Oh," I said. "A few years."

"Were you any good?"

"Yup."

I slid out my toiletry case from under my bed.

"But you don't play anymore?" Charlene asked. "Were you kicked off the team because of your weight?"

I stood up and faced her, heat rising to my face. "You know what Charlene? You don't have the right to ask me those questions, just like you don't have the right to ask any camper questions, even if it's in powwow."

"Powwow is about sharing."

"Well, maybe some people aren't ready to share yet."

I started for the bathroom, but Charlene stood in front of me. "Is that why you haven't shared yet? Because you're not ready?"

"I haven't shared because I have nothing to say, if it's all the same to you."

"What about that junk you're writing in your journal?"

I wanted to tell her to shut up, that the diary was none of her business. It was all I could do to hold my tongue. "I told you earlier—it's all bull."

"You could still probably use some of it to—"

Trish interrupted. "Not every overweight person comes from a messed-up family, Charlene. Everyone has a different story. Besides, you haven't said anything in powwow either. And you were lucky enough to get out of Truth or Dare last night."

"That's not my fault," Charlene said. "It was lights-out by the time Simone came back in."

"How convenient."

"Powwow isn't the same as Truth or Dare anyway," Charlene told her. "That's just a stupid game. Powwow is for getting to the core. For the serious stuff. The sooner you say something, the better you'll feel."

I raised my voice a notch. "Maybe you need to stop getting up in everyone else's business and just deal with your own."

A few girls stopped what they were doing. Marion stepped close to Charlene, and for a moment I thought she would interject. But she did not.

Charlene looked from me to Trish. "What's up with the bitchiness?"

"Why don't *you* say something in powwow, Charlene?" I said. "Why don't you dig deep and let it all out?"

"Maybe I will."

"That would be good. Then you can quit nagging me, and you can quit interrogating the other girls."

"She's just trying to help," Vanessa said, standing next to Charlene.

"Tell them, Vanessa," Charlene said. "Most of these girls don't know what happened to you."

Marion stepped in between Vanessa and Charlene.

"Ness," she said, "it's almost time for lights-out."

"Let her tell it," Charlene said. "It makes her feel better to talk about it. Doesn't it, Vanessa?"

"When I was twelve," Vanessa said flatly, "my cousin raped me."

I wanted to cover my ears. I wanted to stand under the shower and sing out loud so I wouldn't have to hear Vanessa's story. But I didn't move. I stood beside my bed, hugging my folded pajamas and toiletry bag, and listened along with everyone else.

She continued slowly and clearly, like she was giving an oral report in science or history class. "I didn't know that side of the family very well," Vanessa said. "They live in Mississippi. But my dad, he got a bonus at work and wanted to treat us to a family vacation. We got this really cool condo in Ocean City, Maryland near the boardwalk, and I got to buy a new two-piece bathing suit. The kind that makes a girl have boobs, even when she doesn't. I was pretty skinny back then. No hips." She patted her sides. "I sort of looked like a boy, so I don't know why my cousin thought—anyway, we had a totally chill week together, hanging out on the beach all day, swimming in the pool after dark. He's four years older than me. That made him sixteen at the time."

Now, all of the girls from my bunk were standing like statues, listening to Vanessa. Sue stood in her underwear. Sabrina held her bandana in her hands, wringing it like a wet dish rag. Diane stood next to me, her breath heavy, like she'd just run the obstacle course.

"My cousin came into my room while I was half-asleep," Vanessa said. "He said he wanted to take a walk on the boardwalk. I looked at the clock and it was after midnight. I thought his idea was crazy, but I also thought it was sort of a grown-up thing to do and all. So, we snuck out through the sliding glass door in the living room and took the stairs down from the balcony. We walked on the boardwalk for a while, past the bars, down to the pier, where they have rides and stuff, but they were all shutting down for the night. So, we started back along the boardwalk, and he said, 'Let's walk on the sand instead.' Well, we walked beside the ocean, heading back in the direction of the condo, and next thing I knew he was holding my hand. At first I thought it was weird, you know, being cousins and all, but then I thought, what's so wrong about holding hands? My best girlfriend and I used to hold hands when we were little. But then he said, 'Let's stop and rest. I'm tired.' And he fell to the sand, pulling me down with him. We were right in front of one of those big lifeguard stands. It was empty because it was nighttime.

"The beach was pitch-black. About the only lights came from the pier, which was ten blocks away, and the moon, and the stars, there were so many that night. And I remember the sound of the waves, which were a few yards away but sounded closer. And it happened before I knew it. It happened, and I cried, and I don't think he heard me, because the waves were loud. And it was over so fast. One second he was on top of me, and the next, he was wading up to his knees in the ocean."

My jaw was clenched. I wanted to find that boy. Go into my basement and wipe the spider webs off my lacrosse stick, then find him and check the side of his head. I had never felt so defensive before. Especially off the field. I wasn't sure where the feeling was coming from. Just looking at Vanessa, at her sweet brown face and pretty brown eyes, and knowing someone had done that to her…

"Did you tell anyone?" I barely squeaked.

"My mom. But she never told my dad."

"Where's your cousin now?" Diane asked.

"He graduated this year from Old Miss. He's going to become a pastor."

"Tell them what happened last year," Charlene said.

I wanted to deck Charlene as hard as Vanessa's cousin.

"Oh, yeah. Well. Last year, we had a family reunion, and there he was, sitting right across from me, eating low country boil, drinking from a soda can, and it was like he'd never done anything wrong. Or anything at *all.* I started thinking that maybe he didn't. Maybe it was something *I* did. He had told me on the beach how beautiful I was. So, I thought…I mean, I didn't know I'd thought it until later…if I was ugly, maybe he wouldn't have done that to me. If I hadn't been the kind of girl he thought I was, I'd still be a virgin."

She laughed like she was ready to share the punch line of a joke.

"Later that night, after we snuck back to the condo, I walked right into the kitchen and made myself a submarine sandwich out of leftover lunchmeat. I could hardly fit that sub in my mouth. But I did. It makes me feel better to eat, you know what I mean?"

All of us nodded.

"Makes me feel safe," Vanessa said. "I eat to be fat. I *want* to be fat."

"You do?" Sabrina asked.

"Yeah. Because if I'm fat, then no one will think I'm beautiful. And if I'm not beautiful, then no one will look at me. And if no one looks at me, then no one will hurt me."

Charlene placed a hand against Vanessa's back and smiled.

I don't even remember what was said after that. I only remember Vanessa getting ready for bed as though she hadn't just told a bunch of girls she'd been raped by her cousin. And how eerily quiet the cabin became.

After my shower, Charlene and I were the last ones to use the sink. I spit the toothpaste out of my mouth, and whispered to her, "You have no right."

"What are you talking about?"

"You have no right forcing people to say what you think they need to say. You might become a doctor one day, but you're not one yet. Stop practicing on us. We're not your personal guinea pigs."

I swished a handful of tap water around in my mouth, spit one last time, and slammed a stall door behind me. I sat there for a few minutes after I peed, until the last call for lights-out was given.

Half the girls were already snoring as I made my way to my bed. Only the dim yellow light from the porch found its way inside the cabin. Charlene lay on her cot with her back to me. I couldn't tell if she was asleep, but I was sort of hoping she wasn't. I was sort of hoping she was thinking about what I'd said. That it wasn't her place to get people to open up. It wasn't her place to ask questions, to dig so deep. Not everyone was ready to go there yet.

Especially me.

Chapter Twenty-two

The next morning, Charlene and I stood with forty girls between us during yoga, and sat on opposite ends of the table at breakfast. At Café Kamama, she laughed with a bunch of cabin nine girls on the other side of the room as they baked low-fat brownies. During the obstacle course, when she fell hard into the dirt below the monkey bars, I automatically held out my hand to help her.

"No thank you," she said, brushing off her rear end and running to the next obstacle.

I didn't care. I wasn't really thinking about Charlene and her busy-body attitude. I was thinking about my tree. And Phoebe. And her diary.

When our penance at the obstacle course was over, I pulled off my ankle weights, slid the whistle around my neck, grabbed my bag, and nearly tore down the path to the tree.

My reflection spot was quiet. Even the birds seemed to be sleeping. Phoebe had promised to give me time to reflect, so I hoped she meant it this time. Even so, I took a quick glance around before I threw my backpack on the ground and kneeled down on the log.

I pulled out the treasure-filled baggie first, with those delectable squares of chocolate like precious pieces of gold. Gold that was calling out to me. I reached in and grabbed one, then another. I opened the first and chewed it like it was the last piece of candy in the universe. But it wasn't. I ate the second. That one tasted better than the first, as chocolate often does. My eyelids fluttered in ecstasy. I would have eaten a chunk of cardboard coated in chocolate I was so desperate for a piece of home, a piece of normalcy. I felt like Winnie the Pooh, only instead of honey, I'd stuck my hand in the tree and pulled out chocolate! A happy tune played in my head, even though I felt decadent. I sucked down some water, washing the chocolate into my stomach and pushing it into my veins, into the tiny capillaries in my brain that were celebrating with fireworks and party favors.

I glanced around again, buried the goodie bag back in the leaves, pulled the other baggie out, then slid out the diary. Against my lap, it seemed to open by itself, falling to the exact spot I had left off the day before. An encouraging sign, I was sure.

A happy little smile sat on my lips, but my smile faded and the chocolate in my gut began to churn like a mucky river as the words of the strange poem fell before me:

Sick, ill…
Absolutely no will.
Plain Jane, going insane.
A lesson, a game, a freaking shame.
Tired, mad, no pride from your dad.
Cry, fly, and soon maybe die—

A loud snap fell down from somewhere above. I jumped up, startled, but no other out-of-place sounds came from the forest. Maybe a large bird of some kind—maybe even a woodpecker—digging around in the branches. I waited a whole minute before sitting again, realizing that my finger had held its place in the book without my even knowing it.

As I re-read the poem, a few itty bitty words soaked into my brain, pulsating like a headache: *a game…your dad…*

After the poem, the words turned into a journal entry.

If you want peace in your life, you have to share how you feel. Maybe others can help you get your life back on track. Maybe then you'll feel the way you used to. You remember how you used to feel, don't you? Before everything changed? You need to share your feelings with at least one person. Yes. You could do that. Even though you don't think you have any friends, you do. There has to be at least one person you can turn to…but choose wisely…maybe a new friend from across the lake?

Gooseflesh attacked my arms. Who else besides me did Phoebe know from across the lake?

The next pages were blank.

Another snap, this one from the ground. Phoebe. On the path. A tiny wave hello.

I threw her a wave, turned my back, and as quickly as possible zipped up the baggie and pushed it into the earth. As I stood up to greet her, I shoved the chocolate wrappers into a pocket of my shorts and hid my dirty hands behind my back.

Phoebe's hair was pulled back in a white headband, but it was apparent she hadn't brushed it first. She held onto an empty bottle of Gatorade. Her clothes were the same from the day before. Not so unusual, considering I wore my Kamama T-shirt at least two days in a row.

"Phoebe," I said.

"Hey, Simone." Her face had a gray tint to it.

"You don't look so good."

"I don't?" she asked, readjusting her headband and flattening down her hair.

I wasn't really talking about the way she looked. I was talking about the way she *was.*

"Are you okay?" I asked

She laughed, but it was so slight, the average person walking by wouldn't have noticed. "They keep giving us terrible breakfasts."

My stomach grumbled suddenly, loud enough for both of us to hear. Chocolate tried to rise up in my throat. I took another swig from my water bottle to wash it down and tried my best to conceal a belch.

"There's nothing wrong with me," Phoebe said, as if I'd asked. "Anyway, I always feel better as the day goes on." She stepped closer. Even though she looked a bit washed out, she still smelled like honeysuckle. "Did you reflect?"

"Sort of," I lied. "Mornings are hard for me too, I guess." That was a lie as well. Mornings had never been difficult for me. I looked forward to breakfast too much.

She sat on the log with her legs straight and looked up at me. I prayed to myself that she wouldn't notice the harried way the baggies had been buried.

"Did you play Truth or Dare last night?" she asked.

"No," I said, thinking about the mini powwow we'd had in the bunk and how Truth or Dare would have been better. It was strange standing here in front of Phoebe, harboring the secret that I had read her words, that she had mentioned someone from *across the lake* in her private diary.

"I've driven through your hometown on my way to Atlantic Beach," she said.

"Oh?"

"I was really young at the time. Aren't there a bunch of old houses there?"

"Uh-huh."

"What do you do there?" she asked. "I mean, for fun?"

The diary crouched behind Phoebe like a wolf.

"Hang out on the river," I said, trying to keep my voice steady, ignoring the nervous fluttering in my stomach. "Well, I used to, back in middle school."

"Not anymore?"

"I'm not exactly what you'd call bathing suit material."

After a moment of silence, Phoebe said, "A couple of us girls took a walk this morning around the lake."

"You walked all the way around the lake?"

She shrugged. "I like to exercise. Anyway, we heard you all shouting, and we snuck behind a tree and I saw you running around that course. You were amazing."

"You watched me on the obstacle course?"

"I couldn't believe how hard everyone was working," she said. "Is that mandatory, too?"

"Every day. And swimming. In an indoor pool."

"Oh. I would hate for anyone to see me in a bathing suit."

"I thought you all hung out on the beach," I said, trying not to let my eyes move over her shoulder to the hole in the tree. "You know, soak up the sun—"

Her laughter interrupted me. "Hardly."

She didn't elaborate, and I wasn't sure how to respond.

"Are you afraid of anything?" she asked me then.

"I guess so. I mean, everyone's afraid of something."

"Like what?"

I wanted to say I was afraid of back-to-school shopping at Belk during the day, so instead, during one of their crazy midnight sales, I would shop in privacy in the plus-size department. I wanted to tell her that if kept going the way I was,

I'd end up at the Wal-mart in one of those God-awful scooters, with Moon Pies and Doritos and frozen tater tots taking up space in the little basket. I wanted to say, hell yes, I'm afraid. I'm afraid of barely making it through the summer only to go home and eat my way through the cabinets the second I stepped foot in my kitchen. Afraid of Bucky pretending he doesn't know me. Of Mom crying into a pillow behind her closed bedroom door. Of Dad continuing to distance himself from me, to the point where he disappeared from my sight altogether, like the *Incredible Shrinking Man*. I wanted to tell Phoebe—was dying to tell *someone*—how afraid I was of hurting loved ones. Of hurting people I didn't love as well. Of hurting people in general.

But I wasn't sure I wanted to confide in this Felina who had written strange poetry and diary entries I didn't have the right to read.

Instead I said, "I'm afraid of ghosts and demons and stuff. You know…"

"Oh."

"What about you?"

She looked up at me. A beam of sunlight fell through the trees, causing her to cup her eyes with her hand. "I'm basically afraid of everything."

"*Everything*?"

"Well, not the woods. Or tiny animals. Or you." She changed the subject. "What's your favorite food?"

"Meatballs."

"Gross," she said. She moved over an inch on the log so the sunlight was no longer in her eyes. "I hate meat. My father tries to make me eat liver. Ugh. It's disgusting." After a pause, she asked, "How come you wear that lacrosse hat all the time?"

"I used to play."

"Why don't you play anymore?"

"Sort of over the whole jock thing."

"I've never been a jock," Phoebe said.

"You look like a gymnast," I told her.

"I do?" she asked, her cheeks turning pink. "Thanks. I wanted to be a dancer when I was little, but that didn't pan out."

"Why not?"

"My dad, well, he thought the outfits were, you know, skimpy. What he really meant was slutty." After a pause, she said, "I wish our camps were closer together."

"That might not be so good," I told her.

"Why not?"

Because some of our girls would have some of your girls for lunch.

"Some of the Kamama girls don't exactly like you guys," I said.

"Why not?"

Jealousy? Distrust? Worried a Felina might write about them in a journal?

The grumbling in my stomach grew constant. I tried to ignore it.

"The girls from your camp..." I started. "From our camp... we're just too different. You know. The way we look."

"I don't care what you look like," Phoebe said, pouting. "Do *you* have something against the way *I* look?"

"What? No. Of course not. It's just that the girls over here are trying to figure stuff out."

"Who isn't? God, Simone. You make it sound like we're all bitches or something. I don't appreciate being told I'm a certain way or that I fit into a particular category. And I definitely don't appreciate it coming from someone I thought was my friend. Friends aren't supposed to do that..."

A loud rumble came from my stomach just before a spasm attacked me. I doubled over, placing my hands on my thighs.

"Simone?" Phoebe stood up.

My stomach lurched. Heat climbed up my neck and spread across my face. I fell to my knees and swallowed hard, my tongue and throat like the floor of a desert. The ground started rolling beneath me.

"Simone? What's wrong?"

"It's my stomach. It hurts so bad…"

She helped me stand and put my backpack on her back. Along the path we trudged, Fatty-Watty and Pretty-Kitty, all the way back to Kamama, where I barely noticed the worried faces of other campers as they gathered around us, and the ground met my face as I fainted.

***

I lay on a cot under a fluorescent light. A thin sheet covered my body. My head throbbed, and a woman beside me held my hand. Something cool was lying across my forehead. I vaguely remembered someone placing me on the toilet as my bowels let loose, and everything I'd had for breakfast and probably from dinner the night before poured out of me.

"You're in the infirmary," the woman said. "Take it easy. You've lost a lot of fluids." Her hands gently fluffed a pillow behind my head.

I looked toward the woman. Mary's kind face stared down at me. Behind her, a blurred figure stood quietly in the doorway.

"She'll be fine," Mary told the person. "But we have to make sure she gets extra fluids…as well as lunch."

I had missed lunch? Even with my throbbing head, I knew I would die if I missed a meal.

"How did I get here?" I whispered.

"One of the girls from Camp Felina said she found you in the woods. She helped you back to camp."

Phoebe.

"Take a sip," Mary said, placing a straw between my lips. "It has electrolytes to help you get back on track."

I sipped the cool liquid which tasted like lime Gatorade.

"You have to be more careful," she said. "Dehydration is dangerous."

"I was reflecting," I whispered. "I guess I forgot."

"I thought you might have a bug," Mary said, "but you don't have a fever. You didn't eat something you weren't supposed to, did you?"

I prayed there wasn't any chocolate residue stuck in the corners of my mouth, or a tiny dribble on my shirt.

"No, ma'am."

"How does your stomach feel now?" Mary asked.

"Better. I think there was a monster that needed to come out."

Mary spoke to the person in the doorway. "Could you stay with her? Take her to the cafeteria when she's ready. Make sure she gets extra water with her lunch. You'll both be excused from the garden today. You can make up for it another day."

Mary left the room, and Charlene took her place in the chair next to the cot.

"How are you feeling?" Charlene asked.

I wished it was Diane or Sabrina or any of the other Kamama-mamas acting as my guardian angel, not Charlene.

"My head hurts," I told her, rubbing the side of my skull.

"That's because you hit it when you passed out."

We were both quiet for a moment. She placed the cold

compress against my head, gently.

"Charlene..." I wanted to apologize for being mean to her the night before. I didn't like to see people hurt, especially if I was the one who hurt them, and even if it was someone as nosy as Charlene.

"Hey," she said, as if she knew what I was thinking. "No worries. Life is short, right?"

I nodded.

"So," Charlene said. "A Felina. There's one for the books."

"Where's my backpack?" I asked.

"In the front office. You're lucky that girl didn't steal it." She paused and then said, "Your color seems pretty good. You ready to eat?"

I felt my stomach grumble—in a good way—as she helped me out of bed and across the camp to the cafeteria.

Chapter Twenty-three

Instead of swimming, I was asked to go from my late lunch of plain broth and salt-free saltines to Ms. Diggs' office. On the way, Jake passed me.

"I heard about your get-out-of-jail-free card," he said, stopping on the path near the office. "How's your stomach?"

"Better."

"And your head?"

I touched the small but tender bump. "Mary says I don't have a concussion."

"That's good. We'll miss you in water aerobics."

"Thanks."

He continued down the path toward the pool.

Ms. Diggs was standing outside her office, leaning against a post, staring out into the trees and smiling. "Hello, there, Miss Simone. Feeling better?"

"Yes, ma'am."

I followed the director into her tiny office. The room was paneled in golden- colored wood with a set of low bookshelves behind a metal desk. The shelves were loaded with books crammed into every inch of space. Half a dozen rows of framed photos covered the paneled wall to my left of campers, girls from years gone by, laughing or smiling for the camera. I moved my gaze to a photo on her desk. An obese woman stared out at me, her face defiant, as if daring me to say something about her weight.

"Is that your mother?" I asked.

Ms. Diggs and the woman in the photo had the same eyes.

"No," she said. "That woman is me. Back then I was at the top of my weight, around three-fifty. And I'm only five-foot-three." She leaned against the edge of the desk. "See this?" She stretched out her right arm and slid up the sleeve of her extra large T-shirt. "Scars, my darling," she said jovially.

"From what?" I asked. The crinkly pink scars went from just below her elbow to her armpit.

"From too much fat."

She could tell by the look on my face that I wasn't making the connection.

"Fat," she said again. "I had my gallbladder removed sixteen years ago. They sent it off to a college lab for the medical students to ponder over. How 'bout them apples? I could barely keep anything down the first eighteen months. I lost over two hundred pounds in the first two years."

I knew where the gallbladder was located, but I was still confused. "They went into your stomach through your arm?"

She laughed. "No, though they probably will one day. I lost so much weight so fast, all that was left was excess skin. So much of it, my arms swished when the wind blew. I didn't wear short sleeves or shorts for years. Then I saw a report on television about removing the excess skin."

"I've never heard of that before."

"I hadn't either. I went to a specialist, and the following month, I was cut up like a filet o' fish." She laughed again, and I smiled. I liked Ms. Diggs.

"Did it hurt?" I asked. "The healing part?"

"Not as much as it itched. But that was the price I paid for nearly eating myself to death."

I compared her to the photo. "You look awesome now," I told her.

"I feel awesome." She waved toward the desk. "Now, let's get some work done. I'm going to have you prepare mailers for me. We're trying to get a winter camp going this year. For a little extra revenue. See if we can't get some campers up here for a winter wonderland. Grab a chair from the corner, take an address label from this sheet, and stick it on the brochure, like this." Ms. Diggs demonstrated. "Simple, yes? If you feel nauseous, or if your head begins to hurt, just holler. Katharine is in her office next door."

I nodded.

"How about listening to nature's music while you work?" She opened the turn-style windows above the bookshelves, letting in the sounds of birds chirping and wind rustling the leaves. "If you don't have time to finish before the hour is up, no worries. Katharine will help me finish later."

She grabbed a folder from her file drawer before leaving the office.

For the next hour, I peeled labels and stuck them on brochures. This was easy, labeling stuff instead of water dancing. Not a bad swap. But I found myself wondering what the trade-off would be if I skipped powwow.

As I reached the bottom of the pile, I rearranged the pamphlets to organize them better. Beneath the stack, a newspaper page, with a big red circle drawn around an article title, caught my eye. Even though it was upside down, a photo of the lake was clear. I turned the article around: *Camp Kamama closing due to loss in profits; camp director holding out for a miracle.*

I swallowed hard. Camp Kamama was closing?

I read the article:

> *For fifteen years, fifty acres of Appalachian woodland has been a summer home to girls who all have something in common: obesity. Although some locals refer to it as a fat camp, Sandra Diggs, the camp's director, says that since their opening nearly ten years ago, Camp Kamama has evolved into "a place where girls can learn about the joys of living healthily while forming new friendships." Diggs says that through meditation, cooking classes, and tough but regulated exercise, the nearly one hundred young teens can gain control over their choices.*
>
> *"These are a very specific group of girls. All are between the ages of fourteen and seventeen, all have morbid obesity, and all are harboring the key to their own success: self-forgiveness."*
>
> *Diggs says that over the last few years, Kamama has taken a back seat to other summer camps, like those that offer specific sports. She also acknowledges that her camp is more expensive than most, but says that even with the high summer tuition, they barely break even each year. Fire insurance, as well as medical care and ground maintenance, are just a few of the rising costs. Some girls are allowed attend for a lesser cost if they are financially challenged. This year, the camp is taking a huge loss, according to Diggs, which breaks her heart.*

"We are not here to turn these girls into skinny models, or to make them shameful about their bodies. We are here to teach them how to be healthy through exercise, and show them the enjoyment that comes from growing food, preparing food, and sharing it with others. If the camp closes its doors, so many young women will not get the help they deserve." When asked where she and the other directors will go next, she shakes her head sadly. "I just don't know. But it isn't me I'm worried about. It's these young girls who have struggled, not only with their weight, but with fear or anger buried deep inside that only a place like this can help set free."

Jake Stonewolf, the camp's co-founder, explains the word Kamama: "In Cherokee, some words have more than one meaning. A butterfly looks like it has elephant ears when it stretches out its wings, and an elephant has ears like a butterfly, so the Cherokee use Kamama for both elephant and butterfly. These girls are special. They are the epitome of Kamama."

Kamama's last summer camp day will be August 11th. Diggs plans to run a special winter program to help off-set some financial woes, but when their lease is up for renewal in April, the camp will officially close its doors.

My stomach sank as my eyes moved from the framed picture of Ms. Diggs back to the newspaper photo of the lake.

My mind was suddenly spinning with thoughts of the camp closing, of Ms. Diggs and her endless energy, of all the future girls without a place to go the following summer. When Doctor Stan had first mentioned Camp Kamama, all two-hundred-and-fifty-four pounds of me was against it. I still refused to speak in powwow. Had yet to understand the proper way to reflect. And more than my family, I missed my bedroom drawers filled with Little Debbies.

Then how could it be that I found myself wanting to save the place?

I didn't have an answer. I also didn't yet know if saving the camp was even possible. But if it was, I wanted to be a part of it.

***

As soon as I stood up from Ms. Diggs' desk, the door opened.

Charlene said from the doorway, "I am here to inform you that you've been asked to go to the bunk instead of expression time and powwow."

"No way. Really?"

She laughed. "You don't have to be so happy about it. Anyhow, Mary is making me stay with you. So I guess we both win."

"You don't have to babysit," I told Charlene. "I'll be fine by myself. I've been sitting here alone for an hour. What could go wrong in a cabin?"

"Mary said she'd feel better if someone stays with you the first twenty-four hours."

In lacrosse we'd learned the symptoms of a concussion, and I had none of them. My headache was gone; even my stomach felt normal again.

Back at cabin ten, Charlene dropped my backpack on the floor and we each lay down on our beds. With my arms folded behind my head, I thought about that crazy afternoon, what I'd learned about the fate of Camp Kamama, Phoebe helping me back to camp, what the faces of the other campers must have looked like to see a Felina in Kamama territory. Charlene's face, especially.

I suddenly wished I was alone.

"So," Charlene asked, "what's her deal, anyway?"

"Who?" I asked, inspecting a chipped nail in dire need of attention. I chewed on it, then spat out a tiny piece of a hangnail.

"The Felina who helped you back to camp? She had her arm around you like you were best friends."

"So? What if we are friends?"

She shook her head in dismay. "That would be totally dangerous."

"You are so freaking dramatic."

"I am not."

"Yes, you are. She's not as bad as you think, Charlene. Or, should I say, as bad as you *want* her to be."

"So, you know her personally then?"

"As a matter of fact, I do. She's as nice as she is pretty. After hanging out with her for a while, she doesn't look so skinny. And I don't feel so fat."

"You're crazy."

"Why? Because I'd rather hang out with a Felina than—" I cut myself off.

Charlene sat up. "Be careful, Simone."

"Of what? Of offending a Kamama?"

"She's not what she says she is."

I rolled over, facing her, and leaned on an elbow. "Oh my God, Charlene, do you hear yourself? She's just a girl, like you or me. Just a girl at camp who wishes she was…"

The words from Phoebe's diary floated before me. Charlene had no right to hear those words. Then again, I didn't either. They were private. For a fleeting moment, I wondered if I had more in common with Charlene than with Phoebe.

"Wishes she was what?" Charlene asked.

"Nothing," I said. "Anyway, you aren't my mother, and you definitely aren't someone who should be telling me what to do."

"Fine," she said, getting up from her cot and slipping into her flip-flops. "But don't say I didn't warn you. And don't come running to me when that pretty little kitty cat claws your eyes out."

The door slammed behind her, the cold echo hanging in the cabin air a moment, then disappearing.

Chapter Twenty-four

I awoke to the sound of my name.

"Simone..." it whispered. "Simone..."

I sat up, unaware of what time it was, but sure it was well after midnight. The sound of collective breathing, a few snorts here and there, and crickets mingled with the dark in the cabin.

I got out of bed as quietly as I could, trying hard to keep the springs from squealing.

"Simone..." came the voice again.

I pushed my hair out of my sleepy eyes and tiptoed to the cabin's screened door.

Phoebe stood at the bottom of the cabin steps on the outer rim of porch light.

I carefully opened the door a crack, tensed my body for the inevitable squeak, and pushed it a few more inches. Finally, I stood on the porch. I held the door as it softly shut again, then walked down the steps in my bare feet. The nighttime earth felt cool and damp.

Her face was like a classroom's white board, those two blue

round circles like someone had colored them in with a dry erase marker.

"Phoebe," I whispered, waving her to a shaded spot away from the cabin, closer to the bushes. "What time is it?"

She shrugged.

A nocturnal critter ran close by in the brush. Phoebe didn't seem to notice. Her eyes never left mine.

"I wanted to make sure you were okay," she said. "After what happened today."

"I'm fine."

"I wanted to have our director call over here to check on you, but we're really not supposed to come this far, you know, and if anyone found out, well, I might get in trouble."

"I'm fine," I told her again. "I didn't hydrate. Not enough electrolytes and all that jazz."

"You should drink Gatorade. It has tons of electrolytes. So, listen." She touched my arm like we were old lost friends who had suddenly found one another instead of campers whispering in the middle of the night. "I wanted to let you know that I won't be able to meet tomorrow. Our camp is going on a day trip. To the waterfalls."

"Okay."

"I wish I didn't have to go," she said.

"Why not?"

"I feel like we're becoming friends. Like there's some stuff I want to share with you."

The guilt of reading Phoebe's diary was all around me. It was in the crickets' song, the humidity of a summer night, the thumping of my heart.

"No worries," I told her. "We can talk the day after."

She nodded.

"You going to be alright going back?" I asked. "It's so dark."

She held out a small flashlight. "I'll be fine." We whispered goodnight before she disappeared into the dark, back in the direction from where she came.

***

The heat of the day made me feel like I was on valium. My therapist back home had given me a prescription for it once, thinking it might relieve some anxiety, explaining in not so many words that a drug approved by the FDA is a much better solution than crap food approved by Bojangles.

I kept my mind on the task at hand, ignoring Charlene, who was most likely ignoring me right back. She probably thought I owed her an apology, but as far as I was concerned, I owed her nothing.

In yoga, as the mountain sun inched its way into the sky, I performed downward dog until my face felt purple. As we sat in lotus position with our eyes closed, the sound of laughter floated from across the lake. I opened one eye a crack. Clusters of girls moved about beyond Camp Felina's shoreline, too far away to see exactly what they were doing. Every once in a while, a loud "Whoa!" rose into the air, followed by laughter, the way little kids shout when someone does a back flip on a trampoline. I wondered, as I closed my eyes again, how long it took for their voices to travel from their side to ours—two seconds? Less?

I realized I would miss visiting with Phoebe today. She was a strange girl, and entering Camp Kamama on three separate occasions, even if one of those times was to come to my aid, was insanely risky. She seemed desperate and naïve and a bit kooky. Didn't she realize how reckless it was to disappear from camp without anyone knowing? It was that desperation that caused me to feel uncomfortable and her innocence that led me to worry about her.

Across the lake, the crowd of girls was thinning, probably getting ready for their trip to the waterfalls. I pictured Phoebe sitting on the white camp bus with the other girls, staring out the window while they gossiped or sang stupid camp songs, raking her fingers through her pretty hair, nose pressed against the glass as the bus jerked up the mountain.

"Time for breakfast," Jake said, interrupting my thoughts.

We headed to the cafeteria for a bowl of bran cereal with strawberries and low-fat milk. Afterward, in cooking class, we learned how to crack an egg one-handed against a bowl without dripping goop all over the edge, how to separate the yolk from the whites, how to whisk it correctly, how to scramble it in a pan. Afterward, Willie made us painstakingly wipe every inch of the counter with soapy water and a sponge. "It's never worth getting salmonella poisoning," she said seriously, then made us groan when she said, "This day is egg-zactly what the doctor ordered."

After Café Kamama, as I crawled through the obstacle course tunnel and jumped rope, all I could think about was what came next: reflection. The air was super thick with humidity, there wasn't an ounce of a breeze, and there wasn't one cloud to divide the blue sky in any direction. It felt like my legs were moving underwater as I trudged along the path. By the time I got to the tree, sweat had soaked my bra and panties, and I had the urge to jump into a pool or a lake.

I dropped my bag to the ground, then took out my freshly filled water bottle and guzzled half of it, not wanting to take any more chances with dehydration. I removed my hat and retied my pony tail. I glanced around but saw and heard no one, then glanced into the hole. Halfway sticking up through the leaves, a chunk of blue inside the baggie was visible from where I stood. I'd buried it better than that, and now that book was sticking up like a tombstone. A person had to be blind not to see it.

Phoebe's words from the night before whispered in my ear: *There's some stuff I want to share with you.*

It would be wrong *not* to read it, especially if this was what Phoebe wanted. She had come all the way to Kamama in the middle of the night just to tell me she wouldn't be meeting today. She was giving me permission—no, an *invitation*—to know what she had to tell me. This was her way, to write it down instead of coming out and saying it. Her own little personal powwow.

But what if I couldn't help her? What if she shared things I didn't want to know? If her baggage was too much for me? What if I didn't have any advice to give her? Or, worse yet, gave her the wrong advice? After all, I wasn't Charlene.

True. But I am someone that Phoebe trusts.

I reached into the hollow and pulled out the diary, then dug through the leaves until the baggie of goodies was in my hand. Maybe Phoebe had left those little chocolates to thank me for giving her an ear. Or, as it were, a pair of eyes. As I skillfully unwrapped a chocolate with one hand, I opened the book with the other. I put my nose to the paper and took a whiff. Phoebe had definitely been here, probably this morning by the smell of the ink. I popped the chocolate in my mouth and stared at the handwriting again. She really had beautiful script, way prettier than any I'd ever seen except for some early American documents we had in our history books.

I repositioned my rear on the log and got comfortable. Then I began to read the newest entry of her journal:

Your parents sent you here for a reason. You have to trust others...trust that they will not take what happened to you and throw it in your face.

Such simple words, the same way I would have written them if I'd kept a diary, except I would have written in first person, the way diaries are usually written.

I washed down the chocolate with some water. Then I grabbed a second and slowly unwrapped it. The next few lines were written as a list, like she was giving herself a pep talk.

Don't listen to others who say you are weak.

Take charge of your life.

All things are possible.

So far, the list sounded like lines from the posters in my guidance counselor's office.

Only time will help you heal.

Keep the faith.

You won't be fixated on food forever.

I read the last line again. My throat grew tight. I stared down at the chocolate, naked in my hand, just waiting to land on my taste buds.

And now a poem for this crisp blue morning, a little entertainment just in case someone else's eyes happen to read this nonsense.

Someone *else's* eyes?

You're hurting others, fathers, mothers.
You can't help eating, can't help cheating,
Since the heart is barely beating.
At the stadium, everyone knows,
If only in their eyes it shows.
The game, the lights, the start of decay,
Your life was ruined because of that day.

In my palm, the chocolate was beginning to melt.

Food and pain combined with shame,

Everyone thinks you are to blame.
Now you are a fatty-watty,
Trying hard not to hate your Daddy.

What? *What*???

I shook my head. I didn't understand—

Eating, or not eating, doesn't help anything, does it? It doesn't change anything. Damn, girl, be honest with yourself and stop hiding behind food. Food isn't your enemy...

I flicked the gooey chocolate off my palm like a dead bug and it landed in the bushes. My hands trembled. Chocolate had smudged the bottom of the page, but I didn't care.

I stared at the words, the line of them creeping into my head like a snake slithering under a doorway.

And then the words that changed everything appeared before my eyes:

Only you can forgive yourself for what happened that day...only you can pick up where your life left off and start over...as though no one had ever been injured by what happened during the game...

This diary was written in second person because it was *meant* to be read by someone else. And that could only mean one thing: Phoebe knew. She *knew*.

The game...your daddy...you won't be fixated on food forever...

This book was meant for me. Phoebe was talking to *me*. I had been right all along: she wanted me to find it, but for reasons I hadn't thought of until now. Hadn't she made it easy, leaving it there in the hole, like a big fat burger with a side of fries? Or a baggie filled with fancy chocolates? She wanted me to take it. Like bait.

And I had taken the bait.

I tossed the baggie of chocolates back into the hole behind me, and even though I was afraid to read more, I couldn't help myself, the acid in my stomach coming up in my mouth and making my spit taste like metal.

If you want peace in your life, you have to tell others about the truth of how that day affected you. Maybe they can help you get your life back on track. Only then will you feel the way you used to…

But *how*? How could Phoebe possibly know what had happened? I hadn't said a word in powwow. How could she know about that day? Had we met before? Was she friends with someone I knew? What was the connection?

I thought back to our earlier conversations. She'd said she lived in Raleigh—that she had only been to New Bern once when she was little.

The game…the game…

And then it hit me. That particular game, the one that ruined my life, had taken place in Garner, a city that sits between Raleigh and New Bern.

It was like watching a car wreck, where you know you'll regret scoping out the details, the body on the stretcher, the crying driver sitting on the curb, the shattered glass everywhere, but you look anyway. Your brain memorizes all of it. This moment was just like that, only I was an integral part of the car wreck. Smack dab in the middle of it.

The heart and the soul are tarnished now,
But only you know why or how.
You're a disgrace on the outside, skinny on the inside,
The tight rope you walk is on the thin side.
First it hurts, then it numbs,
After a while, you're in love with crumbs.

I couldn't breathe.

I turned the page, but it was blank. No more cruel words, no more sick poems. I shut the diary and looked around, expecting

Phoebe to be hiding in the brush watching me, giggling like a little girl who has just caught her sister making out with a boy. But of course she was not hiding. She was probably standing under a waterfall right now, letting the cascade run over her perfect little summer body.

Her words were making fun of me, of my weight, of the details of what I had carefully tucked away in the tiny recesses of my brain.

I sat on the log, confused and overheated, not knowing what to do, when a loud snap came from up the path. Charlene appeared among the trees.

My words attacked the air as I jumped up. "What do you want?"

"Diane wanted to come," Charlene said, "but Mary asked me. To make sure you don't pass out again." She looked at the book in my hand, then back up to my face.

Heat rose from my jiggly legs all the way to my pudgy cheeks, filling them with fire. "Go away," I said. "Now. Or I swear, I'll…"

What? What would I do? It wasn't even Charlene I was mad at right now. It was Phoebe.

"You know what?" Charlene said. "All I've done is tried to be nice to you, Simone, and for what? For you to treat me like I'm the enemy? I'm not a Felina, you know."

Felinas were the enemy after all, weren't they?

I started crying.

"Oh," Charlene said, cocking her head to the side like I was a rare animal in a zoo. She took a hesitant step toward me. "Hey. I didn't mean to make you cry…"

"I'm not crying because of *you*," I mumbled.

"Then why?"

"Just go away."

"It's that girl, isn't it? The one who brought you back to camp." Charlene put her hands on her hips. "Did she do something to you?"

"Please, Charlene…"

"If she's doing something to hurt you, you have to nip it in the bud."

"There's nothing to nip. Just go away. I don't want to share anything with you. Not now. Not *ever.*"

Charlene licked her lips before squeezing them together, and then pivoted hard enough for dust to rise up from her tennis shoes. She marched away in a huff, back up the trail toward camp, smacking a low tree branch with her hand. Even with her back facing me, I could hear the words like they were right in my ear: "I told you so, Simone. I freaking told you so."

Chapter Twenty-five

Phoebe's brutal words incapacitated me.

I debated taking the diary back to camp with me. It would have been so easy to stuff it in my backpack and toss it into a Kamama bonfire. But I didn't. Maybe there was a part of me, that car crash witness, who *wanted* to read more. Maybe I wanted Phoebe to—what? Help me with my problem? Help me fix things?

She can't do that, I argued. *No one can.*

My body wanted to expel everything. I had to force my way through lunch, some mushy vegetable casserole or another that sent me to the bathroom twice. In the garden, I absently filled my bucket with weeds from the blueberry bushes, excusing myself to use the toilet again. By the time we entered the swimming pool, my gut felt better, but I barely paid attention to the music or the moves. We were forewarned by Jake that the following week we would start competitive swimming.

I wasn't feeling very competitive. I wasn't feeling anything but angst and a hunger from a place deeper than my stomach.

By the time I dragged my drained body from expression time into powwow, the circle was almost filled. Charlene took a chair across from me in between Mary and Vanessa, and I sat next to Diane. Charlene glanced in my direction, but I stared at the crisscrossed lines on my palms.

After a moment of silence, Mary walked to the middle of the circle. "Once a week, we loosen things up. It's incredibly important to recognize the positive in our lives as well as the serious stuff. This exercise isn't to embarrass anyone. It's designed to make everyone feel good. Now, each girl takes a turn standing in the middle, like I am now. We go around the room, one by one, giving the person in the middle a compliment. A *real* compliment. From the heart." She looked around the circle. "Why don't we begin with you, Charlene, since you're in the seat beside me. We'll go clockwise."

Charlene walked to the center of the circle as Mary went back to her own chair.

"Let's see," Mary said to Charlene. "You have an amazing knack for getting people to say what is on their minds."

Charlene smiled, and Mary nodded to Vanessa.

Vanessa said, "You look like you've lost weight. Your shorts are sort of baggy." The next girl said, "Um…you have really pretty hair."

The first half of the circle went quickly.

"Are we allowed to, like, repeat what someone else said?" Sabrina asked.

Mary said, "I can't imagine you'd have to."

Sabrina thought a moment. "Oh, I know," she told Charlene. "You're really good at helping others with their problems."

I almost laughed out loud.

Diane said, "I like your nails."

I think Diane was just making that up, because Charlene bit her nails more than I did.

Then it was my turn, and I pulled from something I thought was true, but I faked my enthusiasm: "You make the monkey bars look easy."

Charlene barely looked at me and went on to the next girl.

When Charlene's turn was over, Vanessa walked to the center.

Each time a compliment was tossed into the ring, the room seemed to lighten a bit.

Soon it was my turn. Except for the fainting thing, it was the first time since coming to Camp Kamama that I'd been singled out for something, and with Phoebe's cryptic words still swirling around in my head, I felt especially vulnerable.

The first girl spoke to me, and then the next, and when the compliments started rolling, my nervousness faded a bit. A positive kind of energy radiated from the group to me and back out again.

"You have the thickest hair I've ever seen."

I used extra-body conditioner four times a week.

"You have pretty eyes."

I got them from my father.

"Your skin is really clear."

I had washed my face with honey and glycerin soap since I was eleven.

"You're totally helpful, like when you helped me up off the ground during the obstacle course our first day."

I remembered that. The girl seemed surprised that someone had stopped to help, especially when there were other feet dangling that could have kicked me in the head.

Mary said, "You're a quick healer."

I smiled at Mary.

Another girl said, "You sing like Adele. I heard you in the shower."

I laughed. I was feeling good. Better than I had all day. All week, in fact.

Thoughts of the stupid diary started to vanish. Standing in the middle of the circle was like magic. These girls were tossing fairy dust over me, helping my angst fade away.

"Your teeth are really straight."

Two years of braces.

Marion said, like she had that first day at orientation, a day that felt like a million years ago, "I love your name. I might use it for one of my daughters one day."

I was flying high.

And then it was Charlene's turn.

"Simone," she said, frowning as she thought about what to say. "You are passive. Just like Gandhi."

The next girl continued the pattern:

"You can almost do the splits. I saw you in yoga."

The compliment should have made me smile, but I barely heard it under the word Charlene had chosen for me: *passive.*

My old lacrosse coach had deemed me The Dragon. When Bucky was six, I protected him from a neighborhood bully. Fought for causes at school. Defended the Special Ed kids. Climbed the Oak tree in my neighbor's yard to free their kitten. I used to be fearless. A leader. A go-getter.

Used to be.

Now, I was no different than piece of trash, a six-pack holder or a water bottle, floating down a stream with no control over where it's going or where it will end up.

I barely heard the rest of the compliments, and then my turn in the middle ended. I went back to my chair feeling worse than when we'd begun.

We continued around the rest of the circle until each camper in the room had received her compliments. Wide grins, pink cheeks. The whole room was glowing.

Except for me. My own glow wasn't bright enough to light up a shoebox.

While most of the girls spent time afterward hugging one another and saying how much they loved the powwow, I hurried out of the room, anxious to walk to dinner by myself. I was supposed to remember all of the positive things the girls had just said about me. Lap them up and hold them close to my heart. After all, it's not every day that someone gets so many compliments thrown at her all at once. But the only word that rang through my mind was *passive.*

***

After watching the movie *Enchanted*, we all went back to our cabins. Sabrina was showing the girls a dance she had learned on YouTube, and most were trying to imitate her, but it was hard without the music playing. Sabrina had taken off her bandana and was using it as some kind of prop, like one of the ribbon girls in the Olympics. Everyone was laughing, except for me. I lay on my cot and stared up at the ceiling. A maze of spider webs was strung across the beams, and I briefly wondered if any daddy-long-legs or black widows came down for a visit while we slept.

Phoebe's face, that sweet, supposedly innocent face, floated before me. Who was she, really? Was she only coming to the tree to torment me? To trick me? Did she know some of my classmates? How could she possibly know details about the game unless she had been there, or at least had heard about it? This last question led me to one conclusion: even if I didn't know Phoebe before this summer, she knew me. It was the "how" that had me baffled.

My brother's face came to me, but I shook it away. Bucky wasn't smart enough to concoct a scheme like this. His creative thinking skills ended with *Super Mario* or *Minecraft*.

I closed my eyes and saw the words drift across the inside of my closed eyelids: *You won't be fixated on food forever…only you can forgive yourself for what happened that day…only you can pick up where your life left off and start over…as though no one had ever been injured by what happened during the game…*

Honest words. Painful words. Words meant especially for me.

Someone sat on my bed. I opened my eyes.

"Talk to me," Diane said.

"What do you mean?"

"You barely said a word to me all day. Are you mad at me?"

"Oh, no. Not at all."

I sat up, crisscrossed my legs, and eyed the other girls to make sure they were still enthralled by the dance Sabrina was teaching them.

I sighed. It might feel good to tell someone, at least a part of it. "I met someone at my reflection spot," I whispered to Diane. "A Felina."

"That's cool," she said, her self-assured voice unable to match my whisper. "I have lots of friends who are bitches. They keep me entertained."

"She's not a bitch."

Isn't she?

"Oh," Diane said. "Well, that's cool, too. I have lots of friends who aren't bitches. Not as entertaining as the bitchy ones though."

In the center of the room, laughter rose as the girls tried to imitate Sabrina's moves.

"There's more," I told Diane.

I glanced down at my hands. Leftover forest dirt had managed to burrow beneath my nails. Maybe it would be stuck there until the end of summer, as a constant reminder...

"She did something," I said.

"What?"

As I was thinking of where to start, the irony knocked me in the head: I had felt guilty reading a diary that was supposed to belong to someone else, when, as it turned out, the book was written for me. Just like an O'Henry story, only without the sparkly combs or the pocket-watch chain.

I summarized everything, minus the actual words Phoebe had written, and my thievery of the chocolates, left for me like cheese in a mouse trap.

"Isn't she the one who brought you back to camp when you fainted?" Diane asked.

I nodded.

"Well," she went on, "that doesn't sound like a person who's out to get you. Plus, this book doesn't sound like a diary, especially if she wrote it to help you."

"I'm not sure it's meant to help me."

As soon as Charlene broke away from the dancers, I knew she'd overheard our conversation.

She sat down eagerly on her bed, facing Diane and me. "I thought you said that book was yours, Simone." When I didn't respond, she asked, "Is that Felina threatening you?"

Even though the words were written for me and had buried themselves deep in my bones, I had no right sharing them with anyone else. Maybe Phoebe, in her own strange way, really was trying to help me. Maybe I was destined to see what other wise words she had bequeathed me. No matter how painful, they belonged to me.

Diane said, "Don't worry about it, Charlene."

"Come on, Simone," Charlene said, ignoring Diane. "Give me something."

Give her something?

Her eyes were eager and one of her top teeth was biting into the corner of her lower lip, as if she were expecting my words to change her life somehow.

"Fine, Charlene," I said. "I'll tell you what she wrote. Life is a merry-go-round and we are the horses…I fancy your XXL T-shirt…I hope we can be pen pals…You're my bestiest friend ever…Let's do lunch sometime…I'll have my secretary call your secretary…"

Diane was laughing.

Charlene was not. Her wide eyes grew narrow, the little brown flecks disappearing. She knelt down in front of me and placed a hand on my arm. "Kamama is a camp for girls who need to stick together. We're family. Don't you feel that way?"

I thought about Mary taking care of me while I was sick. About Ms. Diggs and her kind spirit. About Jake with his undying patience in yoga and swim class. About the fact that Camp Kamama wouldn't be around the following year.

Diane said nothing, but there was something in her look that told me it was up to me. That if I wanted to share things with Charlene I could, and if I didn't want to, well, that was totally my business.

I couldn't. That book, no matter what was written inside, was between Phoebe and me. Adding others to the mix, including Diane, somehow ruined it.

Ruined what? I asked myself.

The possibility of knowing more…

"You don't know about those girls," Charlene said quietly, her hand still on my arm, her eyes glued to mine. "They're high on themselves. Snot-noses. Just like the mean girls at school. You know what I'm talking about. Girls who don't have to worry about anything, ever. Girls who are perfect no matter what they do. And then they shove around other people they think are beneath them."

"I just want to keep it to myself," I said, pulling my arm from her fingers. "It's private."

"Then you should have chosen a different camp," Charlene said, standing up. "Because this one expects you to share."

"You haven't shared yet," Diane reminded Charlene. "You spend all your time asking other people questions."

"You're pretty tight-lipped yourself, Diane. Though it's obvious what *you* have going on."

Charlene pulled out her ponytail. She began brushing her fingers through her thick hair as though it were on fire. Little strands of strawberry blond floated into the air.

"Don't be a hater, Charlene," Diane said.

"This is summer camp," I told Charlene. "It's not a beauty pageant. We're not competing with the Felinas in some contest for a tiara and a ride on a float."

"You should tell that Felina to go to hell," Charlene said.

"Why are you getting so defensive?" I asked.

And why wasn't *I*?

Charlene looked from me to Diane. "Because I have to," she said. "Someone has to." She grabbed her flip-flops from under her cot and made her way to the shower line.

Marion announced there were fifteen minutes until lights-out.

"There's one at every camp," Diane said as she grabbed her toiletry bag and headed to the sinks.

I crawled into bed in my dirty feet and clothes of the day and pulled the thin sheet over my face.

Chapter Twenty-six

In the shadowy morning, I awoke in a panic to an army of footsteps running by our cabin. I looked at my watch. It was only 5:30. We still had another thirty minutes to sleep, so I was confused. I found myself missing the early music blast of music.

Karen flew across the floor toward the cabin door.

"What's happening?" I asked.

"Not sure," Karen said.

We all ran out of the bunk in our bare feet as a voice came over the loudspeaker.

"Kamama-mamas, please get dressed. Head down to the beach, pronto! This includes all staff and all counselors!"

I was frightened. What had happened? Had someone been found floating in the lake? Was the forest on fire?

Within minutes, nearly one hundred girls stood on the beach facing Ms. Diggs and Jake, the lake a quiet backdrop behind them. Unlike a usual morning when it took a few minutes to get everyone settled, no one said a word. Jake looked angry as he paced back and forth across the sand. Ms. Diggs looked like she might cry and kept shaking her head.

"Your garden—*our* garden," she said softly, but loud enough for all of us to hear, "has been desecrated."

Jake used his hands to explain. "Someone destroyed six rows of plants, mainly cucumbers and green peppers. Just wacked them to bits with a shovel."

I didn't like green peppers so much, and I remained neutral when it came to cucumbers, but I couldn't imagine who would go out of their way to destroy the food we ate.

Jake said, "Yoga is cancelled today. You girls should go back to your cabins and try to decipher who did this. That garden is for your pleasure. For your sustenance. I can drive down the mountain anytime I feel like it and pick up some garbage wrapped in cellophane from the grocery store. So this isn't about me. It's about the respect you give your food and ultimately to one another and yourselves."

Jake marched off the beach, his bare feet kicking up sand as he headed toward the path.

I glanced at Charlene. She was looking across the lake. I followed her gaze. A few girls were playing a game of tag or something on the Felina beach, their girlish voices rising up and rolling across the water. I wondered if Phoebe was among the girls, chuckling about whatever it was Felinas chuckled about.

When I looked back to Charlene, Phoebe vanished from my mind and my stomach dropped to my feet. Charlene was grinning.

***

We spoke quietly among ourselves, each of us sitting on our cots, waiting. Marion informed us that one of the directors would be along in a few minutes; the cabins were being questioned in order from one to ten.

Sue the invisible camper said, "My parents would die if someone did that to our garden back home." She started crying. Diane went to her cot and sat beside her, then put an arm around her.

"I can't imagine it was someone from our bunk," Karen said.

Some girls nodded in agreement.

Charlene said, "Odds are, it wasn't someone from *our* camp at all."

"What do you mean?" Karen asked.

Charlene pointed her thumb in the direction of the lake and sang, "Fe-lin-as."

Sabrina said, "What would they do that for?"

"Ask Simone," Charlene said.

I swallowed.

"Tell 'em," Charlene said.

"There's nothing to tell," I told the group, all of whom were staring at me.

Charlene spoke for me. "A Felina wrote some nasty shit about Simone."

"That's not true," I said.

"What?" Marion asked. "Where?"

"In a diary," Charlene answered.

"It's not a diary," I said. "At least, not exactly…"

The girls waited for me to speak, but I said nothing. All that went through my mind was what if Charlene was right? What if Phoebe or another Felina had vandalized our garden?

Diane said, "How do we know it wasn't you, Charlene?"

"Why would I destroy our own property?" Charlene asked.

"To make it *look* like a Felina did it?"

"Not exactly my style," Charlene said. "But it would be the style of a bitchy Felina. Meow!"

"Shut up!" I shouted. "You think you know so much Charlene." I was two inches away from telling her and the other girls about Camp Kamama's plan to close just to change the subject; just to give them something else to worry about. But even though I didn't care about Charlene's feelings, there were other girls in my bunk who didn't need to go through weeks knowing they'd never come back again. For some girls, Kamama was their summer home. "You don't know squat," I finished under my breath.

The cabin door opened. Ms. Diggs stepped into our bunk. Mary followed behind.

Ms. Diggs moved to the center of the cabin. "Please put your suitcases on your cots and open them."

I looked around the room expecting someone to argue that this request was against our civil rights, but no one said anything. One by one we placed our suitcases on our beds, opened them, and stood waiting.

Ms. Diggs started with mine, since my bed sat closest to the door.

"What are you looking for?" Marion asked from across the room.

Ms. Diggs didn't respond.

She went through my bag, opening every little compartment. She finished quickly, satisfied by what she'd found—or didn't find—then moved on to the next. With relief, I sat on my cot and waited as she made her way around the cabin.

When she got to Trish's bed, Ms. Diggs stuck her hand in the bottom of the suitcase and yelped when a tiny gray mouse ran out. It fell to the floor and scurried into the bathroom. Most of the girls screamed, and Sue jumped onto all fours on her cot.

Trish started crying. She pointed to the underside of her bag.

Ms. Diggs opened the false bottom of the suitcase and pulled out a Trader Joe's bag, folded once. Before she'd ever had a chance to open it, the contents came pouring out of a hole in the bottom. A variety of candies rained onto the bed, along with what looked like chocolate sprinkles, but in actuality were tiny mouse turds.

Trish blubbered, "I deserve—to get—sent home."

"The rest of you girls may go to breakfast," Ms. Diggs said.

We went to breakfast without Trish.

Along the way, Marion said, "That girl could have got our whole bunk into trouble."

I pictured Karen from a few nights earlier, her hand chop-chopping her neck, relieved that it wasn't mine.

The word traveled fast around camp: Trish had been sneaking her precious candies out in the middle of the night and eating them in the garden. Rumor had it that she'd had a bit too much energy the night before. Maybe the sugar she was hoarding had attacked her brain. She'd found a shovel on the side of the shed and let off steam on the innocent cucumbers and peppers. She was also sugar-high enough to leave a bunch of candy wrappers lying around the garden.

The joke of the day was this: *the best way to lose weight at Camp Kamama is to destroy the food you grow yourself.*

But no one really laughed when they said it. Especially since when we got back to our bunks later that day, Trish's suitcase, pillow, and thin stack of *People* magazines were gone.

Chapter Twenty-seven

Each girl held onto a rake or broom or sponge. Nearly one hundred campers trudged with heads down as we scrubbed toilets, washed down sinks, swept paths that zigzagged between the cabins, raked leaves from the narrow beach. Our morning activities were cancelled. I found myself missing the obstacle course.

"How come *we* have to pay?" Sue asked Marion while we squirted Windex onto cabin ten's windows. "Trish *wanted* to go home," Sue added. "She *wanted* to get caught."

Marion said in her I'm-a-counselor-so-I-have-all-the-answers voice, "Ms. Diggs believes that some girls knew about the contraband in Trish's suitcase."

Sabrina stopped sweeping dirt from under the cots and leaned against the ratty broom. "No one would have covered for her if they thought she'd hurt the garden."

Marion just shrugged.

For nearly three hours the entire camp remained under probation. At 10:30, Ms. Diggs made the announcement that we were to stop working in order to reflect. "I hope you all think about what happened here at Camp Kamama. Think about Jake and how hard he works to make your garden an integral part of our family. Think about yourselves. About what it is you expect to get out of this camp; what it is you can give back in exchange. We are not here to coddle you. We're here to help you grow wings. But it's a two-way street."

I'd thought about finding another spot to reflect, but *not* going to the tree would show the truth in Charlene's words, that I was passive. I was like my mother after all, a frozen Popsicle too overwhelmed to make a real decision, to take a stand. As I trudged along the crooked path, the same questions that had plagued me for over a day continued to roll through my head, one after another, like North Carolina thunder. By the time I'd made it to the tree, I was physically and emotionally drained.

But I had made a decision.

I would talk to Phoebe directly. I was going to get answers. Even if I didn't want to know them.

This time, I didn't take the chocolate bait. It was obvious she wanted me to eat them, just like she wanted me to read the book. Well, I was learning to do without the extra treats. I didn't need her stupid candies to make or break my day. I leaned into the hole and pushed the baggie of chocolates deep into the earth where I couldn't see them, soaking my hand in wet leaves and dirt.

Sitting on the log, I waited, checking my watch every minute or so. The path leading to Camp Felina was silent. I felt like the only human left on the planet.

I waited some more. When Phoebe didn't show up, I thought, maybe I was supposed to do this without her. Maybe she wanted me to discover on my own how she knew me, and why it was so important that I read her words.

Before I knew what I was doing, the book was on my lap. I opened it. This time, the pretty script seemed to go on forever:

You can get over this. Just because you're at a camp for bad eaters doesn't mean you can't survive in the real world. What do the counselors know? Are they inside your head? Do they even have a clue about what happened that day? Is your father such a bastard that you can't share the truth? Doesn't he realize that if he punishes you, he will end up punishing himself?

This was the second time she'd mentioned my father, but no one knew about my dealings with him, except for the bullshit I'd handed to my therapist, and then later to the doctor who'd interviewed me for Kamama. No one knew what was *really* in my mind. Not my mother, not Bucky, not anyone at camp. *No one at all.*

Except for Phoebe.

My eyes continued to scan the words:

Just forget about what happened. It doesn't need to take over your life. You might look like a freak in the mirror, but you are still beautiful on the inside. Let that beautiful person out every once in a while…

And just when I believed that nothing Phoebe had written could make me feel any more nervous or confused, I turned the page. Like a pair of sharp scissors, the words rammed through my gut:

You are a loser. You are a fat fuck.

A distinct and reverberating snap of a foot landing hard against a twig. I jumped up, impulsively hid the diary behind my back, and stepped to the side of the tree. Phoebe had stopped on the path about thirty yards away wearing her un-summery sweat jacket, a pair of stifling jeans, and those damn Rainbows. She just stood there, staring at me.

Is that how you see me? As a loser? As a fat fuck?

She had to know that I was reading it. That I knew she knew I was reading it. What would happen now? Should I hold the book out like a token of appreciation? Throw it at her stupid pretty face? Scream that she had no right knowing me, when I didn't know her? Would it make her happy I'd read her cruel words? Somehow make her feel vindicated? Superior? A lion among the kitties?

Phoebe continued her walk toward me. "I want to grab my journal," she said simply, as though we were strangers passing each other at a bus stop. Her hands beat nervously against her thighs like a song was stuck in her head. Her words ran together like she'd had too much coffee. "I have some stuff I need to write down. It's sort of important. Timely. You don't have to leave. I know you're reflecting. I can write in it somewhere else so you won't be disturbed."

I barely got the word out. "Journal?"

She came around the tree and stood beside the log. "I'll just grab it and go."

I took a wide step to the left as Phoebe kneeled on the log and swished her hand through the leaves, slowly at first, than more ferociously. She pulled out the baggie with the chocolates.

"Where is it?" she asked. She dug some more, then stood up. Her right eye twitched like it had the first day we'd met.

We stared at one another, this girl and I, as different as night and day, winter and summer. But who was which season, I wasn't sure. I wasn't sure of anything anymore. I brought my hand from behind my back and held the book out in front of me. It looked like I was offering a gift, but really, I was daring her to take it. To grab it from my hand.

Phoebe kept her wide eyes steadied on mine, but she did not

reach for the diary. "Did you read it?" she whispered, pressing her lips together until they looked like one thin pencil line. When I didn't answer, she held up the baggie of treats. "You ate some chocolates, too." She snorted. "How did they make you feel?"

I spoke slowly, deliberately. "You left them here on purpose."

She ignored my accusation. "Did you read *everything*? About being a loser? About—"

"Yes!" I suddenly screamed.

"And are you happy now?" Phoebe asked.

My lips trembled. I could feel my bladder wanting to let loose. My bowels, too. "Are you insane? Why would that make me happy?"

"Because now you know the truth," she said.

"The truth…"

My head was spinning. I watched her, the way her eyes bugged out, the right one still twitching, the way she stood there with her arms suspended in front of her, her hands flopping through the air like they were on fire. The way she stared *through* me instead of *at* me, like she saw who I was on the inside without knowing anything about me.

But she does know you. She knows all about the incident that changed your life forever. How else could she have written words especially for you?

I picked up my backpack and yanked it onto my back. I stuck on my cap, pulling my ponytail through the hole.

"You know what?" I said. "I don't care about your precious book." I threw the diary and it crashed into the hole. *Two points!* I nearly shouted.

Phoebe's eyes moved toward the hollow and settled on me again. She said nothing.

"Don't give me that stupid Felina look," I told her. "I'm done with you. And *it.* I don't care what truth you think you know. I don't care if you talked to my old friends, teammates, or even my family. I don't care if you're a spy or some kind of witch who can read my thoughts. You know why? Because even though you seem to care oh-so-much about me and my life, I don't give a crap. About. *You.*"

I turned on my heels and stormed up the path, my legs pumping harder than they ever had on the obstacle course. I forced my eyes to remain on the path ahead, not to look back. I had no desire to see what Phoebe was doing. If she was laughing, flipping me the bird, or scribbling the recent events in her psycho diary.

"None of it matters anyway," I mumbled, "because you aren't me, Barbie Bitch. You and I are nothing alike. *Nothing.*"

***

As I scraped the little peas into the compost heap after lunch, I thought of a new joke: *if you really want to lose weight, read some nasty stuff about yourself in a Felina's diary and ruin your appetite for good.*

After lunch, we girls spent the usual time in the garden, but no one even whispered. It was as though a black cloud hovered over the camp after Trish was sent away. I hardly noticed, since I was carrying around my own black cloud.

Swimming was even worse since Jake was in a terrible mood. Instead of disco, he had us do laps until I thought I would drown.

During expression time, Diane sketched a picture of Jake's garden—pre-demolition—and I sat across from her, playing with the little beads, counting them, rearranging them, but never making anything. Diane never asked how I was dealing with the whole Felina situation, and I liked her even more for that reason. I figured she'd make a much better psychologist than Charlene.

Powwow was spent with Mary giving us "free time" to discuss our feelings. Even though a lot of girls were chatting up a storm about what had happened to Trish, analyzing the situation, I remained silent, sick to my stomach over what had happened during reflection. My spinning head re-read the words in Phoebe's diary until I knew them by rote. I pictured her bug-eyes, that stupid look on her face that I wanted to smack off, wondering if she had gone running back to her camp to tell her friends what she'd done, if her fellow Felinas had patted her on the back.

That night's bonfire was especially mellow. Most of us sat around in little clusters, chatting about this or that, trying not to let each other see how drained we were from the day. Charlene stayed away from Diane and me, which made me grateful. Lights-out came upon us quickly, and for that I was also grateful. All I wanted to do was let the day go and sleep, sleep, sleep.

Chapter Twenty-eight

Warm air brushed against my left cheek. I lay flat on my back in the dark, the thin sheet up to my chin. Something had woken me up. I opened my eyes and watched the cabin door, heard the muffled thump as it slowly closed behind someone. I pushed off the sheet and ever-so-carefully slipped out of bed, stuffed my pillow under the blanket, and grabbed my tennis shoes from under my bed. From inside the screened door, I watched as Charlene walked down the cabin steps.

I pushed the tiny button on my watch and saw that it was three o'clock. I waited until Charlene had stepped onto the path before I slowly opened the door. The sound of snoring followed me onto the porch.

I'll show you who's passive, I thought, as I quickly tied up my tennis shoes and snuck down the cabin steps after her.

She moved confidently, never looking back, barely pausing to step over a root or a rock. When she got farther into the woods, she disappeared into the dark. Out of fear, I was about to turn around when a flashlight illuminated the path ahead.

I knew the path way better than Charlene, since I took it twice a day to my reflection spot, but her feet moved with confidence. I followed a few yards behind when she suddenly turned around and shined the flashlight in my direction. I ducked behind a tree and froze. She paused a moment before continuing.

Like a soldier, she hiked all the way to the big old tree. *My* tree. With her back to me, she moved the beam of light up the tree's trunk, then side to side, then directly into the hole. She kneeled down on the log. When she stood again, she held a plastic baggie. I wasn't sure if it was the chocolates or the diary, until I saw the square blue in her hands.

Two things went through my mind as Charlene's flashlight hovered over the book. Why would she come all the way out here in the middle of the night just to snoop, and why had Phoebe left it behind after our altercation?

After a minute or two, Charlene tossed the book back into the hole. I prepared to crouch down low in the bushes next to the path, but she didn't come back my way. Instead, she continued moving away from the tree in the direction of the lake, her brisk march announcing, "I am on a mission."

As she disappeared around the next bend, she stole the only available light. I couldn't see anything beyond what was directly in front of me. The moon was bright white, but only slivers of light squeezed through the tree tops.

I had to catch up or I'd be left in the dark. I concentrated on my footing, careful not to trip. Soon, I could hear Charlene's footsteps up ahead as they clomped through the dirt. As stealthily as I could, I followed until she approached the edge of the lake. The moon suddenly ducked behind some clouds, and the lake turned ominous, like a backdrop in a movie with werewolves or zombies. I froze near the edge of the Kamama boundary line, still hidden by some trees, afraid if I followed any farther, my luck would run out.

So what? It's a free country. I have every right to follow her. She doesn't own this freaking camp, even though she'd probably like to.

That was my emotional side talking. My logical side told me I should stay incognito.

As the moon broke its way through the clouds, Charlene strode along the side of the lake and disappeared into the trees on the other side.

And once again, I followed.

***

While stepping behind the widest tree trunk I could find at Camp Felina's border, my foot landed on top of a branch, snapping it in two. Charlene, who was now about twenty yards ahead of me, became invisible as she clicked off her flashlight. I waited, laying my palm against the tree trunk and my forehead against the back of my hand, my eyes squeezed shut as if that would make me one with the tree. When I heard her footsteps again, I came out from behind the tree and stepped back onto the path.

Camp Felina was way better lit than Camp Kamama. The metal pole lamps looked like the ones along a highway. Sad blue light washed over the path and the buildings up ahead on the left.

I moved swiftly behind Charlene, keeping wide swatches of shadow between us. She disappeared for a moment then reappeared as she weaved her way among the buildings. The cabins at Camp Felina were nothing like ours. In fact, they weren't really cabins at all, but two-story buildings made of cement blocks, and none of them had porches. They looked like the buildings found on a community college campus. I wondered with envy if they were air conditioned. Each one had a row of windows along the top, and I stared up at them as I walked, the dark square eyes staring back.

Charlene headed into one of the smaller buildings sitting in the middle of the others, a one-story with a yellow glow emanating from the open doorway.

I hid behind an evergreen just outside the door. If I stepped any closer, Charlene would spot me. I cupped my hand around an ear and listened. At first I believed I heard voices—strange low voices—but then I realized a breeze had kicked up, and some tree branches were scraping against the building's roof.

I waited for what felt like hours, though it was probably less than thirty minutes, and when Charlene came out again, I believed I could see her grin in the dark. I ducked down and held my breath as she passed right by me—the smell of her shampoo came to me in a wave of strawberries—then rounded the bend going back the way we'd come.

As soon as Charlene was out of view, I ran to the building's doorway. Before me was a large bathroom. The *Felinas'* bathroom. The fluorescent lights in the ceiling were off. A yellow bulb that sat inside a mesh wire cage was all that lit the peach-colored walls. Two small rectangular glass windows sat at the top of the opposite wall, both with the slats open. The floor tile was a bland earth tone, and exposed pipes ran across the ceiling.

The room didn't look fancy to me. As a matter of fact, it wasn't any better than ours, and I wondered if even pretty rich girls didn't have a say about what their camp bathrooms looked like. Six stalls sat in a row, just like any other bathroom, except that they were missing doors. In each stall sat a toilet, exposed.

Like a boy's bathroom.

I turned around and, by the dim creepy light, saw the standard row of counter sinks and the long mirror that ran the entire length of the counter. It took me a second to understand why Charlene had come all the way over here just to sneak into a bathroom, especially one straight out of a scene from *Nightmare on Elm Street.* On the mirror, in tall thin letters, a message was left for whatever girl would be the first to see it. Each letter was meticulously written, the handwriting smooth and delicate. The words, however, were not. On the left side of the mirror: "FELINA GIRLS SUCK!" In the middle: "LOSERS!" My heart froze and then cracked into a million pieces when I read the final passage: "PHOEBE IS A SKINNY BITCH!"

Within the eerie glow of the yellow light, I took in the entire scene. I wondered, when Charlene's work of art was complete, had she stood a few feet from the mirror and silently patted herself on the back? Was she proud of herself? Would she sleep tonight?

No one would dispute that what Phoebe had done to me was wrong. But what Charlene had done was worse, because none of this had anything to do with her.

My eyes traveled to the floor. Charlene's muddy footprints had left smears across the tile in front of the sinks. Even more than the vindictive words, those footprints made a scream form in my throat.

I stepped up to the mirror and looked at the word "BITCH!" The toxic smell washed over me before I touched the letter *B.* Charlene had used nail polish. I dabbed at the tackiness and rubbed the polish between my fingers. Would it be possible to wipe nail polish off a mirror with acetone? Or would those awful words be held there for the summer, suspended in time until the camp had the mirror replaced?

I pictured the first Felina walking into the bathroom the next morning, head down, hair in her eyes, having just woken up. I pictured her going into a door-less stall to pee, then heading to the sink. The first thing she'd do is look in the mirror to make sure her face was still as pretty as she remembered, and when she read the words on the mirror, she would…what? Scream? Cry? Maybe she would laugh. After all, these were Felinas.

But what if the first girl happened to be Phoebe?

My knees started to lock. I had lost track of time, losing as well the opportunity to follow Charlene's light back to Kamama.

What would I do? Hide in a stall without a door until sunup? What if a Felina had to pee between now and then?

I hesitated, not wanting to venture back alone, but not wanting to be discovered. I left the bathroom, let my eyes readjust to the blue light that poured like a waterfall over the path, and slowly made my way back through Felina territory. I zigzagged through the other camp's trees, over unfamiliar rocks and foreign tree roots.

I had only traveled a few yards, my arms stuck out like a snowman's twig arms, when my peripheral vision caught something bulky hanging from the bough of a tree. I gasped loudly and covered my mouth. It was a body, swaying lightly back and forth as the wind made its way through the trees. I shook my head and shut my eyes. Maybe I was still asleep on my cot, having a strange dream. I opened my eyes again. Reason told me that I was seeing things. I took a step toward the hanging body. It was a dummy, made from old clothes and stuffed like a scarecrow, the bulges fatter in some areas than others. I touched one of the shoeless feet that dangled just above my head, pressing against it to get an idea of its weight. It must have taken five or six people to string it up that way. The rope was tied to a branch somewhere above me, the knot invisible because of the dark.

Why would the Felinas hang a dummy from their own tree?

I reached up and turned it by the feet. The head lolled toward me. There was no mouth, only a nose and a pair of hollow eyes made from pieces of material either glued or sewn onto the creepy face. An anti-face…

I turned and ran back toward the lake. I didn't want to see any more. I wanted the feel of my mushy cot, the warmth of my covers, the snores of my bunkmates.

I was nearly out of the Camp Felina forest when I tripped over a root. I let out a loud, "Oof!" before tumbling to the ground. My knees screamed out in pain, but I didn't have time to worry about such things. What I did have to worry about was the light that suddenly appeared in a tiny building on the edge of the camp. Compared to the others, the building looked like a shack, the kind a hunter or a fisherman might stay in while out in the woods. As I stood again, I barely made out the wooden plaque on the door: *SECURITY.*

And then the door to the shack was opening, and a dark shadow was suddenly standing in the doorway…

Even with throbbing knees, I sprinted. My legs moved like they were eating up the length of a lacrosse field as I raced toward the nearly treeless edge of the lake. I was in survival mode. My eyes focused on the line of trees that bordered Camp Kamama. I kept glancing behind me, wondering if that creepy body hanging from the tree had gotten loose and was flying above me like a giant bat, or if the creepy shadow in the doorway was on my heels.

As I ran along the curve of the lake, the sun started to rise.

The early air was already filling with humidity and the sky with bluish-pink brush strokes. Birds were chirping. A couple of low-flying hawks soared over the treetops.

I ran until I landed on the beach where Jake taught yoga, and then continued to the trees that protected the path leading to cabin ten, but then I could run no farther. I was spent. My tennis shoes had rubbed blisters into my heels. I walked now, listening as my heart evened out. In the eastern sky, daylight was coming, and I was instantly less afraid. Morning has a way of doing that.

Worried about time, I took a more direct route past the obstacle course, then finally turned onto the trail that led to my bunk.

In front of the cabin steps, my hands gripped the tops of my knees as I bent over. I shut my eyes, taking slow even breaths in and out. I tiptoed up the steps and snuck into the cabin, cringing as the door made a tiny squeak. All of the girls were in their beds, including Charlene. She lay with her back to me.

Was she already asleep? Even after what she'd done?

The sun was barely streaming through the cabin windows as I slid under the sheet and wrapped my body around my pillow. I lay with my eyes closed, envisioning Charlene's hand writing with nail polish on the mirror, her grin wide as she stepped back to appreciate her artistic mural.

The springs squeaked under Charlene's weight as she shifted on her cot. I wondered what was going through her mind, if there was a chance she knew I knew. If she'd even care.

Talk would be inevitable. About what she'd done, and why. Not to mention how she knew Phoebe's name, when I had never shared it.

Truths would come out. I would make sure of it. It would be like a mini- powwow. Right up Charlene's alley.

I rolled onto my back and rearranged my pillow under my neck. I didn't think I'd be able to sleep, but I fell headfirst into a pile of troubled dreams, and for the next hour I was chased through the woods by a giant scarecrow waving a lacrosse stick.

Chapter Twenty-nine

"Up and at 'em!" Marion shouted over the wake-up music. "No yoga today. Breakfast, then weigh-in, then kayak trip. After breakfast, we'll meet at the office where buses will be waiting to take you to the river. Dress in your Kamama T-shirts and a pair of comfortable shorts. Flip-flops or sandals are fine."

I slid out of bed and shuffled to the restroom along with the others, feeling groggy, momentarily forgetting the night before. But as soon as I went to the sink and looked in the bathroom mirror, it all came back to me: the gloomy yellow light, the toxic smell of nail polish, the fake body hanging from the tree like a lynching had taken place.

And Phoebe's name like a message left by a kidnapper.

As I finished making my bed, Marion came up behind me.

"Hey, Simone," she said. "You're supposed to meet Ms. Diggs in her office after weigh-in."

"What for?"

The creepy image of a person in the doorway at Camp Felina came to me. Had they seen me clearly enough to point a finger?

Had the Felina camp director called Ms. Diggs?

"I don't know," Marion said. "Hey. What happened to your fingers?"

I held up my hands. A dark shade of red covered my fingertips like they'd been sliced with a pair of shears. "Oh, I—"

Charlene jumped by my side. "We decided to do each others' nails. Early this morning. Before the sun came up."

"In the dark?" Marion asked.

"I know, right?" Charlene said.

Karen chimed in, "You guys are so weird."

But Marion, who was a few months older than Karen and a whole lot smarter, chewed her cud. "Line up," she said after a moment, taking the clipboard down from the wall. We did as she asked. Then she told Karen, "You go on ahead. Be the first in line for breakfast. You've earned it."

"Cool. Thanks, Marion."

Karen left the cabin, the door slamming behind her, her feet chomping the dirt as she walked up the path toward the cafeteria.

We waited in line as Marion stood in front of the door. She opened it, the high squeal entering the cabin like a wounded animal. "I heard the cabin door early this morning," she said, letting it close again. "It squeaks, in case y'all didn't know."

I could feel the whole room seize, like an engine with no oil.

"Let me tell y'all something," Marion said, setting her jaw, looking back and forth from me to Charlene. "One thing Camp Kamama doesn't do is preach. They don't tell y'all how to treat others. They assume that since we all come from the same place, you know, carrying all this baggage..." She pinched a chunk of skin through her shirt. "...that we will automatically be kind to each other. That we don't need someone to tell us every second of the day what's right or wrong."

A few of the girls whispered to one another. I dropped my eyes to the floor.

"I have no idea what someone is up to," Marion said. "I'm not even sure I want to know. All I can tell you is we're supposed to figure out on our own that we have to take responsibility for our actions. If y'all did something, you gotta own up. Now or later, you'll have to. If you don't, you'll add to the baggage you carry. And maybe add to someone else's."

She opened the screened door again and held it wide. Single-file, we walked to the cafeteria in total silence.

***

I watched Charlene during breakfast, spooning her cinnamon oatmeal into her mouth as though nothing unusual had happened. As if we really had given each other a manicure in the dark.

Except that her eyes never left her food; never met my own.

What if Camp Felina really had called Ms. Diggs? Would I rat out Charlene?

Charlene had taken up for me back at the cabin—even though I wasn't a part of her cruel prank.

I was thinking about all of these things while cleaning off my tray, when someone tapped me on the shoulder. It was a counselor from one of the other bunks.

"It's your turn to be weighed," she said.

I followed the girl to the back of Mary's office, the same place I'd spent time after my fainting spell. An unfamiliar woman in a white lab coat stood next to the scale, and Mary sat at her desk. Rocking from one foot to the other, I stared at the empty metal chair in the middle of the room.

"Simone," Mary said, "this is Doctor Patton from County Hospital."

"Hi, Simone," Doctor Patton said. She was tall and thin and in her forties, and looked like she could have been a catwalk model at one time. Her cheek bones were high, placed just below her dark eyes, and her blackish-blue hair was cropped super short, with miniature sideburns. "Have a seat, please."

I sat on the cold chair.

"First, we're going to check your vitals." She placed her stethoscope against my back and then against my chest. "Your heart is beating fast."

"I'm just nervous."

The words on the mirror passed before my eyes, then the floating scarecrow with its missing nose and lumpy body…

"No need to be nervous," Doctor Patton said, tucking the end of her stethoscope in her jacket pocket. "This will take less than two minutes."

She slid the blood pressure cuff around my arm and pumped up the black rubber ball, then told Mary the numbers to write down.

"I'm going to prick your finger and take some blood. You okay?"

I nodded.

Doctor Patton drew some blood from my pinky, saying nothing about the red nail polish which still dotted the tips of my other fingers, then handed the miniature vial to Mary, who put a label on it and stuck it in a caddy. Doctor Patton gave me a cotton ball to place against my finger.

"Shoes off, please," she said. "Let's get you on the scale."

I stood up and kicked off my Crocs. In front of the scale, I froze.

"What's the matter?" she asked.

"I don't want to know."

"That's fine," Doctor Patton said. "You don't have to know. I, on the other hand, get paid to know. So, up on the scale please. There are still a few dozen girls behind you."

I did as she asked, looking down at my bare feet as she set the counterweight to balance it.

"Thank you, Simone," she said. "Enjoy the rest of your day."

I slid into my Crocs but stopped when I got to the doorway. Both women looked at me. I wondered what they thought. Were they proud of me? Disappointed? It was hard to tell.

"I—"

They waited.

"Did I?"

They both laughed, and I smiled.

"Of course you lost weight," Doctor Patton said.

"I did?"

"Do you want to know the number or not?"

I licked my lips. I felt like the time I'd begged my parents for a couple of gerbils, and they told me no, but in the middle of the night on Christmas Eve, I snuck downstairs to find the cutest pair of black gerbils digging furiously in the glass box. I was thrilled to have the little guys but sad that I'd ruined my own surprise.

But this wasn't gerbils we were talking about. "Yes, please," I said.

Doctor Patton picked up the clipboard. "Two-fifty-one."

"When you first got here," Mary said, looking at a file in front of her, "you were two-fifty-four."

"Three pounds?" I said. "That's all?"

"Actually, that's quite reasonable," Doctor Patton said. "The healthiest way is to lose between two and three a week."

The amount sounded pitiful. Like the weight a fish might lose when its scales are cut off.

The doctor could see by my frown I wasn't impressed.

"Three pounds a week," she said, sounding like Jake. "How many weeks are in a month?"

"Four."

"That's twelve pounds a month. How many months are in a year?"

"Twelve."

She waited.

A smile grew across my face. "I get it." Now that I had lost weight, I really did get it. It wasn't just a bunch of numbers on a piece of paper. It was tangible.

"Good," Doctor Patton said. "Now send in the next girl. We need to get rolling or I'll be here until Thanksgiving."

Chapter Thirty

In slow motion, I made my way to Ms. Diggs's office, the fear of being accused of something I didn't do overriding the thrill of shedding a few pounds.

I opened the door. Ms. Diggs sat with her head in her hands, a large sheet of paper with columns of numbers sitting on the desk in front of her. She looked up when the door slammed behind me. Her face was serious, a deep groove separating her eyebrows.

"Simone," she said.

I started shaking with fear. Tiny erratic heartbeats traveled all the way to the bottom of my feet, pulsing against the lining of my Crocs.

"We have to make up for what happened," she said, standing up. "You know what that means, right?"

I stopped breathing. She was going to send me home. Even if she knew about Charlene, even if I wasn't the one who vandalized, I had snuck across the border to another camp in the middle of the night. I was about to become one of the two percent who wouldn't make it through the summer.

I didn't want to be asked to leave. Choosing to quit was one thing, but being kicked out…

Ms. Diggs put a finger against a schedule sitting on her desk. "You missed both swimming and powwow when you were sent to the infirmary," she said. "When you miss something around here, you have to make it up by working."

"Working?"

I would hand wash all the sheets in the place and clean the bottoms of every camper's shoes if it meant Ms. Diggs didn't know about the night before.

"In the garden," she said. "You'll be skipping the kayak trip."

"Yes, ma'am." I almost shouted with glee, but I contained myself.

"Head on over then. Choose whatever section you want. It all needs work. Be sure to refill your water bottle."

"Yes, ma'am," I said again, putting my cap securely on my head. I stepped through the door and hurried down the steps.

Campers still waiting for their numbers were lined up from the infirmary door all the way past the first bus parked in the dirt lot. I kept my head down and cruised past.

Even in all the mayhem, Charlene spotted me.

"Simone," she said.

I had decided I didn't want to talk to Charlene after all. What was done was done. Ms. Diggs didn't know a thing. I was safe. I didn't want to think about last night, Phoebe, or Charlene. I wanted to celebrate my tiny achievement of losing three pounds. Alone.

Dozens of excited girls carrying life jackets and beach towels and backpacks were gathering around the buses. The air was thick with equal parts of sunscreen and bug spray.

Wide strides separated me quickly from the pack as I left the main path and turned toward the garden. Charlene kept up with my brisk pace.

"You followed me last night," she whispered.

"I have to do some weeding." I walked faster. When I got to the garden gate, I clicked open the latch.

"Please, Simone," Charlene said. "I just want you to understand why—"

I spun around. "Oh, I understand. You're jealous, Charlene. Of the Felinas. They're skinny, and we're fat, and that's that."

I almost laughed out loud at my little unintended rhyme.

"Simone…" She grabbed my elbow but I jerked it away.

"Leave me the hell alone."

"You don't know what happened to me," she said.

"What happened to *you*? Is that all that's going through your mind, after what you did last night? I just about threw up in Ms. Diggs' office, I was so worried she'd found out. You could get us kicked out of this camp for that stupid stunt."

I walked to the outdoor sink and grabbed a pair of thick gardening gloves.

"*You are a loser*," Charlene whispered. "*You are a fat fuck.*"

I turned to her in slow motion, one hand in midair, the glove halfway on. "What?"

Jake suddenly appeared to our right from behind a long row of raspberry bushes. "Morning, girls."

"Morning," we both mumbled, never taking our eyes off one another.

He walked over to the sink, washed his hands, and wiped them on a bandana hanging out of the back pocket of his shorts. He eyed both of us as he headed through the garden gate, toward the buses.

"I can't believe Phoebe would write something like that," Charlene said, shaking her head.

"How do you know her name?"

"She wrote it in the back of her diary."

"Don't say her name out loud," I said. "*Ever.*" I stormed over to the tall stack of white buckets.

"I warned you."

"This is between Phoebe and me," I said, believing the depth of my words, but not understanding why. "You had no right."

I grabbed onto a metal handle, pulled a bucket from the stack, and headed toward the sunflowers. I plunked the bucket down near the collection of stalks and began raking my fingers through the dirt, looking for any fallen leaves.

Charlene crouched down next to me. "You read it first," she said.

"It's about *me,*" I told her, digging into the dirt with my hands until I could feel the soil pile up on my gloves' fingertips. "She left the damn thing at *my* reflection spot."

"She has no right messing with you."

"But it's about *me*! Not *you*, Charlene. You had no right going over there, into their camp."

"She was trespassing. I just wanted to show her what it feels like to have someone do the same."

"She didn't trespass. She…I…"

"This is what happens when you share personal junk with the enemy," she said. "If you share with a Kamama, with one of us, you'll feel better. I promise. You can talk about what happened at the game."

I suddenly felt like I did that day on the field: exposed, with everyone in the stands watching me; judging me; abandoning me.

"Did you get kicked off the team, Simone?" Charlene went on. "Is that why you lost your scholarship?"

My jaw clenched. My face burned. "They didn't kick me off the team, Charlene." I hoped she could see the red in my cheeks, the sweat on my upper lip. "You might want to get your facts straight."

"You told me you'd lost your scholarship—"

"If you're going to become a psychologist, you need to start listening better. I told you I'd lost my scholarship. I never told you why."

"You told Phoebe why."

"No, I didn't. I barely know her."

"Well, she sure knows you," Charlene said. "You can't let someone talk smack about you. She needs to learn that you can't mess with girls who are trying to get their heads on straight."

Is that what I was doing right now? Trying to get my head on straight?

"FYI, Charlene, I was not *kicked off* the lacrosse team. I *quit.* I quit as one of the best players my school ever had. I used to be a jock. How crazy is that? I was popular and had tons of friends and parties. I was even sort of pretty, in a sporty way. My parents adored me. Bragged on me every chance they got. Now I'm fat. I'm a loser. Phoebe's right." I stood up with my bucket. "You really shouldn't make assumptions, Charlene. Someone could get hurt. What you did last night was the meanest thing I've ever seen."

"At the very least," Charlene said, "she owes you an apology."

I pictured Charlene, bending over in front of the tree in the middle of the night, reading the journal with her flashlight like it held the magic key to life's answers.

"I'd say she's not the only one."

"I was only defending you," Charlene said.

I threw my bucket away to my left. It crashed into a row of green beans, causing dozens of little green sticks to rain to the ground.

"Why, Charlene?" I asked. "Why do you feel you have to defend me? Why can't you just leave me alone? Why do you have to get up in my business? In everyone's business? I never asked for your help. I never asked you to do anything for me."

Charlene looked at me as if I were a homeless person. She said, "We need to let the Felinas know we're strong, that we can band together to protect who we are. We've had enough crap in our lives, don't you think?"

"What crap?" I asked.

Charlene didn't answer me.

I watched her face. Her eyes were still clear, but there was something behind them that told me she was not defending me, she was defending something else. Something buried deep, like all the girls at Kamama.

And then I had an epiphany.

"You have way more baggage than me, don't you, Charlene? That's why you're here a second time."

Ms. Diggs' singsong voice came over the loudspeakers: "Counselors, please line up your girls. The buses will be leaving in fifteen minutes..."

My voice grew calm. "I agree with Mary, you know. You can't save other people without saving yourself first."

I turned away from Charlene and picked up the bucket from where it had rolled onto its side near the green bean vines. I hugged it against my body as I disappeared among the berries and flowers, becoming one with the garden.

Chapter Thirty-one

In the garden, Ms. Diggs spoke to me as I wiped my dirt-covered hands on the back of my shorts. "It's nearly two o'clock," she said. "Why don't you call it quits? You've been going at it since the buses left this morning."

I'd only taken one short break for a cup of vegetable soup in the empty cafeteria. I was happy to have been left behind, to weed in silence. For a few hours, I pushed away Phoebe's mean words and Charlene's buried issues. Instead, I concentrated on the plants that fed me and the news I'd received that morning. Losing those few pounds was like opening a door to possibilities—for the first time in two years.

Ms. Diggs tossed me a power bar. "Go reflect."

"Can't I reflect while I weed?"

"You can reflect in everything you do. But physical breaks are important, too. So take one."

She smiled warmly and walked out of the garden, leaving the gate open.

Ms. Diggs had dedicated the last half of her life to helping girls who were on the same destructive path she used to know. She had taken the negative and turned it into something positive, offering a refuge for obese girls to rediscover, or maybe discover for the first time *who* they were beneath the fat. Where would Ms. Diggs go if the camp closed? What would her life become?

I stood next to the sunflowers, yellow-rimmed and black-faced, reaching high into the afternoon sky like tall willowy children. Every once in a while I spotted a smiling face on one or two. I put my bucket back in the stack, stepped out of the garden, and latched the gate behind me. In less than a year, Jake's garden—berries, nuts, sunflowers, veggies—wouldn't be tended to anymore. Everything would wither and die and turn into one large compost heap.

Cabin ten sat lonely in its silence as I walked along the quiet path. I pictured Kamama in ten year's time, full of cabins but void of human activity, earthy vines taking over, pulling the buildings under. I thought about the campers without a place to go in the summer, the baggage they all carried that only a place like Camp Kamama could help unburden. Especially girls like Charlene.

Was it possible I carried just as much?

Of course I do, or I wouldn't have been one of the lucky girls chosen for Camp Kamama.

I'm not the one who snuck over to the Felina camp in the middle of the night.

But you read the diary. You're the one who opened the can of worms.

I kept walking. Even if my mind had fought against it, my feet would have taken me there by rote. And even after all that had happened, it was still my reflection spot, the only thing I could call my own. I was sure Phoebe wouldn't be there. I had confronted her, had left her standing next to the log, caught in her own web of cruel deceit. She'd be a fool to show her face again. A fool not to fully understand the warning beneath the words Charlene had written on the mirror.

I rounded the last corner. My rotting log welcomed me. The nearly overgrown path stretched beyond it toward the lake, sunlight pouring through the trees like yellow rain. I looked up. The tree seemed lonely, like an old man who had been waiting years for a friend to come and visit. It let out a sigh as the breeze rustled through the leaves overhead. Maybe it knew this might be the last summer a Kamama would enjoy its cool shade.

I sat on the log and took off my cap. I pulled my hair from the pony tail holder, shook it out, and retied it.

Creature of habit, I thought.

Over my right shoulder, I casually peeked into the hole. The baggie with the chocolates was gone, but the dark blue plastic rested on top of the leaves where Charlene had carelessly left it. Why Phoebe had not taken it back was beyond me. Maybe she'd had enough of the book as well; had taken her mean prank as far as it could go. She would move on to other things for entertainment, messing with other girls, maybe from other camps scattered about the mountainside.

Charlene had removed the diary from its plastic covering the night before, the only thing to protect it from the elements. For some reason, this made me more sad than angry. The empty baggie was caught in a nearby branch. I plucked it free and shoved it into the pocket of my shorts.

Before I knew it, the book lay on my lap. I rubbed my hand along the damp blue cover. I didn't need to open it to see the words inside.

Who was truly guilty here? I wondered. Phoebe for writing

it? Me for reading it? Me again, for not turning in Charlene? Was there an invisible abacus up in the sky, adding points for what each of us had done wrong, like the lighted scoreboard in a bowling alley?

In school, if I received a bad grade on a test no matter how hard I studied, I'd become despondent. If I failed to help my old lacrosse team win a game, I'd chastise myself for days. Conversely, I forgave others too quickly, often making excuses for their behavior. My brother—too young to know what he was doing. My father—disappointed that I wasn't living up to his expectations. Charlene—consumed by her own angst.

And Phoebe—perhaps unaware of how she was affecting others.

Cruelty doesn't turn into kindness just because a person doesn't know what she's doing.

What did the book matter in the great scheme of things anyway? Would I, years from now, even care about these words? Would I share them with anyone? My future husband, if I ever got married? My future daughter, should I be lucky enough to have one?

I breathed out a warm puff of air, frightening a tiny rabbit that ran across the path and into the brush on the opposite side. Then I placed the diary back in the hole. I gathered a fresh pile of leaves and buried the book like a dead family pet. I had perfected the art of burying things, of pretending, so I would simply pretend the diary wasn't there. And maybe soon it wouldn't be. Without the protective baggie, it would probably rot.

Good.

As the blue disappeared beneath the damp blanket of leaves, I understood something profound: that book didn't belong to me. Maybe it didn't even belong to Phoebe. It belonged in that hole. In the belly of an old tree.

***

The sun hovered above the tree tops a little to the west. I moved my bottom until it was comfortable on the log, stretched out my legs, and let my faded baseball cap cover my eyes.

I breathed deeply, taking in the smells of evergreens and soil, flowers and leaves, which all together smelled like a lush summertime forest. Birds in the branches fluttered their wings, sang and chirped in the late afternoon. The occasional nut or seed fell from somewhere high, hitting one branch, then another, until it finally plopped on the ground like the silver ball dropping to the bottom of a pinball machine. Squirrels chased each other up one trunk and down another, their tiny claws digging into bark and tapping across the branches.

I felt myself relax, felt my mind go deeper into itself.

I had let the book go. I had let Phoebe go. Maybe these were precursors to letting *everything* go.

With my eyes shut, I soon felt myself floating high above me. Like a drone, I glided, letting my eyes travel down the path leading away from the tree. In and out of shade and light, my vision moved down the narrow trail as it snaked its way through the trees of Kamama. There was Jake, sitting in lotus position on the beach; Ms. Diggs, running like a maniac around the obstacle course; Mary, helping girls get to the root of things, even though I had yet to—

Shuffling sounds from something bigger than a rabbit entered the stillness, pulling me from my thoughts. My eyes flew open. I pushed my cap back and stood up.

Along the path on the other side of the tree, Phoebe walked

in a pair of faded jeans and tennis shoes, a brown zippered jacket with the hood up, and a long black shirt hanging below the jacket's hem. A shock of blond bangs stuck out from the hood, which was tied beneath her chin and tight around her face. Her steps were choppy, like a robotic bridesmaid walking down the aisle in a pair shoes too small for her feet.

I said her name, carefully, like I was speaking another language: "Phoebe."

As her name entered the air, the cruel words from her book pummeled my brain to dust, obliterating any earlier hope of liberation.

Ten feet from my tree she stopped in her tracks. With narrowed eyes, she peeked at me through the hole in her hood. Her head tilted back. She stared up into the trees. She was taking her time, contemplating…

Something was wrong. My heart pressed an irregular rhythm against my chest. I wanted to run away. I could move fast even though I still weighed a lot—I'd proved that the night before, running back from Camp Felina.

But I did not move.

Phoebe started walking again. Her face grew clearer. She wore a thin sheepish grin that seemed to come from somewhere else, like another person had let her borrow it for a while.

The palms of my hands grew damp, and the hair on my arms rose, a strange feeling to have goose bumps on such a hot day. She stopped again, this time next to the tree only a few feet away from where I stood, but said nothing. My throat clicked loudly as I tried to swallow.

I will not be passive. I will tell Phoebe the truth about the bathroom mirror, how I knew who it was but had said nothing. If I hand her an admission of guilt, she will follow with one of her own, because that's how girls do it…tit for tat…even Steven…

"I'm sorry," I told her, the sentence like a dead leaf suspended mid-air.

She didn't respond. She was going to make me say it.

"For what happened last night."

Sadness spread across her face like a shadow, that strange pout pulling her pale skin downward. She untied her hoodie and pushed it back. It fell away from her head, exposing a tousled mess of blond hair that a few days before had been shiny and flaxen, but today looked like it belonged on the head of a discarded Barbie. One of her dangly earrings was missing.

Phoebe's uneven voice broke through the pretty forest sounds. "Sometimes we get so caught up in our own messed-up worlds we forget there are others dealing with the same kind of BS. Right?"

I didn't know what she was talking about, but I nodded.

"Things that have to do with other people, Simone. Like all the girls you go to camp with. Or, like me, for example." She pushed her hands into the front pockets of her jeans and leaned a little to the right. After a moment, she said, "You still don't know, do you?"

The word *off-kilter* popped into my head. I felt like Alice in Wonderland, stuck in some underground world with the Queen of Hearts, trying to answer a riddle I had no desire to know the answer to.

"Know what?" I whispered, barely recognizing my own voice.

"About Felina."

Charlene's chant came into my head: *The girls at Camp Felina love to eat their canned Purina; they purr and meow and cry like cats, but deep inside they're really rats.*

Phoebe pulled something out of her pocket and held it out in front of her in a fist. Her fingers slowly opened and I saw what lay in her palm: a piece of chocolate, cozily wrapped up in foil. I stared at her hand, confused about what chocolate had to do with anything, other than the fact that she knew I'd eaten some. And as I thought about the taste of that tiny morsel, my stomach grew nauseous. Like once, when I got food poisoning from a cream-filled donut, for a whole week after it was all I could do to say the word *donut* without throwing up.

"Maybe you should know," Phoebe said. "Maybe you should know everything."

She shoved the candy back in her pocket and rolled up her sleeves to her elbows, exposing her chalky white skin. With her arms outstretched, her palms facing down, she walked toward me. She reminded me of Frankenstein or a zombie. A chill attacked my neck like a lightning bolt and rode down my spine, spreading wide and grabbing onto my hips. I pictured the Felina scarecrow, hanging from the tree by moonlight, swaying back and forth in the breeze.

Phoebe shoved her hands closer to my face. I stepped backward and tripped over a root. I grabbed her by her skinny arms to keep my balance. She didn't flinch.

"I have a whistle," I told her, gripping her arms harder, standing firmly on both feet. "I'll use it."

"Turn my hands over, Simone," she said, ignoring my tiny threat.

"What?"

"Turn them over!"

I placed my hands on the back of hers. Her pink polished nails were chipped and dirty. Slowly I did as she asked.

"Do you see?" she asked.

I let my eyes move from her shaking fingertips to her palms, up to her elbows, and back to her hands.

"I don't—"

And then I *did* see.

Thin white scars. On both wrists. Even whiter than her milky skin, like barely traceable lines on a road map. The slices had been done the way I'd read about in health class, running the length of the wrist instead of across. That was the real way. The way that said, *This is no joke. This is not a cry for help.*

I released my grip, but her arms remained in the air, two skinny bridges floating between us.

"I tried it two years ago," she said. "Just went *swish.*" She moved an invisible blade along the inside of her wrist. "My mother saved me. Just in time. Maybe you hate yourself as much as I do. Something we have in common, right?"

I shook my head.

"Of course you hate yourself," she said, lowering her arms to her sides. "Look at you. Look at me. Two strange peas in a very oddly shaped pod."

She laughed and I noticed her teeth for the first time, teeth I had assumed were as white as any Cover Girl's. But they were light gray, like a drizzly afternoon.

She said, "I wanted to make it all go away."

"Make what go away?"

"The pain," she said.

"Pain from what?"

"From what happened to me. To my family. My life. It would be so easy to try it again. Just because we don't have any knives or blades over there, doesn't mean I can't find a way."

"No, Phoebe. Maybe if you talk to someone, let it out—"

"You sound like the Felina doctors."

"Doctors?"

She unzipped her jacket and slid to the ground, leaning her

back against the log. Her eyes had lost their shine, yet she still offered a shy thin smile. She stared up at me. "Ever wonder if it's too late for us?"

"It's never too late," I said, not really sure if I meant it.

Tears were suddenly sliding down her cheeks.

I sat on my bottom beside her. As she cried, I brushed a loose strand of blond hair from her face. The smell of honeysuckle wafted over me.

"The other day, you called yourself a loser," Phoebe said. "But between the two of us, I'm definitely the bigger screw-up."

"I didn't call myself a loser. *You* did." The vicious words nearly stuck in my throat.

She shook her head. A lonely silver earring jiggled like a little Christmas ornament.

"In your diary," I said.

"You weren't supposed to—"

"And the game," I said, the image of the crowd jumping to their feet now clear in my mind. "You wrote about the game."

"The soccer game." Her words fell to a whisper. "That's where it happened."

I corrected her. "A *lacrosse* game."

Phoebe looked confused. "I told you before, I've never been to a lacrosse game."

"What about my father?" I asked.

"What about him?"

"You wrote about him."

"Why would I write about *your* father in *my* diary?" she asked.

"I saw it for myself."

"I wrote it," Phoebe said, "but I was writing about me, Simone, about *me*, about *my* life, about *my* dad. Not about *you*. Why would you think that?"

"The words you wrote, they're the same as—"

"I had a feeling you'd read it and it pissed me off at first, but then I remembered we'd made a pact to keep our secrets between us. Didn't we?"

"Yes, but—"

"I've been keeping diaries since I was little," Phoebe said. "This one's sort of different, because it's filled with—well, with stuff that if I don't write about it, if I don't let it out, I'll die."

"But you wrote it like you were talking to someone else. And you said things—"

"It's my diary. I have the right to write it anyway I choose. Don't I?" She got on her knees and leaned into the hole. She dug out the book. "I wrote in it early this morning," she said, fluttering the pages, exposing dirt in the creases. "I couldn't find the baggie."

I stared at the ground, ashamed for what Charlene had done, but way more ashamed of myself.

"Take it, Simone," Phoebe said, holding out the book.

"What?"

"I've decided I want to share it with you. I *need* to. It's better if I write stuff down instead of talk about it. It's sort of how I deal. Really. It will help me for someone else to know. Besides my shrink."

She handed me the diary. It felt differently in my hands than it had before. It felt vital.

"Are you sure?" I asked.

"As long as you promise to bring it back tomorrow."

"I promise," I said. "Promise you'll be here when I show up? That you won't do anything, you know…"

She nodded slowly as we each traced an invisible *X* across our chests.

Chapter Thirty-two

That night, an hour after lights-out, I stayed awake while the other girls, who had spent an exhausting day kayaking, deeply slept.

Lying on the cot under my covers with my flashlight two inches from the page, I re-read Phoebe's diary. Charlene had dog-eared it, as if to mark the pages she felt the most fascinating. Those itty-bitty triangles made me want to cry. I smoothed them out by bending them the opposite way, and then rubbed my fingernail across the tiny creases. This time I pretended I was Phoebe, writing in second person, even though my teachers had said it wasn't the best way to write. But there are no rules for diaries; they can be written any way the writer chooses.

I turned to the back of the book. Her name was right where Charlene had said it was, in that pretty script, with a tiny daisy drawn underneath: *Phoebe Vincent.*

I re-read her sad poem on the first page, trying to grasp whatever pain she was feeling beneath the words:

You walk with your head first high, then low.

It bobbles sadly to and fro.
It moves with grace, it writhes in pain, its will is gone, there is no shame…
And yet you are the one to blame.

I turned the pages, reading one entry after the next, lingering on the meanest sentences—which, of course, were not about me, but about Phoebe. Funny, if I'd kept my own diary, it might have come out exactly the same.

In the still of the night, I made my way through the book, afraid the inked words would disappear if I didn't get to them right away:

You can not tell your mother…she will tell Daddy. If she tells him, he will blame you. He will disown you. He will stop loving you. Therapists think they know you, but how can they know you if you don't tell the truth? But they will tell your parents, won't they? If you tell a friend, a confidante, things might get a little better…if you let it out…

There are not enough kind words. Not enough hugs. Not enough forgivers. Not enough friends. The world is upside down, and you are the reason…

Then finally, the pages that spoke the truth of what had happened to Phoebe poured over and through me, her ultimate surrender ringing as clearly as a bell. I wondered if the ringing would ever end:

It was your fault for teasing him. You should have obeyed Daddy. All the makeup. Those tight clothes. He warned you what would happen if you dressed like a slut. You're dirty. You can't shower enough to get the dirt from under your nails, to get him out of your skin…

All you had to do was turn the other way. But no one had ever looked at you that way before, like a woman. If Daddy had seen you when you left the house, he would have killed you, and that would have saved you…

All you had to do was look the other way when the boy smiled, and then asked you to follow him under the bleachers, that there was something he wanted to show you. He was a senior. You were a freshman. A baby. He knew the difference between right and wrong. "I could fall in love with a girl like you," he told you as he sipped on a can of Pepsi, as if those words would make you believe in his sincerity. And they did. "I just want to show you something…"

Only three sentences stretched across the next page, as if in that moment it had taken too much strength or courage for Phoebe to write any more:

He touched your arm. It was the first time any boy had ever touched you. And it felt good.

Then the next ten pages unfolded like a movie stuck on fast-forward. I flipped from one page to the next, crying, reading the words as though they were my own, as though what had happened to Phoebe had happened to me:

The stands were packed during the soccer game, you could barely hear yourself think. Feet stomped above your head. You thought you were so cool, following him. It was dark under the bleachers, behind all that sports equipment. Day turned to night in an instant. He took you to his cave and told you to lie on a dirty mat. You saw the used condoms and cigarette butts and beer cans littering the ground, and wondered how many were his. You wondered why, when another boy's voice suddenly said, "Oops, sorry, dude, didn't know this spot was taken," you didn't scream for help. The other boy had a girl with him. You heard her giggle. You should have screamed. Maybe she would have helped you. He didn't put his hand over your mouth until after they'd left…you had your chance…

It's you're fault. You didn't listen to your father. He will blame you. For all of it. For that boy putting his hands under your tight sweater and into your tight leggings. Then doing to you what some girls expected him to do.

But not you. You were Daddy's Little Girl.

Huh. Not anymore.

If you weren't here, your parents wouldn't argue about you every night. They might even fall in love again. Daddy wouldn't offer looks of hopelessness for the only daughter he has.

How can you tell them why you can't eat? That to eat would be like accepting a gift, and you don't deserve any gifts. That to eat would make you human again, and you feel anything but human.

It's time to stop pretending things are the same as before. It happened. It still happens, over and over again in your head. If you tell someone, you just might get it out of you once and for all and move on with your life.

Let her into your heart. Maybe she will listen and be a good friend. She has secrets too. Maybe we all do.

And the final entry, the words sitting alone as though they had no business following the others:

In the woods you sit and talk, laugh a bit, take a walk.
You were alone till you met Simone.
Now you and she are a perfect we
As you share your fears beneath the tree.

That was it. Fifty-plus pages lay blank, waiting for the future.

I shut the book and held it tightly in my arms like a stuffed bear I had once loved. The tears which had made it difficult to read were coming harder now, like ocean waves breaking through idle levees. All the memories from the last two years were clamoring to be free.

And for the first time in what felt like forever, I welcomed them.

Chapter Thirty-three

I barely remember the next morning, the wakeup music blaring through the camp and kicking me out of bed. I barely remember yoga, what we had for breakfast, or running the obstacle course. What I do remember is worrying a lot. That Phoebe wouldn't be at the tree, that I'd never hear from her again, that I'd read about her in an online obituary.

I trotted along the path to the tree—*our tree*—the diary tucked neatly in the front compartment of my backpack. My shorts kept slipping down past my hips, and I had to hike them up a couple of times, which I thought for sure would slow me down. But when I looked at my watch, I saw that I had made it to my reflection spot in record time.

As soon as I dropped my backpack to the ground, a sound traveled from down the path. I stepped past the wide tree trunk and sighed with relief. Her hair glistened in the late morning sun that streamed through the branches overhead. She wore a pretty long-sleeved pink blouse with a pair of newer jeans, along with her old Rainbows. She looked fashionable, yet simple. A bottle of lemon Gatorade dangled from her hand.

"Morning," Phoebe said, a sliver of a smile on her face.

"Hey."

She took a wide step forward and hugged me. I hugged her back. She sat on the log and tugged on my hand to follow.

"Did you read it?" she asked, licking her lips like I was a famous book reviewer.

I nodded as I pulled the diary out of my backpack and handed it to her.

"So now you know," she said, placing the book on her lap and laying her hands on top. "Everything." She let out a whiff of air.

"Where is he now?" I asked. "The boy, I mean."

"I don't know," Phoebe said. "I switched schools. I told my parents I wanted an all-girls school so I could focus on my studies. They jumped on it."

"I don't understand why you can't tell your parents. I mean, they know something's wrong or they wouldn't have sent you to Felina."

"My dad. He's a police officer. And he's the strictest parent on my street. And not always so nice. If he knew what happened, he'd find him and kill him. I'm not kidding. My dad's friends are all cops. It would not be good. Trust me."

We sat in silence a moment, listening to the sounds of the forest, but I could feel the unasked question swirling in the air, taking on weight, like a growing swarm of bees.

"What happened to *you*?" Phoebe asked, her voice soft and caring.

It came to me that the planet needed someone kind like Phoebe. She needed to finish high school, go to college, get married, have a couple of kids she could be sweet to.

"What happened isn't a secret," I told her. "It was in half the newspapers in North Carolina. I think it was even on the news. It's only a secret the way I feel."

Not once in the last two years had I found the courage to share my feelings, but sitting on the log with this miniature girl from an enemy camp, I suddenly couldn't wait. *The truth will set you free,* I had read somewhere. *As long as you trust the one you're telling,* I added.

I pulled my cap off and held it in my hands. "My nickname used to be The Dragon."

"Why?"

"Lacrosse," I said, touching the cross-stitched lacrosse sticks on my hat. "I was a pretty good player, especially for a freshman. That was two years ago. We made State that year. I played offense, an attack position called 'first home.' I was a total threat in my position, but I was hoping to play center the following year."

"I've never played lacrosse," Phoebe said. "Is it hard?"

"Not if you practice all the time," I said. "And if you love playing. Which I did. Anyway, the stands were packed that afternoon. Home field advantage. The game was hardcore, tied twelve to twelve until the last few minutes. I had no doubt we could win. We were an amazing team. The ball was passed to me. I caught it with no problem and ran down the field, cradling that baby, waiting for the right moment to pass."

I think my eyes closed as I told Phoebe my story, because all I could see was me on the field.

"I remember running and sweating and loving it. The crowd was crazy, there was only a little time left. I knew if I got it to the right girl, we'd grab the final goal. The opponent's goalie was sort of a wimp. I found my girl, made eye contact, and knew she was ready. I pulled back my stick and pushed that ball through the air. The pass should have been complete. But it wasn't."

I opened my eyes. Phoebe was watching me. I chewed my cheek a moment.

"She came out of nowhere," I finally said. "I mean, she just appeared smack dab between me and my teammate. In between me and the ball, which was moving like a torpedo. But it didn't hit the pocket. It hit the opponent. In the head. You don't want to get hit by a lacrosse ball. Ever. Sometimes they fly at a hundred miles an hour."

"Don't you all wear helmets?" Phoebe asked.

"My old team does now. But back then, only the goalie. Boys' teams wear helmets because they tend to be more aggressive."

"Oh."

"Anyway, the player fell to the ground. She was out cold. Our head coach called 911. It took a few minutes for the ambulance. By then everyone was gathered around the stretcher: the school photographer, the fans, her family, and my own. I watched as the stretcher moved toward the locker room. I fell to my knees in the grass. Someone put their arm around me, I don't know who. My head was spinning. I thought I'd be sick, right there on the field…"

I twirled my cap in my hands. Tears mixed with sweat slid down my cheeks. Phoebe gently placed a hand on my arm and left it there.

"I remember the assistant coach trying to keep me on the field, telling me we were going to keep playing, it was a state championship. But how could I play after that? I had to know if she—if the girl was going to be okay. I didn't know what I would do if she wasn't. My father dragged me to the sidelines and gave me a pep talk from his college football days. But I never heard a word. All I could see, over and over, was that ball leaving my pocket, flying through the air like it had it in for the girl, and whacking her in the head. I walked out of the stadium. My mother drove me to the hospital. I didn't bother to change my clothes. I think I still had my stick in my hand. I didn't care about the game, and I couldn't understand why anyone else would. It wasn't professional lacrosse. It was freaking high school. Anyhow, at the hospital, they wouldn't let me see her, but I saw her parents sitting in the waiting room, her mom was crying, and I wanted to go up to them, to tell them how sorry I was, that the whole thing was crazy. That she'd come out of nowhere. That she'd made a crucial mistake."

I breathed in deeply and counted down from ten as I let the air out.

"So," I said, "that's what happened. I smashed a lacrosse ball into another girl's head."

Phoebe whispered, "Did she die?"

I wiped my wet cheeks with the bottom of my shirt. "Almost. She was in a coma for a week, and when she came out, she couldn't walk or feed herself. She had three surgeries. She was in rehab for eighteen months. She could have died."

"But she didn't," Phoebe said.

"But she could have."

"Does she play sports now?"

"No," I said. "She has a permanent limp. She can hardly talk."

"Did she forgive you?"

"She doesn't remember ever playing lacrosse. A lot of her memories disappeared. I sent her family a card, and they sent me one too, and they were almost identical. With an apology and everything. Telling me they knew it was only an accident, and how sorry they were that I had to live with what had happened."

"They forgave you," Phoebe asked. "But you couldn't forgive yourself."

"I tried to. I really did."

"What stopped you?"

Say it. Let it go.

"My father," I said. "He never forgave me."

"For accidentally hurting someone?"

"For quitting, Phoebe. I quit lacrosse after that. I was terrified I would hurt someone else. Afraid that the next time could be worse. That someone could die because of me. I went to practice the following week, but I threw up the second I stepped onto the field. I couldn't do it. And my father, he hates me for it. He hates that his Dragon up and quit."

I began sobbing. Phoebe slipped an arm around my shoulders and left it there until the tears subsided.

"Our dads sound a lot alike," she finally said. Then she added, "My mother suffers from anxiety because she doesn't know what's wrong with me, which makes me worry about her. It's sort of an ugly cycle. But I wouldn't be here if it wasn't for her. And if I hadn't come here, I wouldn't have met you."

I smiled.

"You understand about Felina?" she asked.

"I do now, after reading your diary. Do you have group sessions like we do?"

"Uh-huh. Three times a day. Talking about our diets, what we eat each day, what we don't eat each day, how many calories we need to survive..."

"You can have some of mine," I said, patting my belly.

"That's my problem," she said, laughing sarcastically. "I don't want *any*."

"I don't think I want them anymore either."

"Well, whatever you do, don't do it my way."

I nodded. "Think we'll ever get our act together?"

"It's hard," Phoebe said. "*Really* hard."

I thought about all the crap food I'd shoved into my body over the last two years, all the sodas and breads and desserts. For such a glutton, it was a wonder I wasn't diabetic.

"If you aren't a foodie like me," I said, "why did you hide those chocolates in the tree?"

"They're not *real* chocolates, Simone. They're laxatives. To help me…you know…I didn't know you'd find them. Sorry they made you sick."

"Yeah, well, I got out of a couple of activities that day," I told her. "But those things are pretty harsh, Phoebe. You shouldn't be eating them either."

Phoebe didn't respond to my advice, and I wondered if she regretted sharing so much.

I changed the subject. "I really am sorry about what happened to your bathroom mirror."

I told her about Charlene and how I'd followed her over to Felina in the wee hours of the morning.

Phoebe said, "Our security guy was pretty sure it was someone from your camp, but our director said to let it go, that camps did that sort of thing from time to time. Apparently, something like this happened last year, too."

I apologized again, picturing the bathroom swathed in that strange yellow light and the creepy scarecrow, hanging from the tree.

When I asked Phoebe about the scarecrow, she said, "That's Effy. Our effigy."

"Effigy?"

"A dummy. You know, an image that represents something else. We made it on the first day of camp. From scraps of old rags and stuff. Then we hung it from the tree after we stuffed it with pieces of paper. It's supposed to look like a girl, but we didn't do a very good job."

"What's it for?"

"On the scraps of paper, we each write out everything we hate about ourselves, about the secrets that clog our heads, the stuff we can't talk about, or don't want to talk about. We can write as many and as often as we need to. Some girls stuff it twice a day or more. At the end of the summer, we'll cut it down, drag it to the beach, and set it on fire, supposedly to get rid of our negativity. Very symbolic. We do a lot of stuff like that. We do trust exercises where the girls stand in a circle on the beach and one girl stands in the middle, then falls backward with her arms at her sides, praying that whatever direction she chooses to fall, someone will catch her. At first it seems silly, but by the end, everyone feels pretty good."

I thought about Kamama's compliment circle in powwow. I wanted to tell Phoebe something nice, maybe about how pretty her hair was, or how good she looked in jeans, but those seemed especially superficial. Instead, I said, "After camp is over, you can call me anytime."

"Maybe we'll come back up here next summer," Phoebe said. "And we can hang out again."

My stomach fell. "That's not going to happen. Camp Kamama won't be here. They're closing next spring."

I told her the details I'd read in the article.

"That's messed up," Phoebe said.

"I'm afraid to tell the other girls. I'm not sure how some of them will take it. So I've been thinking about ways to keep it open. There should be a place for some of them to come if they need to."

"Yeah. That's how I feel. What do you think we ought to do?"

"*We?*"

"Maybe we could put our heads together and come up with a plan."

"Well," I told her, "I do have a few ideas..."

For the rest of reflection time I shared my thoughts with Phoebe. Not only was she a good listener, but she had some interesting ideas of her own.

A short while later, after hugging goodbye and promising to meet the next day, I walked to lunch with a spring in my step. As I made my way over the slight rise, I thought, *Reflection time might just be the best thing about Camp Kamama.*

Chapter Thirty-four

I brought a couple of pens, and Phoebe turned her diary into a planning book. In her blue journal, we jotted down gobs of ideas. Most of them bordered on idiotic, like stuff a couple of elementary school kids might come up with: a car wash (there were hardly any cars up here in the mountains); a bake sale (we weren't allowed to bake anything with sugar); or an auction (highest bidder gets this tacky orange bracelet!) But by the time a week was up, we'd hit on a couple of ideas that sent the good kind of goose bumps up and down my arms.

One day at Kamama, while on our way to the garden, I left my group and stopped by the office. I looked through the screened door and knocked. Ms. Diggs wasn't inside, but Jake was standing next to the large desk going through a ledger.

"Can I talk to you for a second, Jake?" I asked through the screen.

"Don't you have garden detail?"

"It has to do with your garden," I told him. "And the pool. And the obstacle course..."

He waved me inside and pulled out a chair for me. I sat, and he leaned against the corner of Ms. Diggs' desk.

Jake listened as I told him about the article I'd read regarding Kamama's closing. Then I shared how I'd met Phoebe the Felina at my reflection spot and that we'd become good friends. Without telling him the sordid details, I explained how Phoebe and I had more in common than we'd ever suspected.

"We confide in each other," I said. "She's made me think about things in a new way. It took the two of us together…and a little bit of time…and I think we've come up with an idea for how to save Camp Kamama."

Jake smiled. His teeth were straight, and especially white against his smooth tan skin. "We all are required to be a messenger from time to time."

"A messenger?"

"You met Phoebe to learn from one another. Everyone is lucky enough to meet someone in their lifetime that changes them in some way, but not everyone is astute enough to notice, Simone."

Jake went around the desk and sat on the office chair.

"When I was in my twenties," he said, "I lost both my parents to diabetes. They were full-blood Cherokee, and so am I, in case you didn't know. My immediate family eats like there will be a famine at any moment. I watched my parents slowly kill themselves with bad food. I left home when they died. I couldn't bear to see anyone else live—or die—that way.

"A few years after my parents had passed, a friend of mine asked me to come with him on an outing. He'd found a spot up here in the mountains he believed would cause visions. I was skeptical. I had given up the folklore of my people. I had dropped out of society. More specifically, my society. Because I thought if I stayed, I'd end up like my parents.

"But I was young enough to be adventurous, so I went with my friend. After a few hours of hiking, we reached a cave. I followed him inside. My friend sat down on the hard floor with his legs crossed and I did the same. He showed me how to relax, and within a short time, we were deep in meditation. My eyes were only closed for what felt like a few minutes when I sensed another person enter the cave. But I couldn't open my eyes. The person, a man, sat right beside me and said, 'You must come back to your land. You must show your parents that they did not die in vain.' Then he said, 'You are Cherokee, and you will always be Cherokee. No matter what you do, you will not escape the hands of your people which wrap around you and hold you tight. If you want to make the memory of your parents a positive one, then you must show others the way.'

"A few hours later, after meditating, my friend and I left the cave, and when I told him what had happened, he said, 'He is the man of the mountain. Dead for centuries, in a battle between the Cherokee and the early government. Only those who truly need his help and are willing to listen will hear his words of wisdom.

"You and I are very lucky, Simone, to have met someone who offers words of wisdom—and visa-versa. Do you understand?"

Before I had a chance to respond, the door opened and Ms. Diggs stepped into the office.

"Everything alright?" she asked. For the first time since I'd come to Kamama, Ms. Diggs looked tired. There were soft dark circles under her eyes, like she hadn't slept well in a few days. She grabbed a smaller chair from the corner, brought it over to the desk, and sat.

"Simone knows about Kamama's future," Jake told her.

"You haven't told anyone, have you?" Ms. Diggs asked me. "I wouldn't want to put a damper on the remainder of the summer."

"I have," I said, "but not anyone from here."

Once again I explained how I'd met a Felina, and how we'd been discussing the camp's closing.

Ms. Diggs said, "I'm happy you've made a new friend, but what does she have to do with Kamama? Does this young lady have a trust fund she's willing to give us? Because at this point, that's about the only thing that can save us."

"We came up with a few things that don't require a trust fund," I said.

When I was done sharing our ideas, even the silly ones, Ms. Diggs leaned back and placed her hands behind her head. "There are definitely some possibilities here. What do you think, Jake?"

"If you want my honest opinion," Jake said, "I think it might be better to share what's going on with our campers. Maybe get their input."

"You really think that's a good idea?" Ms. Diggs said.

"Don't we promote honesty and openness here at Camp Kamama?" Jake asked.

Ms. Diggs nodded. "Of course."

"Well," Jake said, "nothing we've come up with is feasible. Either we close next year without telling anyone, or we allow the girls to help us decide how to save the place."

Ms. Diggs nodded again, this time more passionately. "We could give flyers to the head counselors to share with their bunks."

"Or, for starters," Jake said, smiling at me in a mischievous way, "Simone could talk to the girls during powwow."

***

Those red scripted words across the wall stood out like a billboard advertisement:

O' Great Spirit, help me always to offer the truth,
to listen with an open mind when others speak,
and to remember the peace that may be found in silence.

Silence, I thought, *will not be part of my existence today.* The fan overhead spun around. Metal chairs squeaked as girls took their seats. I whispered to Mary that I needed to speak first, that I had an important announcement to make. Then I stood in front of a chair in the circle, and when the girls settled, I shared the truth about Camp Felina (wide eyes all around), my friendship with Phoebe (a roomful of gasps), and Kamama's fateful future (even more gasps). Then I told them that it was up to us Kamama-mamas to find a way to keep the camp open (excited whispers).

Mary said, "Girls, I know you all will come up with some wonderful ideas, but let's save the discussion for the end of powwow. Simone still has the floor."

Mary smiled approvingly. The chatter dwindled. Eventually the room grew quiet. I left my chair and moved to the center of the ring directly under the ceiling fan, nervous but ready. Nearly twenty pairs of eyes waited patiently. And then it just happened. Bits and pieces of the last two years rose up from within my belly and began falling into the room. Sharing my story with Phoebe had given me some practice, but sharing it with my Kamama friends was something else.

Slowly and carefully, like unwrapping a special gift, I told the girls all about that fateful game. About my fears. My angst. My guilt. I told them how my father couldn't stand to look at me, and worse, how I couldn't stand to look at myself. They nodded with understanding, because they, too, had let a particular moment in their lives define who they were, what they had become. I no longer wanted to be defined by the guilt eating me alive on the inside and the fear responsible for adding layers of protection on the outside. It was as though with every exposed detail, a tiny little pound melted away.

"It feels so good to finally let it out," I said, fighting back tears of relief and joy. "I know that sounds cliché, but it's true." I met Charlene's eyes. She sat like stone, her hands folded in her lap. "Only each person can decide for herself when the time is right," I continued. "Having another person or a group is great for support. But having them tell you *when* or *how* to do it...well, that doesn't work at all..."

***

Two more girls spoke after me, and the rest of powwow was spent coming up with ideas. Girls broke into clusters, weighing pros and cons, asking me what I thought. I felt like a politician with a really cool agenda.

"Maybe we can sell stuff from the garden at a farmer's market," one girl suggested.

"We could publicize Camp Kamama in the schools," said another.

Diane said, "I'd be happy to sell some paintings."

Toward the end of powwow, Ms. Diggs stopped by. The girls nearly pounced on her with their ideas.

Ms. Diggs calmed everyone down and said, "I will take all of your proposals into consideration, as well as the other campers'. Naturally, this will take some time to figure out. In the meantime, I want to say how proud I am of each and every one of you for showing your maturity in this matter. If the camp does stay open, it will be because of all of you."

She smiled at me, and I beamed.

As the other girls talked excitedly over one another while we walked to dinner, Charlene made her way through the small herd.

"Simone," she said. "I need to talk to you."

Diane hung back with me.

"In private," Charlene added.

"It's okay, Diane," I said, appreciative of her desire to protect me. "I'll catch up in a sec."

Diane hesitated before falling in line with the rest of the girls.

Charlene and I stepped off the path. She looked down at her feet, sucked in a deep breath, and then met me square in the eye. Tears were forming. "I didn't know Felina was that kind of camp. I…didn't know…"

I let her cry it out, since out of all the Kamama girls I'd met so far, she seemed to need it the most.

"Can I meet her?" Charlene asked as she wiped her wet face with the back of her hand. "I want to apologize in person about the mirror."

Charlene meet Phoebe? My knee-jerk reaction was a big fat no. I felt like a mother cat, wanting to protect Phoebe like the fragile feline she was; like the runt of the litter.

But how can someone learn a lesson if no one gives them the opportunity?

"I'll leave it up to Phoebe," I told Charlene.

She responded with a hopeful smile.

The next afternoon, Phoebe and I sat on the log together.

"Charlene wants to meet you," I told her. "She wants to apologize for what she did to your bathroom mirror."

"Oh," Phoebe said, nervously twisting an earring.

I gave her a moment to process.

"Okay," she finally said. "Why not? I'd sort of like to meet the person who had the balls to visit her enemy's camp in the dark."

Phoebe had been brave enough to visit Kamama in the dark, but I said nothing.

The following afternoon, I handed Charlene a stern warning on the way to the tree.

"No lectures. No assumptions. You may not analyze her. You may not dissect her. Give her your apology and then listen. That's all."

The moment Charlene saw Phoebe, she began to cry. "It was me," Charlene said. "I'm the one who wrote…well, you know. I'm so sorry."

"It's okay," Phoebe said, shrugging. "I am a skinny bitch."

Charlene laughed through her tears as they hugged.

I thought I would be jealous, knowing they could be forming a friendship, but I wasn't. By the time they were finished hugging, I had my arms wrapped around the two of them.

Chapter Thirty-five

A few days later, as the camp buzzed with the possibility of being saved, and ideas flooded the box outside the office door, Diane came up to me after finishing the obstacle course. She wasn't out of breath like she had been the first week. Her cheeks radiated heat, but they also radiated pride.

"Can I come with you and Charlene to your reflection spot today?" Diane asked as we hiked up the path. Charlene had given up her reflection spot in favor of spending time with Phoebe and me, and even though she hadn't disclosed any secrets yet, we didn't mind. Diane, confident as she seemed, hadn't shared her story either, in powwow or otherwise.

"Let me check with the boss," I told Diane, hoping Phoebe would say yes.

She was thrilled. "If she's anything like you and Charlene," Phoebe said, "then sure."

Our threesome became a foursome.

It was drizzling the day Charlene opened up. The thick branches full of leaves kept most of the rain away, but the drops that found their way through the canopy felt wonderfully cool. There wasn't enough room for all four of us to sit on the log, so Diane and I sat on the ground on Phoebe's spread-out hoodie, and Charlene sat next to Phoebe on the log. Phoebe had brought two bottles of blue Gatorade, which we passed around like drunks on a curb.

Everyone in our little group knew what had happened to both Phoebe and me. I figured it was only a matter of time before Charlene felt left out, and I was right.

After talking about food, the weather, movie stars, singers, the general stuff girls talk about, Charlene whispered, "I want to tell you about my older sister."

No one said anything. After a few weeks in the calmness of the mountains, we had become experts in the art of listening.

"Cheri was one year older than me," she said. "Our mom worked a lot, and Cheri became my second mom. She was always there for me, before school, after school, helping me with homework, or laundry, or cooking. She was a great big sister. But she was really heavy. Even heavier than I am now." She paused, visibly trying to muster the courage.

"You don't have to tell us," Phoebe said.

"Yes, I do," Charlene said. "I feel like I owe you. I owe all of you." Her lips trembled and she started crying, her shoulders shaking with each heavy sob.

I understood how that can happen. How a well can be dry for so long and then suddenly fill with water, causing a flood without your permission.

After her tears subsided, Charlene took off her baseball cap and fanned herself with it. "Cheri was in the ninth grade when I was in the eighth. Our private school was K through twelve, and most of us had known each other forever, so we were pretty tight.

Even so, there were a few mean girls, especially in the sophomore class, one grade above my sister. These girls were really good at kissing the teachers' asses, then pulling stuff without getting caught. You know the type."

We all nodded.

"They stuck together and protected one another. One clique in particular made it their daily ritual to pick on anyone who wasn't living up to their Snob Hill standards. For some reason, in the middle of the school year, they made it their mission to destroy Cheri. They'd wait for her when our mom dropped us off in the morning. They'd say hello to her at the curb, so from where my mother sat in the car, it looked like Cheri had tons of friends. But she had none. Zero. Even *I* didn't want to hang with her in school. She embarrassed me."

"Because of her weight?" Diane asked.

Charlene said, "I know you're wondering how I could be embarrassed by that, considering I'm the same way, right? There's something you don't know about me. I used to be average weight for my age and height. Before everything went to hell."

I took a better look at Charlene, trying to see how she would have looked back then. She must have been beautiful with her hazel eyes and clear skin and wavy strawberry-blond hair. She still was beautiful, really, but her features sort of disappeared in between puffy cheeks and extra chins.

I saw Charlene's throat move up and down as she tried to swallow. I handed her the Gatorade, and she drank from the bottle. It was interesting how when she cornered a girl in cabin ten, she looked like a grownup standing at a podium, speaking at the Hilton in front of an audience of psychologists. But sitting here at the base of the tree, she looked like the rest of us: a lost girl desperately trying to find her way.

Charlene continued. "There were a lot of times when the mean girls really messed with my sister. Like, one time, they stole her clothes from her locker while she was in gym class. Cheri ended up walking around for the rest of the day in her sweaty gym shorts. Another time, I was walking in the hallway between classes, and Cheri was right in front of me, and there was this red blob on the back of her sweater. It was paint, like from art class, or something. And I had this weird feeling she knew it was there. Like she had accepted this was who she'd become and was wearing an ad to prove it. It made me sick to see people make fun of her, but it made me even sicker that she didn't do anything about it."

"Did *you* make fun of her?" Phoebe asked.

"No. But I never took up for her either. I mostly ignored her. Especially during school. In a way, I wasn't any better than those bitches. I was passive."

I knew that word.

Charlene said, "She killed herself that Christmas Eve. Overdosed on a prescription drug. No one knows where she got it. I went to her room to see if she was ready for midnight mass and found her lying on her bed."

"Oh, Charlene..."

"How awful..."

"Beyond awful. And the weight thing, well, that just sort of crept up on me, you know?"

I nodded, understanding that creeping.

"I've tried to analyze it all," Charlene said. "Maybe I'm fat to punish myself. Or maybe it's because I want to be like Cheri so I can tell all the mean girls to eff off—which is what I should have done for my sister." She looked up at the leaves over our heads. A drop of rain fell on her forehead, but she didn't wipe it away. "The saddest part is there were signs. Her grades went from honor roll to D's. I knew something bad was going on, but I was too selfish worrying about my own life to care about hers."

"What happened to the mean girls?" Phoebe asked.

"I started home-schooling right after Cheri died," Charlene said. "I told my parents who the girls were, but there was no real proof. Besides, I'm the one who should have been punished. I'm the one who should have taken up for Cheri." Charlene took Phoebe's hand in her own. "I thought you were a bunch of mean girls hurting one of my friends. That's why I did what I did."

I said, "I'm really sorry about your sister, Charlene."

"I think becoming a psychologist will be good for you," Diane said.

Phoebe added, "Maybe you can help people like Cheri."

"Do you think so?" Charlene asked.

It was raining harder. Tears mixed with raindrops streamed down Charlene's round rosy cheeks. Her forehead was wrinkled. She looked like the cabbage patch doll my mother had bought when I was four, thinking I would like it. But it only frightened me, and I'd stuffed it headfirst into the recycling bin.

"I'm worried I'll never make up for it all," Charlene said. "I'm worried that so many girls will slip through the cracks. That no one will know their truth. I worry that I won't be able to defend all the people who get picked on. All the underdogs. All the losers who are really just sad people with big hearts and no hope that things will get better."

I thought about the powwows, how opening up had instantly made me feel lighter, and I hoped that Charlene would soon share her story with more than three people in the middle of the woods. That by sharing with many would bring her back to herself.

***

Like Trish a few weeks earlier, Sue, the invisible camper who wore a ring as a sign of abstinence, left Camp Kamama. Just disappeared into the ether. Naturally, it was Charlene who shared the news.

"Did you know that Sue had a baby?" Charlene asked. "Her parents made her give it up for adoption. I heard someone say she left because she wanted to hire an attorney to get him back. So much for being married to your virginity."

Who knew what was true or what wasn't? I was starting to discover that it was way more beneficial to share the truth than to let others make up a story about you.

As our cabin whittled down to just seven, our private powwows grew. Eventually, Sabrina and Vanessa joined us at the tree. We never invited Karen or Marion to come along. We agreed that this had to be a group without hall monitors; that we could monitor ourselves just fine.

We learned so much about each other, sitting beneath that big old tree. And our rules were simple: no judgment and no advice unless someone asked for it. Questions were okay, as long as they weren't like the Spanish Inquisition.

Like a bunch of onions, we began to peel away the layers.

Sabrina, with her tie-dye obsession and bandana collection, had a story that would have made a great Netflix movie:

"I was thrown into my first beauty pageant when I was four. It was fun, at first, wearing all that makeup and getting my hair teased. I got to wear all kinds of frilly clothes. What four-year-old doesn't like to play dress-up? But it got crazy. My mother, well, she freaked out whenever I didn't win, sometimes in front of other contestants. I looked like a child hooker with all that junk on my face and my hair woop-de-wooped. She made me exercise all the time and stuck me on a low-carb diet when all my friends were eating McNuggets. I didn't have my first soda until a few years ago."

"Soda is awful," Phoebe said. "It can eat right through a car battery."

"When I turned thirteen," Sabrina went on, "I concocted a plan to keep my mother from putting me back on the stage. I decided to eat my way through puberty. I was sick of starvation diets and clown makeup. My nerves were shot with all the pressure of winning. I got to a point where I wanted to throw up every time I went out on stage."

"What was your talent?" Charlene asked.

"I play the flute. Or, I did. One day, I put my flute on the railroad tracks by my house and the Number Seven turned it into metal toast."

Sabrina laughed a little, and we all nodded to show we were on her side.

Diane's story didn't enter our circle for a few weeks. Then, out of the blue, and in her blunt Diane way.

"I came out of the closet at twelve, and my mother has never gotten over it."

"Who cares if anyone's gay?" I said. I'd known more than a few lesbians over the years from playing sports. It didn't bother me on the field, and it certainly didn't bother me now.

"I thought it was fashionable to be lesbian," Sabrina said jokingly.

"Sounds like your mother's problem," Phoebe told Diane. "Not yours."

"She makes it my problem every time she tries to fix me up with some dorko named Junior or Stanley from church or the country club. She thinks I just need to meet the right guy. Do you know I've had sixteen first dates? That's a record, even at my school where half the girls are ho-bags."

"Why does your mother have such a hard time with it?" I asked. "These days, everyone's coming out of the closet for one thing or another."

"She wants grandkids," Diane said, laughing sarcastically. "Give me a break. She's thinking of grandchildren, and I barely have my driver's license. I told her, 'If you're so hot on having babies around, get your tubes untied,' but she didn't see the humor in that one."

A few weeks after we began our private reflection-time powwows, Phoebe brought another Felina along, a girl named Ginny who was a toned-down version of a mime. Thick pale makeup covered her face, dark eyeliner circled her eyes like an early 1900's film star, and her hair was divided into chunks of pink and yellow stripes. Ginny suffered from bulimia.

"I've only eaten two meals since the day before yesterday," Ginny told us with a slight lisp. She didn't share her back story with us, and no one, even Charlene, insisted she need to. I thought it was nice that Phoebe had another Felina she could trust.

"What do you do with the food they give you?" I asked Ginny.

"Hide it underneath my clothes and then toss it out in the woods. I've started naming the raccoons." She smiled proudly.

Diane told Ginny, "You have my permission to bring any extra food over to our camp."

Vanessa said, "No doubt."

We all laughed in spite of our ridiculously messed-up selves. But what's really funny is, if a girl happened by and saw us sitting together under that big old tree in the middle of the woods, all she'd see was a group of oversized and undersized girls, and she'd never know by looking at us just how much we really were alike.

Chapter Thirty-six

Mountain time wrapped itself around us as we continued through the seemingly endless summer. I conquered meditation while standing in tree pose. I learned to like beets, make blackberry jam, and cook with olive oil instead of fake butter. I won a trophy for breaking an all-time record in the obstacle course. Jake helped me gain strength in the 400-meter breaststroke. I excelled at rolling through the water with a kayak attached to my butt. We hiked a twelve-mile section of the Appalachian Trail, a place close to where Jake had grown up, where the air was thick with the smell of earth and the trees were taller than the ones at Kamama. Diane taught me to paint a watercolor of oranges sitting in a bowl, though by the time I was finished, it looked more like fuzzy chickens sitting in a life raft. I hung it above my cot.

Summer's end, though it took a long time to come, was suddenly knocking at our cabin door.

Camp Felina ended a week before Kamama.

I made a point of saying goodbye to Phoebe alone. She'd

made me a card. On the front she had drawn a picture of an elephant, complete with huge ears. On the inside her pretty script flowed across the cardboard: *First you hide, then you grow, then you share, then you go. I will miss you more than anything. Love, Phoebe.* I gave her one of the bracelets I'd made in art expression, complete with little butterfly charms dangling from it. Phoebe said she might get a butterfly tattoo when she got back home—without her father's permission, of course.

She left me standing at the tree, never looking back as she meandered one final time down the winding path toward Felina. Tears rolled down my cheeks as I whispered goodbye. Then I looked up at our tree. I wrapped my arms as far as they could go around that big old trunk, and told it how much I loved it. I thanked it for being such a wonderful part of my summer. As I cried, I rubbed my hands up and down the tree's bumps and lumps and wondered if it would miss us. Miss *me.*

After a while, I dried my eyes and turned back toward camp. I didn't look back. I wanted to remember the tree exactly as it was, tall and old, supportive and patient. I figured, after all that summer's drama, the poor thing needed a breather. Hopefully, it would be well-rested by the time another weary traveler decided to sit on the log to reflect, write in a diary, or share in a special powwow.

***

By the time our parents came back to Kamama to collect us, I had lost a total of twenty-eight pounds.

Two-twenty-six.

My mother hugged me until I thought my lungs would collapse.

"Oh, Sissy, you look totally awesome!"

She didn't know it yet, but we had a lot of talking to do. About our co-dependent relationship. She had as much to learn in the coming year as I did. But I also had a lot of great new recipes I wanted to share, and none of them included grease or butter or cheese. They did, however, include the two of us spending quality time in the kitchen together. I couldn't wait to fill our baskets with veggies and hormone-free poultry at the local farmer's market. To show my mother how to make jam and smoothies from fresh fruit, and how to pan-fry chicken in olive oil instead of eating it out of a bucket.

My brother Bucky came along and didn't complain about the long day or make a rude comment about the fact that all of us girls were blubbering like babies. He even smiled a couple of times.

While my mother and brother got lost in the crowd, I turned to see my father, standing like an island a few feet away. Then he did something that surprised me. He stepped forward and wrapped his arms around me.

I surprised myself even more because I didn't hug him back. My tongue was a frozen Popsicle in my mouth.

"Simone?" my father said, dropping his arms. He looked around at groups of campers with their families, girls hugging their moms and dads, talking, laughing. "I thought this camp was supposed to work on the inside as well as the outside." When I didn't respond, he said, shaking his head, "Honestly, honey, you need to let it go."

I was angry. I had worked my ass off for eleven weeks to lose twenty-eight pounds. I had given up my Krispy Kremes and DQ shakes and Hardees french fries. Had run the obstacle course over one hundred times, swum enough laps to enter the Olympics, powwowed enough to get me into the *Guinness Book of World Records.*

"You want *me* to let it go?"

My father's face was a combination of sadness and confusion.

While I'd learned to share with strangers, I still hadn't shared with the person who needed to hear it most. It was time to do it; time to come clean. I was suddenly packed with two years of everything I wanted to say, filled to the brim like an effigy stuffed with hundreds of Post-its.

I sucked in warm air and looked my father square in the eye. "*You're* the one who hasn't let it go, Dad. *You're* the one who's spent the last two years hating me."

"What are you talking about?" he said.

"Like you don't know. Isn't that why you sent me here? As punishment?"

"Your mother and I sent you here so you could learn to work through—"

"I came here because you think I'm a fat loser."

He lowered his voice. "Don't say things like that."

"It's true, Dad. You're mad at me for quitting lacrosse. You can't stand the idea of losing your little jock daughter. A mini-you."

He clenched his jaw, took in a deep breath, then let it out again. His cheeks turned bright red, making it obvious who I'd inherited those genes from.

"I have *never* thought of you as a loser, Simone. *Ever.*" My father paused when a group of laughing girls walked past. "And I was never mad about anything. I was *upset.*"

"Because I quit lacrosse."

"No."

"Then why?" I asked.

"Because you quit *life*, Simone. You just...gave up."

"But you pushed me away from you..."

"No, honey, I didn't. You pushed food in between us like a wall. In between you and the whole family. I'd take you on hikes and all you talked about were the drive-thru's you couldn't wait to hit on the way home. We'd go to Bucky's soccer games, and you'd spend your time at the concession stand instead of sitting with us. All you did was talk about food, how much you wanted it, where we could go to get it, how wonderful it would be once you had it. You even convinced your mother to make you second breakfasts."

I looked at the ground.

"Didn't think I knew, did you?" He paused, waiting for an answer, but I said nothing. "You used food as a crutch, instead of coming to us. Do you know how that made me feel, knowing you were keeping things bottled up? Knowing my little girl was in pain but there was nothing I could do about it? Do you know how many times I tried to get you to open up? To let it out a little? But you were so mad at yourself, even I couldn't get past your anger. I didn't know what to do. What could I have done, Simone? What would have worked?"

I started crying.

He placed a hand on my shoulder. "You used food to get even with yourself, Simone. Not with me. I feel sorry for you. For what happened. I know how it feels to hurt another. I injured my share of guys playing football."

"You did?"

"I tried to tell you, but you wouldn't listen. All you could hear was your own self-chastising. I wasn't mad at you for one second. Is that what you've been thinking all this time?"

I nodded as tears spilled down my cheeks and onto the soft earth.

He handed me a folded bandana from his back pocket. I wiped it across my face.

"Simone, those pounds have been your protection from yourself. To help you deal with what happened. Your mother wasn't helping, though she means well. And we both understood that this camp might be our last ditch effort to see our only daughter become healthy again."

"So you don't blame me?"

"Absolutely not."

"And you don't care if I play lacrosse again or not?"

"You're getting healthy, Simone," my father said. "That's what I care about most."

He wrapped his arms tightly around me, this time hugging me hard enough to crack my ribs, and I let him. I'd take a set of broken ribs any day in exchange for that kind of hug.

***

Our parents were invited to hang out in the cafeteria, where healthy snacks were served and eleven weeks of photos and artwork decorated every inch of wall space. While most campers and parents cooed over paintings of trees and lakes, and kiln-fired sculptures of people, elephants, and butterflies, I wandered off to say goodbye to Jake's garden. To wish it well.

Diane and Charlene tagged along.

"If the camp doesn't close, will you come back next year?" I asked the girls as we made our way past the sunflowers.

Charlene reached out and caressed the petal of a white rose. It was the first time I'd noticed that flower in the garden, and I thought about Jake's bonfire story of the Cherokee Rose.

"I told Mary I'd want to be a counselor," she said. "But I had to promise to work on sharing."

"I haven't decided yet," Diane said. "All depends on how the year goes."

I thought about something then that Mary had said at our final powwow a few days before:

"You all are going to have to work independently for the rest of the year, even if it feels like no one else supports you. You are going to have to deal with what you have acknowledged about yourselves, forgive yourselves for going astray, and celebrate getting back on track."

She'd made me excited about the prospect of rediscovering the road I used to be on.

But then, as if Mary had read my mind, she'd said, "Beware. The road won't look the same as the last time you walked it. You ladies have changed, so you will see the path that lies ahead of you with different eyes and a renewed spirit. Remember to pace yourselves. Each girl has her own clock, and some clocks move slower than others. Do not waste precious time comparing yourself to those around you; only compare yourself to the person you want to become."

There were tears in Mary's eyes, and ours as well, because no one was sure of Kamama's fate. Even with all the great ideas we'd passed along to Ms. Diggs, there were no guarantees. It was possible that the following year we'd all have to find somewhere else to go for the summer.

After a time, the three of us left the garden and walked back toward the office, where crowds of campers and families gathered out front. Suitcases were dragged across the dirt and girls exchanged numbers.

Diane said, "There's my mom, AKA *Grandma*. Gotta go." She hugged Carlene and then me. "Tweet me. I'm online all the time. Devout Pringles *and* Cyberspace junkie."

We watched as she headed through the mob.

"What's the first thing you're going to do when you get back home?" I asked Charlene.

"I lost twelve pounds," she said. "That's more than last year, so I need to buy some new clothes. How 'bout you?"

"I'm going to call my school and see if there's room on the swim team this winter."

We hung out in the garden a little longer, neither one of us saying a word as we wandered slowly back toward the gate, lost in what the summer had given or taken away.

After hugging Charlene goodbye, I said my farewells to Jake, Ms. Diggs, Katharine, Mary, Willie, the counselors, and my other bunkmates as we joined our families in station wagons, SUV's, and sedans. One by one, the long line of cars drifted out of the parking lot, down the dirt driveway, and onto the winding mountain road.

Epilogue:

The Following Summer

"Kamama-Felinas over here!" Ms. Diggs shouts. Next to her stands Mr. Reynolds, one of the four co-directors.

"Do you think they're doing it?" Charlene had asked the week before, when Kamama-Felina had the first-ever camp orientation. She was referring to Ms. Diggs and Mr. Reynolds, who obviously had a thing for one another. The two camps weren't the only thing to merge into a perfect union.

I had smacked Charlene in the arm. "It's nobody's business."

Charlene looks healthy and seems much happier this year. But that busy-body thing…that's something she hasn't managed to curb yet.

Diane is the only one besides Phoebe and Charlene that I've kept in touch with over the year. Diane didn't come back to Kamama-Felina. She told her mother she was willing to try a Bible camp if that would shut her up. What she *didn't* tell her mother is that there is another Protestant by the name of Hailey that Diane made friends with online. Someone who understands exactly what Diane is going through. Someone who is just her type.

Now, among the nearly two hundred girls, I sit at a picnic table next to Phoebe. I notice her arms. I had caught a glimpse of them last summer, back when they were thin and frail and white like milk. This summer, they are tan and sculpted. Her hair is a little shorter, and it cups her much rounder face.

I don't know how much she's gained. One of the new rules at Kamama-Felina is that we are not allowed to talk about our weight in numbers. We still gear up for the loud music that bangs through our skulls in the morning and sit lotus-style on the beach before breakfast, though we take up way more room now while sitting on the side of the lake that joins the two camps. We still swim, run the obstacle course, and dig in the garden. We still have healthy meals three times a day. But weight is *never* to be mentioned. Powwows are available, but only if girls want to go, and some do. There is very little pressure at Kamama-Felina.

Phoebe and I are counselors in separate cabins, so we try to get together as often as possible, like during movie night, or bonfires, or team-building exercises. The garden is still luscious, filled with berries of all kinds, and sunflowers that stretch as far as the eye can see. The first time I stepped foot in the garden this summer, I was amazed by its beauty, and I beam when I think that I was part of the reason it didn't turn into compost.

Jake passes by my table, and we smile at one another. I'm pretty sure he never shared his Old Man in the Cave story with any of the other girls. Secrets are okay sometimes, as long as you confide in someone you trust.

Phoebe turns around on the picnic bench with her back toward me.

"Lift up my shirt," she whispers.

I lift her pink T-shirt—mine is light blue again—and see the tattoo, just above the hip-hugger waistband on her shorts. It is a majestic elephant with a butterfly delicately perched on the tip of its trunk. On the back of the elephant lies a curled up kitty cat.

"I love this," I tell her. "It's beautiful."

Snacks are passed around, a cup of vanilla yogurt with granola and raisins on top. I eat mine slowly, taking my time to enjoy it. I watch Phoebe out of the corner of my eye. She stirs the mixture around for a moment, takes a deep breath the same way I did before taking that first dive on the swim team last winter, and puts a heaping spoonful into her mouth. We finish at the same time.

After everyone is accounted for and fed, we are divided into two groups. Because the activity is weight-sensitive, only half of us are allowed to participate—the other half has to stay back, hanging out by the creek or hiking along one of the trails.

"Stay with me," Phoebe says, grabbing my arm as we are again divided, this time into groups of ten.

Two older female guides who look as healthy as mountain climbers take us to an area under a large tent where piles of gloves and helmets and harnesses sit. We each choose what fits, then follow the guides' instructions on the correct way to put everything on.

"I'm nervous," Phoebe says, putting a yellow helmet on her head.

"Me, too."

She and I help each other with our harnesses. A guide moves through the group to make sure they are secure. She tightens one of my straps, and my butt cheeks rise by a few inches. They tell us to make sure our tennis shoes or hiking boots are secured tightly to our feet.

After additional instructions, do's and don'ts as well as what to expect, we follow the two guides up a long trail that resembles the ones at Kamama-Felina. We stop at an area with a short cable suspended between two trees, but the cable is so low I can almost touch it. This line is for practice only, to make sure we know exactly what to do when we get to the *real* line—the line draped between the trees a few hundred feet in the air.

After we practice on the baby line a few times, we hike to an open area where we are told to follow a steep staircase that leads up into the trees. I look up. I know that a wooden platform sits somewhere over my head, but I can't make it out with all the leaves surrounding it.

We are all panting by the time we make it up to the platform, where the sun beats down on us. My palms are sweating and my feet are soaked from being trapped inside socks and tennis shoes. My heart races as one of the instructors introduces us to the cable, which stretches like a long thin spider web from where we now stand, to another platform about six hundred feet away. We will travel along five lines today, flying from platform to platform between the trees.

But this one is the first.

"Be sure to look down," one of the guides says. "There is so much to see, we don't want you to miss anything."

She shows us how the harness attaches to the cable. "See ya'll on the other side!" she shouts as she grips the line, jumps off into space, and slides away from the girls in our group, who watch after her with awe.

"You can go before me," Phoebe says.

"Gee, thanks."

The second guide has stayed behind to help us onto the line. A few girls volunteer to go first, and I watch as they, too, float away over the tops of the trees. Before I know it, it's my turn.

I can do this. I used to play lacrosse. I can swim like a dolphin. I eat beets! I give a big smile to the guide to show her I am fearless. I am The Dragon!

In reality, I am not ready to look down. If I can see the creek below and the tree tops that look like giant clumps of broccoli, I think I'll wet my pants. I keep my head up. The helmet nearly blocks my view of the cable above me.

I hold my breath, tighten my gloved grip on the line and wait, my lips pressed together, my stomach moving up and down like tiny ocean waves.

"You ready?" the guide asks.

As soon as I nod, I hear a loud click as she locks me in. I look up, even though I trust her, just to be sure. After all, it's not every day a girl flies through the air with only a carabineer between her and a newsworthy death.

"Go free," says the guide.

I step off the platform into nothingness. I can feel the slack of the line as my weight pulls my body downward, then I start giggling uncontrollably as I move forward, sliding along the cable like a sheet being pulled in on a laundry line. I feel like a sheet—as light as one, anyway.

I make myself look down. What does it matter? It won't change anything. Whether I look down or not, I am still a few hundred feet up in the air. I spot an eagle below me, floating on the wind, and below the eagle I see two otters playing in the creek. As I pass over a leafy tree top, I see a nest filled with baby hawks, their little mouths opening and closing. I wonder if they think I'm their mama.

I am crying now, for what reason, I'm not sure. Maybe it's because I have made it to this point in my life, when only a year before I never thought it was possible. I had heard Jake's speeches, how cooking fresh food and eating well and getting off my butt would change my world, and took to heart Mary's promise that I would find a way to forgive myself.

My father's face comes to me as I slide along the cable. *I wish he could see me now.* But that doesn't matter. He saw me this past year, watched me swim like a fish in the 400-meter, took countless photos of me with my letter. He even made a point of hugging me in front of my teammates, including Joey, a senior, who glanced at me in a very cool way more than once during swim season.

Everything fell into place after last summer. I started cooking nearly all of our meals at home. Bucky and I started shooting hoops again in the driveway. Mom stopped taking me to get fast food. Actually, I had stopped asking her and, to my surprise, she never offered.

Now, here I am, hanging from a cable high above the forest. I let go of the line and turn my arms into steady wings. Phoebe's laughter bounces to my ears from somewhere behind, and I find myself flying with my mouth wide open, stuck somewhere between a scream and a laugh, happy tears running down my face and falling toward the ground like raindrops.

For the next few minutes, we zoom through space, and I can hear my campmates as they holler their way across the line. "Woo-hoo!" they shout, like younger versions of Ms. Diggs. "Go Kamama-Felinas!"

One by one, we slide along the zip line, the earth far below, making our way to the other side, floating through the mountain air like a colorful stream of butterflies leaving their chrysalises and venturing into the world for the first time.

I Am Elephant, I Am Butterfly
Food for Thought

DO NOT READ THE FOLLOWING UNTIL YOU HAVE FINISHED THE NOVEL!

1. The word "Kamama" has a double meaning. How does this word relate to the novel's title and the plot?

2. *I Am Elephant, I Am Butterfly* is about harboring secrets that cause us pain and the change we often experience when relinquishing those secrets. Have you ever had a secret that you buried deep inside? How long did you keep it to yourself? Did you ever share it? If so, what kind of relief did it offer?

3. Have you ever spent time at summer camp? What are some great things you remember? What are some negative memories? How did you grow that summer?

4. The United States is a country that revolves around food: super-sized fast food, overwhelming holiday meals, magazine covers, commercials, social gatherings, sports events, cook-outs, dinners out, hot-dog-eating contests, reality shows on cooking competitions, grocery store aisles dedicated to candy…the list goes on and on. How do you think our concept of food directly or indirectly affects our overall health? Do you think food advertising

has a direct effect on the obesity epidemic in our country? What other factors come into play? How can this be remedied?

5. Does someone you know have an eating disorder? Have you tried to help this person? If so, how? Were they open to your advice?

6. *I Am Elephant, I Am Butterfly* represents girls from different backgrounds and with different personalities. Who can you relate to most/least?

7. A major underlying theme in the novel is forgiveness, not only for others but for oneself. Do you think forgiveness is the key to a happy life? How would the novel have been different if Simone had never forgiven her father? Charlene? Herself? Why are so many of us quick to forgive others but not ourselves?

8. Compare/contrast Camp Kamama and Camp Felina. Compare/contrast Simone and Phoebe.

9. Why do you think I decided to create an all-girl camp (except for Jake)? Were you satisfied with this choice? Why or why not? How would the book have been different if boys had played a role?

10. The book takes place in the Appalachian Mountains. How did this particular setting affect the story? Would it have been just as effective to place the story somewhere else?

11. Cherokee sayings are found throughout the novel. Do you have a favorite saying? If so, what is it and what does it mean to you?

12. The girls in the novel are required to "reflect" in order to tap into their deepest feelings. Have you ever reflected or meditated? How did it make you feel? Name some other ways a person get in touch with his or her innermost thoughts.

13. Exercise is an integral part of the book. Does exercise play a role in your life? Do you think people today are more or less active than in the past? How does this affect our country and world?

14. Look up the words "co-dependent" and "enabler" online. Once you have an understanding of their meanings, discuss these terms regarding the relationship between Simone and her mother.

15. Ms. Diggs plays the role of cheerleader/optimist in the story. Why is she so optimistic? Why does she believe the girls have it within themselves to achieve whatever they need to in order to be happy?

16. During Truth or Dare, some of the girls are not comfortable playing, yet feel pressured to do so. Have you ever been pressured into doing something you didn't want to do? How did it make you feel? Have you ever pressured someone else? How do you think it made that person feel?

17. Simone and the other girls must attend the camp's powwows in order to heal. Although these help Simone in the end, they do not help everyone. How do you feel about the powwows? Would you have the courage to bare your soul in front of near-strangers?

18. Female empowerment is a major theme in the book. What does it mean to be empowered? Have you ever felt this way?

19. Who do you believe is the novel's antagonist? Explain.

20. While there are myriad underlying factors for obesity, I chose to use emotional eating as a catalyst for *I Am Elephant, I Am Butterfly*. What are other causes of weight gain in young people today? Do you think obesity is an epidemic? What are ways besides the ones mentioned in this book that can help young people stay healthy? What do other countries do that are the same or different regarding nutrition?

21. Making assumptions can be harmful. What were some of the assumptions made in the book and how did they affect the characters' actions? Have you ever made an assumption you later discovered was incorrect?

22. Continue the book beyond the Epilogue. Where does Simone go from here? What will her future be like? What about the other girls?

Author's Note

If you believe you may have an eating disorder, or you just need someone to talk to (as we all do from time to time), the following resources may be helpful:

http://www.recoveryranch.com/treatment-issues/eating-disorders/over-eating/

http://www.wellspringcamps.com/why.html

https://www.remudaranch.com/

http://rosewoodranch.com/adolescent-program-800-845-2211/

https://Teenspeak.org

https://teenlineonline.org/category/through-ups-and-downs/

http://teentherapycentersv.org/

https://www.teenlife.ngo/blog/

Acknowledgements:

I Am Elephant, I Am Butterfly was nothing more than a tiny spark back in 2009. From the moment I shared the first draft with my agent to watching it become a finalist in the 2012 ABNA Competition, I knew this book would remain in my heart even as it temporarily took a back seat to other projects. Although writers create mostly in isolation, it takes many to help their stories reach an audience: Thank you thank you thank you, Uwe Stender, my literary agent at TriadaUS, for your undying support. You are the first pair of eyes to read my work and the last pair before it is catapulted into the publishing empire. Here's to another nine years! Eternal hugs and kisses to my husband and brilliant artist, Jay Kenton Manning, who never rolls his eyes when I make suggestions regarding book covers and never stops believing in me. I would die without our coffee clutches and our life together. Thank you, Maria Gomez, for offering the best notes in the universe while working as Associate Editor at HarperCollins. This novel lives today because of your wisdom. Detailed research was made possible by the following organizations, respectively: NC State Extension; US Department of Health and Human Services; National Institute of Health; Alliance for a Healthier Generation; Mayo Clinic; and the United States National Library of Medicine. I cannot overlook Polgarus Studio, for without their expertise in formatting, this novel would look like a four-year-old had pieced it together! A special shout-out goes to Patty Howard, Tracie Barton-Barrett, and Denice Josten for giving *I Am Elephant, I Am Butterfly* a thorough onceover before it hit the presses. I am forever grateful for your speedy and insightful feedback. When it comes to sharing stories, no one supports local authors more than Alice Osborn, facilitator of the Wonderland Book Club in Raleigh, NC, and Mary Jo Buckl, owner of the Next Chapter Bookstore in New Bern, NC. And last, but not least, I give thanks to you, kind reader, for supporting authors by buying, reading, reviewing, and sharing books! Artists could not eat, breathe, create, or live without your continued benevolence.

ABOUT THE AUTHOR:

Leslie Tall Manning loves writing about teenagers who believe in independence, often stumbling into it headfirst (UPSIDE DOWN IN A LAURA INGALLS TOWN). She also writes about grownups who crave change and often discover it in ways they never expected (GAGA and MAGGIE'S DREAM). She holds a BA in Theatre from Cal State Long Beach and is thrilled that a play she wrote and produced in college—KNOCK ON WOOD—will become a novel in 2019. As a private English tutor and study skills expert, Leslie spends her evenings working with students of all ages and her days working on her own writing projects. When she isn't clacking away at the computer or conducting research for her books, she loves traveling with her artist husband, bingeing on Netflix, or walking along the river in her historic Southern town. She is happily represented by the TriadaUS Literary Agency.

FOLLOW, SAY HELLO, OR JOIN LESLIE'S EMAIL LIST:

Website:

www.leslietallmanning.com

Amazon Author Page:

amazon.com/author/leslietallmanning

Goodreads:

goodreads.com/author/show/8118702.Leslie_Tall_Manning

Facebook:

facebook.com/pages/Leslie-Tall-Manning-Writer/236448826562926/

Twitter:

https://twitter.com/LTManningWriter

Instagram:

https://instagram.com/leslietallmanning

What readers have to say about
Upside Down in a Laura Ingalls Town

"Brooke's voice feels authentic as she struggles to reconnect with her fractured family, and Manning's historical research shows…an entertaining novel with realistic characters readers should find it easy to invest in."
~ Publishers Weekly

"A gem of a book…"
~ Novel Gossip

"…an eye-opening story for people who think their life is tough and for people who need to appreciate what is right in their lives."
~ B. Lynn Goodwin, Story Circle Book Reviews

"…equal parts humor, angst, grit, and charm…"
~ Padgett Gerler, author of *What Does Love Sound Like*

"Few novels are crafted as creatively as this delightful novel…"
~ Katherine Sartori, author of *The Chosen Shell*

"A wonderful journey back in time."
~ P.A. Moed, author of *The Incident at Montebello*

Turn the page for a sneak peek at
Upside Down in a Laura Ingalls Town
Winner of the Sarton Book Award, 2016

At one o'clock the doorbell rang. Rebecca Lynn ran to the door like the house was on fire. Dad and I waited in the living room.

"You didn't take out your hoop," he said.

I was saved by Ricardo's voice in the hallway.

"Well, if it isn't Miss Rebecca Lynn Decker. A movie star name if I ever heard one."

My sister skipped into the living room like stupid-ass Goldilocks, followed by Ricardo and the same cameraman from the audition. The lady with the red hair and weird grin wasn't with them, and for that I was grateful.

The cameraman's name was Carl. With his skinny arms and neck, and that *Swamp People* goatee, I pegged him as more of a "Bubba," or "Skeeter," but I didn't say anything.

"Please, sit down," Dad said. He fanned his arm to the two overstuffed chairs across the coffee table from the couch. Ricardo sat, but Carl the cameraman, whose camera was already on, stood behind Ricardo.

I thought it was best to jump right in. "Are you going to tell us what kind of reality show this is?"

My dad shook his head. "Brooke—"

"It's alright," Ricardo said. "That's why we're here." He sat back in the chair and crossed one leg over the other, making himself right at home. The bottom of his leather sandal was scuffed. "There are moments in time that can never be understood, at least not fully. Times we only read about in history books, or see in movies, barely a re-creation of the truth. But it takes more than reading about it or putting on the costumes to understand what history really means." He sounded like a PBS host. "This is the opportunity to go back in time."

Carl the cameraman inched closer to my dad's face, but it should have been my face, since I was the one who was about to freak out.

"Ever hear of Laura Ingalls?" Ricardo asked.

"I have her books!" Rebecca Lynn shouted excitedly. She started counting on her fingers, "*Little House in the Big Woods, Little House on the Prairie*—"

"Sit down, Rebecca Lynn," I whispered.

Ricardo turned to me. "Do you know who she is?"

"Of course I do."

I thought of my mom, sitting on the sofa on a rainy Saturday afternoon, watching cable reruns of her favorite *Little House on the Prairie* series. Sometimes she'd cry. She would hold onto a tissue, and she would sob as she sat there on the couch. I asked her once why she was crying. She told me it was because the show made her happy.

Ricardo wiggled his fingers at Carl, who moved with lightning speed to my side. I could feel the camera sending invisible waves through my cheek. It took all my strength not to flip off that large glass eye.

"It helps that you know who she is," Ricardo said.

My dad cleared his throat and clicked his neck. "The show is about modern-day pioneers?"

"Not exactly," Ricardo said. "It has nothing at all to do with *modern*. In order for us to mean what we say when we call it a *reality* show, we plan to keep it as true to the era as possible."

"Which era?" I asked, even though I knew the answer, and even though I knew I would have to do whatever it took to get Dad to see that these people were out of their flipping minds.

"The mid-1800s. Eighteen-sixty-one, to be exact."

I started doing the history lesson in my head: mid-1800s meant no electricity. Without electricity, there would be no lights, no television, no computer…

"You're going to shut off our electricity?" I asked, shocked that this could be legal. I pictured our king-size suburban house gutted of all its modern appliances. "You can't—"

"No," Ricardo said. "The show won't be filmed *here*."

"Then where?" Dad asked.

"I can't disclose all of the information until we narrow down the participants, but the families selected will be part of a community in the North Carolina backcountry."

"Laura Ingalls didn't live in North Carolina," I smugly told him. Didn't these people do their homework?

"The lifestyle is comparable," Ricardo said. "Historians have accurately detailed the way it was then, and we've followed their guidance to a tee."

"Dad—" I whispered, the panic creeping into my throat.

Ricardo kept on yapping. "We are choosing families from different backgrounds, and giving each of them a different backstory, mostly for variety."

"Like Williamsburg," Dad said.

"Except that at the end of the day, you won't take off your costume and go home to a microwave dinner." Ricardo laughed and I wanted to slug him.

"Dad," I said, pulling on his arm. "We can't do this."

"Brooke, not now."

"But—"

"When does it begin?" he asked Ricardo, cutting me off.

"Third week of May. So you have time to become acclimated to your new home before you plant your crops."

"Crops?" A horrifying picture of the three of us picking cotton under the afternoon sun slid through my brain.

"You'll be responsible for growing much of your own food," Ricardo said. "Have you ever had a garden?"

"My wife," Dad said. "She had an amazing green thumb. I think we can figure it out."

"No, we can't," I said.

"Yes, Brooke," Dad said, never looking at me. "We can."

Rebecca Lynn said, "I want to be like Laura Ingalls, Daddy. Can I? Can I be like Laura?"

"You can if we get chosen."

My sister was smiling, my dad was smiling, and Ricardo was smiling. I faced the cameraman. Behind his creepy goatee, Carl was smiling too!

But I was not. My smile had crawled into a hole and died.

Upside Down in a Laura Ingalls Town is available now!

Made in the USA
Lexington, KY
19 February 2019